SKYWALKERS

Dorothy Shorne

WINSOME
Books

Australian English is used in this book. Spellings will be different to standard spelling used in the United States. Some of the terminology may be unfamiliar to readers outside of Australia.

Copyright © 2024 Dorothy Shorne

ISBN 978-0-648297260

Cover Design: GetCovers

Images: DepositPhotos

Published by Winsome Books 2024

WINSOME Books

Adelaide, South Australia

Acknowledgements

Gratitude to Dr Vicki Jones for her patience in waiting for this book to see the light of day.

Thank you to Trish Morey for your review and advice.

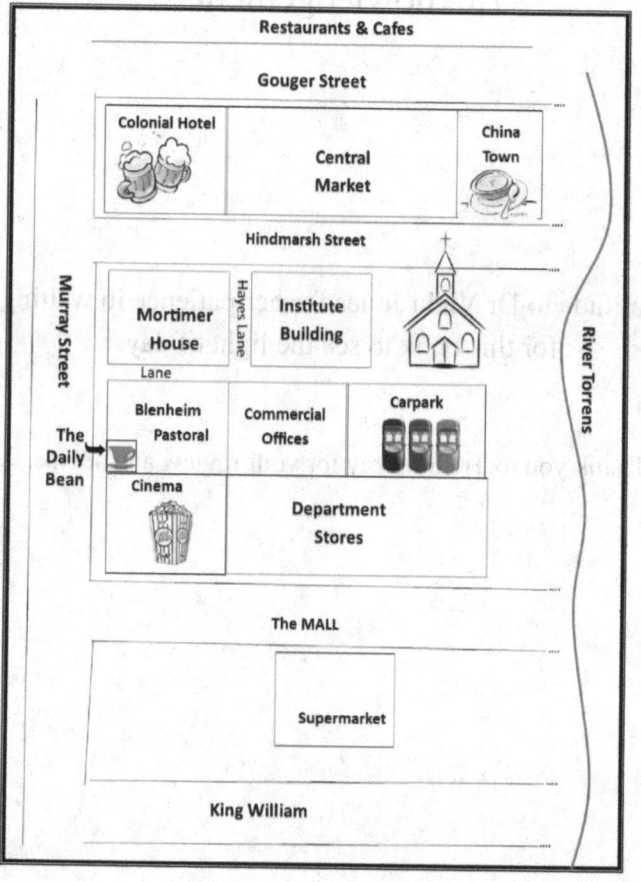

1 The Storm

RILEY LISTENED, LEANING against the parapet. He cocked his head to hear more clearly. The music, building to a crescendo, provided the sound score to the ominous clouds rolling overhead. The temperature had dropped noticeably and he suppressed a shiver. Across the divide that separated their two buildings and unaware of her audience, Phoebe played at her most dramatic, responding to the primal cues from the elements. Her fingers commanded the keys, alternately caressing and emphasizing with passion. The music spilled from her open doorway, enticing, goading and daring the skies to do their worst.

As a challenge, it was pointless. The low rumbling percussion signalled the opening bars of a stronger event. As the sky darkened, Riley had the perception that he and Phoebe were the only two people isolated in a world of their own. Not many would be out on a night like this.

The first fat drops fell. The music came to an abrupt stop. The balcony door across the gap slammed shut as Phoebe closed out the weather and secluded herself. The noise echoed off the surrounding buildings. With it went the light that had spilled out from her open door. Now he stood alone, the sole survivor in their world. The rain morphed into a drenching downpour, and he turned and fled for the door of his flat.

Once inside, he towelled his hair and draped his wet jacket over the back of a chair. The weather had changed so quickly. A noise interrupted his contemplation, unrelated to the rain and the tempest that drummed on the roof. The insistent scratching made the door rattle. Riley strode to the door and threw it open. A large ginger cat fell over the threshold. The animal paused and lightly shook itself like a dog. The tom was larger than some smaller breed pooches. A name tag clinked against the collar around his neck. A flick of the tip of his tail indicated annoyance at being caught in the rain. Its demeanour said the cat had expected the door to be wide open, ready and waiting for its entrance.

After a cursory glare around the room and refusing to acknowledge Riley, the cat skirted the kitchen to its bowl and sat. Whenever it came inside, the cat considered it to be food time. Riley liked to show the cat who was boss. He put on the kettle and fussed with coffee and milk, attending to his own needs.

"Wait your turn, Ginge."

The cat responded with a tail swish and a curt miaow indicating limited tolerance for this sort of behaviour. Ginger Puss followed Riley as he carried out his caretaking tasks, but then would disappear for hours on end, with no indication as to where he had been. Riley suspected that the cat occasionally left the building when the roller door to the basement carpark was opened. He was of the view Ginger probably found someone else to supervise.

Riley flopped down on the couch intending to watch the evening news. He liked to monitor local and world events. He read the online sites, but preferred to sit back and be told what was happening. He moved a pile of clothes aside, unearthing the remote. *Bugger.* The clothes made him remember. The other half of the washing still hung outside.

It was probably soaked through again, so there wasn't much point bringing it in. On the other hand, it could be windy on the roof top. With weather like this the washing would be at the mercy of the elements and might be blown away. Riley didn't have clothing he could afford to lose.

The clothesline was a piece of wire with one end attached to the flag pole and the other connected to a hook attached to the wall of the flat. It wasn't much of a debate. He sighed and levered himself off the low, saggy couch, using the side arm for support.

A baseball cap hung from the hook behind the door. Riley jammed it onto his head, opened the door, and peered outside. Although sheltered by the doorway and technically still inside, the wind whipped the rain against his face. He assessed the weather and the speed at which he needed to move. Heavy clouds blanketed the sky, limiting visibility. Even the lights from Southern Cross Tower were dimmed by the rain.

While he debated, the clouds shifted allowing a glimmer of light to penetrate from the shielded moon. It provided a band of semi-light over the cityscape. A movement caught his eye. Probably shadows. Boxing shadows. It looked like three men on the roof top of the neighbouring Institute Building.

Strange. They were engaged in a weird dance. Who would be out there on the roof in weather like this?

He peered through the rain, willing his eyes to focus. Two. It was only two figures. The clouds closed in again and the boxing shadows were gone. He watched a moment longer but couldn't see anything else. Most likely there had been nothing to see in the first place. Just shadows. He looked back at the clothesline, with his clothes doing their own boxing dance. Too late. Too wet. He shut the door.

2 What Happened?

SIRENS WAILED IN the street below. Riley groaned. The wake-up call was all too frequent. He rolled over and reviewed the coming day. Nothing special on the agenda. Check if there was any damage from last night, wash the bins, scrub the front steps. Usual stuff. He threw back the covers and eased himself out of bed.

He opened the door of the flat and stepped outside to assess the impact of the storm. Small puddles of water lay on the uneven surface of his outdoor area. A wet muddy smell rose from the streets below. Patches of clear sky indicated the night's storm had blown over. The washing on the line hung limply. It should dry throughout the day.

He stretched, easing the cricks in his shoulders before picking up the mop and bucket and one of his pot plants. The storm had sent them flying during the night. The strands of the mop head were wet and dirty. Time to replace it. Like the mattress. He told himself that most mornings.

Phoebe opened her curtains to her balcony door of her apartment over on Mortimer House, with her shape fleetingly discernible as she passed across the window. "Morning Phoebe." he bellowed across the gap. Sometimes she waved, but not today. Probably hadn't heard him; more focused on the morning news rather than the immediate world beyond her enclave.

Ginger rubbed against his legs, weaving figure eights.

"Okay, mate." Riley reached down to scratch the cat between the ears. Ginger rose on hind legs, presenting his head for the rub while supporting himself with one paw braced against Riley's leg. As he complied, Riley's gaze wandered to the rooftop of the Institute Building. Whatever he'd seen last night, or thought he'd seen, there was no evidence anyone had been there in the rain. The parapet obscured his vision anyway. There was no sign of Winston. He was probably still asleep in his own rooftop flat. He was never an early riser.

Ginge gave an insistent yowl. He returned inside, with the cat hard on his heels. He threw a handful of dry cat biscuits in the bowl and before flicking the switch on the kettle. He didn't wait for it to boil, but jumped under the shower, towelling himself dry and trailing wet footprints on the kitchen floor when he returned to the kitchen. The water was still hot enough to pour over his teabag. While it brewed, he grabbed the milk from the fridge and topped up the mug.

"This'll tide me over too," he muttered to the cat, who glanced up briefly and then returned to chasing the remaining biscuits around the bowl. Riley carried the mug back to the bedroom and put it on the bedside table, while he pulled on his jeans and t-shirt.

The day was divided into units of activity and started with the *before* tasks. These were the jobs he did before the tenants arrived for the day. He jogged down the stairs to the level below and then took the elevator to the ground floor and unlocked the solid front door. Two granite steps led down to the footpath. The bundle of daily papers sat there, but that wasn't all. The steps were covered with a layer of congealing vomit. Regurgitated pizza perhaps? A discarded cigarette packet sat on the bottom step. Riley looked around, but the perpetrator had long gone. What would he have done anyway if a suspicious-looking person still lurked? Demand they clean it up? Yeah, like that would work.

The two Ferals sat propped against a planter box in the street, but there was no point in asking them anything. As he watched, Alex took one last drag on a cigarette tightly pinched between thumb and forefinger and ground it into the dirt in the planter box. It was one butt of many. No wonder the poor bloody plants never thrived.

The Ferals didn't look in his direction. They never did, not openly, unless it was to sneer. A stench rose off the steps. Trying to only breathe through his mouth, Riley scooped up the cigarette packet. The wheelie bins for the building sat on the edge of the footpath. He raised the lid of one a fraction and peered in. It might hold the rest of the pizza, and if so, he didn't want to know. They hadn't been emptied. No pizza, but there was the empty box, and a coke can, as well as general office rubbish.

That wasn't all. Something protruded from under the cardboard box. Shoving the box aside, he found a pair of functional leather gloves. They could be interesting. Riley dropped the cigarette packet in and fished the gloves out. They looked good. He could always use more work gloves. They were sticky. Probably from the dregs seeping out of the coke can. Riley stuffed one in each back pocket.

Taking care to avoid the puking mess, he picked up the newspapers and dumped them on the reception desk and unlocked the door to the utility room, tucked away behind the lift well. He uncoiled a hose and connected it to the tap before dragging the nozzle end through the terrazzo hallway to the front door. He directed a jet of water at the offending deposit, chasing lumps over the footpath towards the gutter.

The final clean-up had to be with a mop and bucket. As he worked, he whisper-sang the *Monday, Monday* song from the Mamas and the Papas. He did this most Monday mornings and sometimes when it wasn't Monday. Some days could have been *Friday on My Mind* by the Easybeats. The Monday lyrics sort of stuck with him. Both tracks were from his mother's record collection, still sitting in pristine covers beside her turntable.

Oh, Monday mornin' you gave me no warnin' of what was to be...

He looked up once towards the Ferals and thought they were smirking. That'd be right. Couldn't be sure though. If he was, he might turn the hose on them. He wouldn't really, but there was satisfaction in thinking about it.

He wound up the hose and dragged it back inside. That left the polishing. He sprayed and buffed the door handles and the brass plate on the wall beside the front door. He stood back and surveyed his handiwork. It was a matter of professional pride that for a while at least, they were gleaming and fingerprint free.

Ginger waited by the door on the rooftop when he emerged from the stairwell. The elevator only rose to the top tenanted floor of the building. A flight of stairs took him to the rooftop and his flat.

Pulling the gloves from his pocket, he threw them on the table. The cat followed him inside and watched as Riley soaped and rinsed his hands and then dried them. The tip of his tail twitched, indicating impatience.

Riley grabbed his wallet from the dresser, and after opening the door, held it wide to allow the cat to exit. Ginger bounced down the stairs behind him, and then rubbed against his legs as they waited for the elevator to respond to their call. It was a journey often taken, and the cat stalked into the cabin when it arrived with the assurance of a seasoned traveller.

Back down on street level, he locked the door behind them both, and looked around before stepping down onto the footpath. He couldn't see the Ferals. They must have disappeared down whatever hole they sheltered in through the day. You never knew when they were going to show up again. There was something about them that made Riley uncomfortable. Sneaky. Watchful. Unnerving.

He pushed open the door of the Daily Bean, occupying the ground floor retail space of Blenheim House.

"Morning Riley," Bruno called with offensive cheeriness from behind the hissing coffee machine. "Flat white and poached eggs on toast?"

"What else?" Riley asked, "and the usual for Ginger."

The early morning crowd sat hunched over at their usual tables. Riley nodded a greeting and grabbed a copy of the paper from the rack by the door before making his way to a table in the window. From that vantage point, he could keep an eye on the building and any early morning deliveries needing him to unlock the front door. The regular drivers knew where to find him, but sometimes a rookie who didn't know the ropes.

Ginger did his rounds of the café, pausing for head rubs, and checking under the chairs in case anything edible had been dropped. There was the chance that someone would slip a snippet of bacon off their plate or perhaps a bit of sausage. When Bruno carried the mug of coffee and the bowl of milk to Riley's table, the cat made a beeline for him. It was a regular ritual.

"Thought you might be washed off the roof last night. That was some storm. I expected the gutters to overflow."

"In that case, you would've been at more risk than me," said Riley. "This place would have been flooded out first."

"Perhaps. The building has leaks all over the place." This was called over his shoulder as he returned behind the counter. "It's a wonder that fleabag of yours didn't drown."

The cat's tail twitched as though aware of the disparaging reference, but it didn't look up from its bowl. Riley resumed reading the paper, with some relief. He didn't have a lot of time for general chat. He had skimmed it and reached the Sudoku by the time Bruno returned with his eggs.

"Lotta noise this morning. Sirens and cars—musta been a bit of a rumble somewhere."

Riley pushed his paper aside to make room for the plate. "Probably. There are always more accidents when it rains. People don't slow down."

He was pleased when Bruno didn't stay to chat, but merely agreed with a scrunched-up face and a nod before hurrying back to his station. The morning crowd needed feeding.

The eggs were good. Bruno's wife, Maria rarely emerged from the kitchen, preferring to stay behind the scene. She was a good cook, and one of the reasons Riley often had his breakfast in the café. Only on weekdays. The Daily Bean, in spite of its name, was not open on weekends.

"Did ya hear about last night?"

Riley looked up, but knew who it would be. Winston plopped into the seat opposite, keyed up with the excitement of someone who had a story to tell. He didn't wait for Riley's response.

"Someone jumped from the top of my building. The garbos found the body early this morning. The laneway's all roped off and full of police. The garbage truck's still there."

So that was why the bins hadn't been emptied. Riley cleaned up the last of the yoke with a crust of toast. "That's a bit sad. Who was it?"

"Dunno. Nobody's talkin'. The media are staking the place out."

"Ghouls. They should leave the poor bloke alone." He looked up. "I suppose it was a bloke?"

"Dunno. Like I said, nobody's talkin'."

"Didn't you hear or see anything?"

"Not a thing. I was inside with the telly on. Why would I be outside on a night like that?"

There wasn't an answer to that question so Riley let it slide.

Bruno called from behind the counter. "Winston, my friend—are you ordering today?"

"Nah, mate. Already had my Weetbix. Just dropped in to speak to Riley." He stood up, pushing his chair back in against the table. "You still on for tonight?"

"Tonight?" Riley stared blankly, his mind still on Winston's news.

"The barbecue at Phoebe's; her birthday."

"Oh, shit yes. I hadn't forgotten, just a bit distracted. I guess that rules out tonight's yoga class." He pushed his plate aside. Ginger had finished his milk, and sat where morning sun hit the window, engaged in a fastidious washing routine. "Foul weather last night. Hope it stays clear for this evening."

"It will, according to the forecast. Don't forget to bring something. I always like those meatballs you make." In truth, Winston liked any food that was free and he hadn't made or bought himself. "I'll see ya t'night."

Winston ambled out, either to find someone else with whom to impart his momentous news, or to start on his own morning chores. He was building manager for the Institute Building, colloquially known as just the Institute. It housed a similar mix of tenants as did Blenheim House, except that several floors were leased to Excellerate Training Academy, a privately registered training organisation, mostly focussed on international students. Winston lived in a rooftop flat also.

Riley stood, reaching for his wallet. He knew how much the breakfast cost and carefully counted out the exact amount in notes and coins. He stepped up to the counter and poured the money into Bruno's outstretched hand. Bruno didn't bother to count it.

"And the milk's on the house," he said, as he did most mornings. "'bout time that cat earned his keep and caught some mice around here."

Usually, Riley had a retort along the lines that if Bruno looked after the place better, there wouldn't be any mice to catch, but he didn't bother today. His mind was still on Winston's news. He unlocked the door to Blenheim House and let Ginger inside. Locking it again, he walked down to the corner of Hindmarsh Street and peered around it towards the lane at the side of the Institute.

Winston was right. The street was full of police and media vehicles. The entrance of the laneway was cordoned off with blue and white striped tape, and a couple of police officers stood guard. Winston was in the crowd. He spoke to a couple of window washers who had been working on the building the day before and had turned up for work again.

An earnest-looking reporter was doing a live broadcast, with the cameraman alternately zooming in on her face and sweeping over the crowd, resting on the policemen.

"The distressing scene was discovered shortly after daylight," the woman said. "There were no witnesses and police are still making their enquiries."

Walking down to the entrance of the lane and the restriction imposed by the police tape, Riley pushed past the crowd of onlookers. Surely it wasn't one of theirs; not one of the Skywalkers? "What happened?" he asked one of the policemen standing guard by the tape. "Do you know who it is?"

The man was disinterestedly officious. "Nothing to see here, sir. You might as well go home."

No, there wasn't anything to see last night either. I didn't see anything. Or did I? Riley debated saying something, but he wasn't sure what he saw and even if he did see something, he couldn't identify anyone. They were only shadows. Another reporter bustled up, searching for information, and the momentum was lost. The last thing he wanted was media attention.

As he left, the coroner's van arrived. Time to make himself scarce. Whatever he thought he saw last night, he didn't want to see the results this morning. Not just after breakfast. Not keen to get caught up in discussion with Winston again, he turned and made his way back to the front of Blenheim House.

When he let himself in, Ginger made his displeasure known at being abandoned and left in the foyer area all alone.

"Sorry Ginge. Couldn't take you with me—not to something like that. C'mon, we've got work to do."

The doorbell rang and the first of the morning deliveries arrived. Riley signed for them and piled them behind the reception desk. Diane would distribute them later to the various offices. That taken care of, he slipped down to his workshop in the basement to pick-up some tools and plumbing gear. There was a leaking tap in the kitchen on the fourth floor.

By the time he'd fixed that, the receptionist had arrived and was placing newspapers in pigeon holes and taking care of the parcels. Diane worked for Blenheim Pastoral, who occupied the first four floors, but she provided a basic concierge service for the tenants on the upper floors as well.

"A lot of activity in the street," she said. "Must have been a drama of some sort. Did you see anything last night?"

"Not a thing. It was a miserable storm in case you hadn't noticed. I was firmly ensconced inside.'

"I don't blame you. Don't forget the electrician is coming today. He'll want access to each of the floors and a parking space in the basement." She glared at Ginger Puss. "What is that animal doing down here? You know he's not allowed in the reception area, or anywhere other than your flat, for that matter."

"He's just going." Riley pressed the elevator button. Best he took Ginger home. He'd want a snooze now anyway.

He didn't make his way onto the street again before mid-morning. Driven by morbid curiosity and a fear of what he might have seen, he edged his way towards the corner and into the neighbouring street. The media and police cars had gone. So had the police tape.

There was something ghoulish about staring at the scene of a tragic death. Riley started walking down the street as though he had somewhere specific to go. As he passed the entrance to the lane, he glanced in that direction. As lanes went, it was unremarkable. A road sign on the narrow footpath advised parking was not permitted. A couple of wheelie bins sat at odd angles as they straddled the edge of the kerb, their red and yellow lids providing relief against the shades of grey. A trough of straggling geraniums sat on one window ledge. A sign fixed to the side of the Institute declared it to be Hayes Lane.

A council truck parked there, and an employee hosed down the surface. It was the truck used for watering street trees. A frothing tide of water with a pink tinge gushed down the gutter towards the grated drain at the entrance to the lane.

Riley paused, fixated by the scene in front of him. The council worker nodded in his direction. They knew each other by sight, both being city workers.

"This is what it all comes down to, mate." the worker said. "Just a stain on the pavement, someone hoses it all off and then you're gone. Nothing to indicate you were ever there." He spoke with morose satisfaction.

"Do you know who it was? Did he jump?"

"He was gone by the time I got here, so I didn't see him. No idea who he was." The man shrugged. "Perhaps his missus left him, or he gambled away all his money. Why else would someone do something like that?"

Riley had no idea. As the water in the gutter disappeared down the drain, glittering fragments caught his eye. He peered closer. They were thin pieces of glass. The worker saw him looking.

"His glasses. They smashed. Bits of glass where he fell. Odd that."

"Why? What's odd about that?"

"I'm no expert in these things, but this is the third jumper since I've been with Council." He cleared his throat importantly. "Usually, jumpers take their glasses off first. This bloke left his on. He could see what was coming."

3 Phoebe's Birthday

RILEY GLANCED AT his watch. If he was quick, he could dash to the Woolworths supermarket and get some minced beef and pork before the electrician arrived. He could make the meatballs at lunchtime. Shopping for ingredients the day before had slipped his mind. He grabbed a shopping bag hanging behind the door of his flat and jogged down the stairs to the next level and stepped into the elevator. No need to lock his door. Nobody else ever came up to the rooftop. Only him and Ginge.

The elevator did its usual groany thing as it approached, dinging loudly when it reached his floor. The elevators were serviced each year, and the mechanic assured him they were perfectly safe but as they jerked and trembled on their vertical journey, he often wondered where the mechanic got his qualifications. Once, the cabin stopped about thirty centimetres higher than it should have, and the door refused to open. An elderly couple were in the cabin with him, and the man had tried to prize the doors open with his walking stick. Riley had already pressed the alarm button when the elevator suddenly jerked and completed the last portion of the decent. On returning to his flat, he had puffed his way up the stairs from the ground floor instead of risking the elevator.

"Back soon," he called to Diane as he dashed through the foyer.

"But the electrician—" she called.

The door slammed behind him and he didn't hear any more. If he stopped to explain, she'd only grumble at him and that would waste time. He didn't answer to Diane, though she behaved as though he did.

He took off at a jog down the Mall, dodging groups of tourists and people who ambled along the footpath while staring at their screens. He saw the Ferals, Jodie and Alex, sitting on a corner behind a cardboard sign declaring them to be homeless and asking for any spare change. Jodie had put on her most woebegone look, and Alex stared at the ground, as though lost in the depths of dismal depression.

A group of Asian tourists skirted around them, but a middle-aged couple paused briefly and dropped some coins into the take-away coffee cup that sat beside the sign. It was akin to extortion, but Riley didn't have time to dwell on that. He sprinted past and did his best to ignore them.

The inevitable cluster of children played on the pigs—four brass sculptures that attracted delighted attention. While the kids clambered over or rode the pigs, their parents snapped photos on their phones, or else retreated to the seats installed around the Mall planter boxes and stared at their screens. The elm trees in the planter boxes provided the shade.

On any other day, Riley would take his time, absorbing the ambience of the street scene. He reached the supermarket, pushed his way down the escalator past those who rode serenely, and managed to exit the facility with his bagged mince in just over five minutes. He had the same pedestrian-dodging obstacle race on his way back to Blenheim House.

The electrician stood in the foyer scrolling on his phone as Riley huffed back through the front door.

"About time." Diane said. "I had to allocate a parking bay myself."

"I'm sure you did that very well, Diane. Thank you." Riley tried not to roll his eyes and directed his best benign smile in her direction. Diane's harping could drag anyone down.

He turned to the electrician. "Follow me. We'll start at the bottom and work our way up... or would you prefer to work your way down?"

The man looked bemused and shrugged his shoulders before bending down to pick up his tool kit and hoisting his ladder onto his shoulder. "Whatever. It's all the same to me, mate."

Riley decided to start at the top, because then he could slip up the last flight of stairs to his flat and put the meat in the fridge. The smoke alarms in each strata office and in the passages needed their annual check. Some of the offices were locked and Riley had to use his master key on those to give the man access. Once the tradie was established on the top floor, Riley left him to it and dashed up the stairs to the flat.

Winston was right. Meatballs were his speciality. He didn't need to check the recipe. Each batch was slightly different, depending on what spices and condiments he had on hand. This time he added a dessertspoon of French mustard to the mix, plus some chopped basil he picked from the pot at his back door.

When people asked him for the recipe or wanted to know what he put in his mix, he would tap the side of his nose with the pointer finger of his right hand and say in an exaggerated whisper, "State secret. If I told you, I'd have to kill you."

The response would be a bemused laugh, but some people still persisted. "No, really—what's that underlying flavour? Is it a dash of brandy?"

Riley would give a practised enigmatic smile while raising one eyebrow as if to say, *what is it, I wonder?* and would either change the topic of conversation or would walk off. The regulars at the Skywalker events had learned not to ask anymore, but Riley took note of the suggested ingredients for future reference.

He made the batch while the electrician had his lunch break. Because the evening's event was to be a barbecue, he didn't have to cook them, which was a relief. He could take a container of meatballs ready to grill.

Ginge wanted to be in on the action. He'd been sleeping on his favourite sofa cushion, but lifted his head as the lovely smell of fresh mincemeat hit his nose. The transition from supine feline to prowling, yowling cat happened in a microsecond. Riley anticipated this and had reserved a spoonful of un-spiced mixture to give Ginge a lunchtime treat. The ginger puss was not keen on French mustard.

The gloves he'd picked up that morning lay where he'd thrown them earlier. After washing the bowl and utensils he'd used on making the meatballs, he gave the gloves a quick clean-up. He didn't want to immerse them, but sprayed them with a liquid cleanser before scrubbing them and rinsing under hot running water. He left them out in the sunshine to dry.

Before checking on the electrician's progress, Riley supervised the delivery of a new massage table for the therapist on level six, having reserved one of the lift cars for this purpose. Then he made arrangements for the annual steam cleaning of the hall carpets.

Early afternoon after the electrician left, Diane stopped him as he tried to slip past her desk. She leaned forward in her seat and eyeballed him, as though daring him to try walking past her.

"Why didn't you tell me? I had to hear from the postman that a man died around the corner this morning."

"You know I'm not one for salacious gossip," Riley said in his best holier-than-thou voice. "Anyway, I thought you would have seen all the commotion on your way to work."

"Well, I didn't. I walk to the office from the other direction; you know that." Her voice took on a curious note, almost wheedling. "Do you know who he was? Why did he jump?"

"I've no idea who he was, and who says he jumped? Perhaps he just slipped or was pushed."

Diane snorted. "You've been watching too many B-grade movies. Nobody gets pushed off buildings around here. It's just not done." She patted a stray hair into place.

"You're probably right." It was not a conversation Riley wanted to prolong. Too much time with Diane always made him feel as though life was being sucked out of him. He escaped to his workshop in the basement, wiping finger prints

21

off the brass plate behind the lift buttons as he went. The cloth that hung from his back pocket was always handy for that.

The workroom was his refuge. If he was in there, he was working and nobody would challenge that. It was where he kept his tools, a trolley, and useful bits and pieces. Sometimes he could repair things in the workshop. That was step one. Consulting a technician was step two.

Now he perched on his stool in front of the work bench, and pulled a door lock towards him. The mechanism jammed occasionally and perhaps with the use of some lubricant, he could get it working smoothly again. Daily tasks had diverted his thoughts from the incident that morning, but Diane's questions reminded him of his own confusion.

Why would the man choose such bad weather in which to jump? Had he jumped, or had he slipped on a wet surface? That was unlikely, because there was a parapet around the edge of the roof. It would be difficult to simply slip over. Why was he on the roof in the rain anyway? It hadn't been a light drizzle. It was a drenching deluge.

Then there was the question he hadn't wanted to think about. What had he seen last night in that brief moonlit window of time? Had there been more people on the roof? He tried to recall the detail of those dancing shadows, but it had only been a glimpse and even then, he wasn't sure what he saw. It had probably been imagination and the whole thing was a weird coincidence. He abandoned the sticking lock and slipped back upstairs for an afternoon cup of coffee. The lift bypassed the reception area.

The GPO clock struck six as Riley punched in the after-hours access code to Mortimer House. The storm from the evening before had blown over, but he carried a jacket with him in case the weather turned cold. The temperature at Skywalker level was usually cooler than ground level. He swiped the security pass in the lift allowing him access to the penthouse. Phoebe's son, Charles, insisted that she give Riley the pass in case of emergencies. If Riley didn't see her curtains opened by nine in the morning, he could slip around the corner to Mortimer House and do a welfare check

Footsteps approached in response to his rap on the door of the penthouse. It swung open to reveal Winston.

"I came early to see if Phoebe needed a helping hand," he said by way of greeting. Usually, his help entailed opening the drinks.

Charles and his wife Christine had arrived also. Charles poked at the barbecue and Christine was making a salad, but both looked up when Winston let him in. Christine gave him a brief smile and waved her hands at him indicating they were too messy for contact. Charles strode in through the door leading from the balcony with outstretched hand.

"Riley—good to see you. I hope you're more expert with this grill of mother's than I am."

Riley shook the man's hand, surprised at the enthusiastic greeting. He knew Charles, but not well. *You'd think a dentist would have some experience at handling a pair of tongs and a few sausages. Surely these eastern suburbs types had barbecues all the time?*

"I don't cook on one often," he said. "There doesn't seem much point when I'm only cooking for one, but I'm happy to

23

help." He prized the lid from the container holding the meatballs and put them on the small table beside the grill. "At least I know how to cook these." He looked around. "Where's your mother?"

"Here I am." The voice came from behind him. Spinning around, he almost knocked Phoebe over. She had approached quietly, and was so thin it would be easy to knock her flying.

"Phoebe—happy birthday! I've brought you a present." He held out a medium-sized pot of mixed herbs which she could grow on her balcony. It contained chives, basil and parsley, and he'd got around the gift-wrapping requirement by tying a length of wide red ribbon around the rim.

"Thank you, dear. That's lovely. Put it down over there."

Phoebe pointed to a location outside, clearly not wanting to handle the heavy pot herself. She looked frail with her slight figure, but she was always immaculately groomed, with her hair swept up into a French Roll giving her an air of sophistication. She held herself as though wearing a back brace, and would give people a deathly stare if they upset her or overstepped one of her boundaries. This evening, she wore a pair of earrings which Riley guessed featured diamonds. Probably a present from Harrison Mortimer.

He carefully placed the pot of herbs where she indicated, and looked around. Winston had followed him onto the balcony, and now he leaned over the parapet, looking down towards the roof on the Institute. That building was lower, allowing him to see it clearly. He looked lost in thought, and Riley left him that way. Who wanted to know what went on in Winston's head?

"Would you like a drink? I'm having a sherry." Phoebe gestured towards the kitchen bench inside, where he could see an opened bottle of sparkling wine and also a red. "I have beer if you would prefer."

Charles had a glass of red and Winston clutched a stubbie of beer. It looked like a wild night, as much as a seventy-sixth birthday ever would be.

"I'll have a beer; thanks Phoebe."

She fetched him a Corona from the fridge but left him to open it.

"How have you spent your birthday?" he asked by way of making conversation.

"They don't make much difference, once you get past the first fifty," she replied. "I had a lovely lunch with a friend at the Boatshed Restaurant down by the river, and then this afternoon I attended a matinee performance at the town hall put on by the Adelaide Symphony Orchestra."

"Sounds like you had a good day then. Anyone else coming tonight?"

"Lucinda, my granddaughter is dropping in, but otherwise it's just us. I didn't invite any other Skywalkers. It's not such a big deal."

Riley could have sworn he heard Christine snort, but when he looked in her direction, she was focussed on shredding a cabbage. Phoebe stepped out onto the balcony to supervise her son.

"*Everything's* a big deal with you, Phoebe."

The words were muttered into the coleslaw, but Riley caught them. The relationship between Phoebe and Christine was often strained. Much as he admired Phoebe, he recognised that having her as a mother-in-law would not be easy.

"Can I top up your drink, Christine?" The champagne flute on the benchtop was almost empty.

She looked up at him and unexpectedly smiled. "Thank you, Riley. That would be lovely. Not too much mind. I don't want to get tiddly."

That could be interesting, but he topped up her glass and then went out onto the balcony to watch the action out there. Winston was giving Charles advice on the art of cooking the perfect sausage, which revolved around the position in which they should be placed on the hotplate, and when and how to turn them.

"There's a science to it, you see," Winston said. "I've cooked a few sausages in my time, so I've become a sort of sausage expert."

Charles probably didn't look as impressed as he was expected to, but he appeared to recognise an opportunity when it arose.

"That's fantastic, Winston." He shoved the tongs in his adviser's direction. "You need to show me how it's done. I recognise your superior knowledge about the fine art of grilling a snag."

Charles gulped a mouthful of his red and turned towards Riley with a gleeful wink. "Those meatballs should go on now. I'm sure Winston will know how to cook those."

"Absolutely." Riley opened the container and offered it to Winston. "Make sure they're cooked right through. Yell out when you want another beer."

"Hey, I'm not a cook," Winston protested.

The two men just laughed and stepped back, leaving Winston in charge. Whether the heat of the barbecue or annoyance caused his red face, Riley couldn't be sure. Serve him right. Winston was always proclaiming expertise in something. Now he could prove it.

The sizzling smell had already begun to tantalise the taste buds, when the downstairs intercom buzzed. Phoebe pressed the connection button, and Lucinda's image appeared on the tiny screen.

"Hi Grandma. Beam me up!"

A few moments later, the elevator on the penthouse level pinged and the door flew open to reveal the young woman with another figure hovering behind her.

"I hope you don't mind. I brought Finn with me. We're going onto a fundraiser for Canteen this evening and it was easier to bring him with me, rather than arrange to meet up later."

Without waiting for an answer, she bounded up to Pheobe and hugged her before thrusting a gift-wrapped present at her grandmother. "Happy birthday, Grandma."

"Thank you, darling. I'll open it in a moment. Aren't you going to introduce me to your friend?"

"Of course." Lucinda turned to the young man, and seizing him by the hand, drew him forward. "Grandma, this is Finley Thornton. Finn, this is my grandmother, Phoebe Eilish."

"Pleased to meet you, Mrs Eilish. Happy birthday" He held out a bouquet of roses in peachy creamy colours.

27

"Thank you—how lovely," Phoebe said, burying her nose in the blooms and inhaling deeply. "Just Phoebe will do. I've never been missus anything."

"Phoebe it is. Luci has told me a lot about you, particularly your reputation as a pianist."

The older woman waved a dismissive hand. "That was all a long time ago. Nobody remembers me anymore."

Riley saw she stood a little straighter if that was possible, and knew she was pleased at the recognition. In one of her candid moments, she told him she still had regrets about giving up her career at the request of her lover. Such was the power of love, and Harrison Mortimer had been the love of her life.

While Phoebe rummaged in a cupboard for a vase for the flowers, Lucinda introduced Finn to her parents. Christine wiped her hands on a towel before extending one, and Charles pumped the young man's hand with an alpha grip.

After the flowers were arranged to her satisfaction, Phoebe turned her attention to her granddaughter's parcel. It contained a beautiful pashmina in shades of lilac and soft greens. She wrapped it around her shoulders.

"Thank you, Lucinda. The breeze gets a bit nippy out on the balcony. It's just what I needed."

The colours sat well with her white hair and blue eyes, which had never lost their intensity and sparkle. With drinks in hand, they all moved outside to the balcony where Winston still performed maestro actions with the barbecue tongs. Riley wasn't sure on the nature of the relationship between the young couple, but assumed the association had begun only recently. Charles drew Finn towards the parapet for some friendly grilling, not of the barbecue variety.

"So, you and Lucinda are going on to the Canteen fundraiser? Do you have a strong interest in childhood cancers?"

"Not from personal experience, but otherwise, yes." Finn replied. "It's a worthy cause, but my father is sponsoring the event and it's expected that the family attend."

"Does your father have connections with the Association?"

Finn shrugged. "He supports a variety of causes and he considers this one to be particularly worthy."

"Is sponsorship a personal thing, or is it through his company?"

"Don't be so nosey, Dad," Lucinda interrupted. "Finn's father is Tray Thornton. He has a successful business and likes to give back to the community."

Tray? Does she mean Tremaine Thornton? Lucinda's moving in elevated circles. Riley knew the general story. The family had come to Australia during the post-war migration boom and had worked hard and done well. Finn's grandfather had started with a corner store and progressively built up a portfolio of retail properties.

Tray Thornton had expanded into commercial and industrial real estate, and the family fortunes grew accordingly. Their philanthropic activities were often reported in the media. Finn appeared to be a polite young man, so perhaps the family's fortunes hadn't promoted a heightened sense of his own importance.

Charles' eyebrows elevated slightly at learning of Finn's background. "Good of you to make time in your busy schedule then to attend my mother's birthday celebration."

29

Finn's smile was without guile. "I knew it was important to Luci, so of course we made time for it."

"Done, I reckon." Winston turned off the burners and brought a platter laden with meatballs, sausages and chicken kebabs to the table. Christine had set the balcony table earlier, and she now brought out bowls of salad and a loaf of sour dough bread, already sliced. Riley noted that the settings included a place for Finn. Christine must have been forewarned he was coming, even if nobody else was.

Charles bustled around with the drinks, topping up glasses and fetching Winston another beer. Riley opted to swap to red wine, now that the meal was about to start. Luci and Finn requested a small glass of sparkling wine, with water on the side. They still had a long night ahead of them.

Charles remained standing at the opposite end of the table to where his mother was seated. "I'd like to propose a toast. To the woman who raised me, and kept me on the straight and narrow all my life. May she have many more years. To Phoebe."

"To Phoebe," they chanted, raising their glasses initially and then clinking them with everyone else around the table.

The grilled offerings tasted as good as they smelled, and conversation became disjointed while they filled their plates with selections from the platter.

"I'm surprised you didn't bring that cat with you, Riley," Phoebe said. "He would have enjoyed what we're eating."

"I'm not sure where he was when I left," Riley said. "He leads his own life, and visits other people in the building. You're right though, he would have enjoyed it. Perhaps I'll take him a small doggy bag, or should that be a pussy bag?"

Charles gave him a withering look, and Finn looked bemused.

"We're talking about Riley's cat," Phoebe explained. "He turned up one day and never left. He follows Riley around like a shadow, and sometimes comes visiting as well. I'm not sure if the animal knows it's a cat. Its behaviour is more dog-like."

"Pest-like if you ask me," said Winston. "I found a dead bird on the doorstep of the Institute last week. My bet is that animal was responsible. Made a horrible mess, it did. Feathers all over the place."

He speared another meatball on his fork and smothered it with tomato sauce. "That isn't all that turned up dead, either."

"Is this dinner table conversation?" Christine asked in a resigned tone. Winston was unlikely to be deterred, once he got going.

He glanced at her dismissively before turning his attention back to Finn and Luci. "We had a jumper this morning. A bloke threw himself off the roof of my building."

"Luci paused in the middle of serving herself some coleslaw. "That's terrible! The poor man. What made him do a thing like that?"

"There are a few theories. I heard he had a lot of debt, but…" Winston shrugged, indicating that the jury was out on that issue.

"Do you now know who it was?" Riley asked.

"I do, as a matter of fact. It was David Barton. He is, or rather *was* the Finance Officer for Excellerate. They lease several floors in the building and run the training college there."

There was a moment's silence while they digested this news. Riley tried to recall if he'd ever met the man. He knew various people to nod to from the adjoining building, but didn't know all their names. Perhaps there would be a photo in the papers.

"I thought I saw something last night," he said hesitantly. "During the storm; I thought I saw some people on the roof."

"You mean my roof?" Winston demanded. "How would anyone get up there? Access is restricted and I didn't see or hear anything."

"I don't know. It was dark, and rain was bucketing down. It was only a glimpse but I thought I saw a couple of people moving around. It looked like they were fighting. I can't be sure."

He turned to Phoebe. "Did you see anything, perhaps when you were shutting your curtains?"

"No, I didn't," she answered slowly. "I was looking at the sky rather than at the city and the surrounds. The storm was horrific. It came on so suddenly. I don't think I would have seen anything in that downpour."

"You must have imagined it," said Charles. "Shadows plus imagination can encourage you to see all sorts of things. Did you have a drink before this?"

Had he had a drink! What a ridiculous question. Riley ignored it. How had an artistic, flamboyant woman like Phoebe managed to have a conservative dentist for a son? Perhaps he took after Harrison Mortimer.

"I'd keep that to yourself, son," said Winston. "Like Charles said, it must have been shadows. If there was anything to be seen or heard, I would have seen or heard it, and I didn't."

He eyed the platter of meat, as though contemplating snaffling the last kebab. "The last thing we need is officials poking around. They'll start restricting who can live on the rooftops, and impose all manner of health and safety regulations. We don't want that, do we? They'll threaten our way of life."

A light breeze rippled over the group, sending a couple of paper serviettes flying. Phoebe wrapped her new pashmina a little more snuggly around her shoulders. Riley looked over at his building, wondering if he could see Ginger Puss on the rooftop. The exterior light wasn't on, so the outside of his flat was in darkness.

Then he looked towards the roof of the Institute. It was a little lower than Mortimer House but he couldn't see much of the roof from this angle. Winston was right. There was nothing to tell.

"Grandma, we have leave soon, but could you play something for Finn before we go? After everything I've told him, he's looking forward to hearing one of your pieces," Luci wheedled.

Phoebe didn't need asking twice. She wiped her mouth with a serviette before jumping up. "Stay there, everyone. Have some more wine. You'll hear perfectly well from out here." She moved inside and soon after, the sound of rippling music was heard. It was not the storming crescendo Riley had heard the previous evening but was lighter and more tantalising.

"Claire de Lune," Charles said. "It was one of Debussy's better piano pieces."

"Did you bring your violin, Dad?" Luci asked.

"No, I didn't. I wasn't expecting to provide a musical recital tonight."

That discussion bemused Riley. He'd never considered Charles as having a musical side to him, but given who his mother was, it shouldn't be a revelation. The music ended, and they all clapped. Phoebe appeared in the doorway and gave a small bow.

"I hope you enjoyed that," she said to Finn. "There is still some life in my arthritic fingers."

"It was beautiful, Phoebe. Thank you for that special performance."

"Grandma, we must go. Save us some cake."

Luci pushed her chair back and moved around the table to embrace her grandmother. Finn followed and kissed the elderly lady on both cheeks. Phoebe flushed with pleasure. "Enjoy yourselves, you two. Thank you for coming."

There was a moment's silence after Finn and Luci shut the door behind them.

"He seems a nice young man," Christine remarked. "Very polite. That's quite refreshing today."

She fetched the cake from inside, but Phoebe insisted that singing Happy Birthday was not necessary. This was a relief to Riley, who hated singing unless in a large crowd where his efforts could be drowned out. Offers of port or Drambuie as well as coffee followed the cake.

It wrapped up what had been a pleasant evening. No storms, no dramas, and no dead men. That was how Riley liked it.

Shortly after ten, he made his farewells. Phoebe was ever the gracious hostess.

"Thank you for the herbs, dear. That was very thoughtful of you. Would you like to take some left-overs home for your cat?"

"It's a nice offer, but I'm sure you can put it to better use than Ginge."

Charles stepped forward with an offered handshake. "Thanks for keeping an eye out for mum. She's a bit isolated here."

Not really, Riley wanted to protest. *We Skywalkers look after our own. She's got a larger community than you realise.* With unspoken agreement, it wasn't discussed much with the Flat-earthers, as some of the others called them.

"My pleasure," he said. "Phoebe is company for me as well."

Christine offered him a cheek to kiss, before he made his way out the door and into the foyer. The journey down to ground level in the lift was quick. There was a dedicated lift to the penthouse, providing direct and secure access for Phoebe and her guests.

The after-hours door that Phoebe used slammed behind him, echoing in the street now largely devoid of traffic. The distance around the corner to his own building in Murray Street was short, but Riley paused for a moment in the doorway entrance and looked around. Checking the streets was a habit when out at night. You never knew who might be loitering and with what intent. Cities were like that.

He noticed a few people, but they were engrossed in clustered conversation or walking with purpose. None looked in his direction. He stepped out of the doorway and walked up Hindmarsh Street towards the corner with Murray Street. He passed the entrance of Hayes Lane, glancing down its length quickly as though there might still be something terrible to see. There wasn't.

4   You Dirty Rat

A BLEAK SKY greeted him the following morning. With a cup of tea clasped between his hands, Riley wandered to the wall around the rooftop, as he did most days. From here, he could survey the city and activity below. He took the temperature of the day by what he observed—the traffic, the horizon, and anything else he could see. He yawned and idly scratched his stubbly cheek while looking out over the view.

Ginge couldn't see over the wall, but he usually followed Riley around the roof top, sitting patiently at each stopping point and occasionally winding himself between Riley's legs. He added head-bumps to his routine this morning, reminding Riley of his presence and that it was time for food.

Riley bent down and scratched the cat's head between its ears. "What did your last slave die of, Ginge?"

The cat's only response was to emit a loud chirping purr, and after what he hoped was an acceptable period of petting, Riley resumed his inspection of the world at large.

The early morning air smelled fresh, unsullied by city traffic. Mostly, the street-level pollution didn't reach this height, and even on a bad day, the breeze soon dispersed it. A low haze sat on the horizon, giving a soft filter to the coast in one direction and the hills in the other. He could see a faint patch of blue in the sky to the north. Probably the view would clear by mid-morning.

Sometimes he saw Winston on his rooftop, and then they could exchange a morning wave. He always checked Phoebe's curtains, though sometimes they weren't opened until later in the morning. Hot air balloons occasionally drifted into view when the weather was favourable. They didn't float immediately above, but close enough that he could see the burner when it flared. They took off in the pre-dawn from the park lands east of the city, and travelled lazily over the skies as the sun rose.

Winston wasn't on his roof today, but a team of window washers was. They usually made an early start, while Winston dragged his feet in the mornings. In keeping with safety requirements, the men donned hard hats and secured themselves to the gantry with safety harnesses. Two of them clambered into the box, and descended to a lower level. The spotter stayed on the roof, occasionally calling out to his colleagues working below.

As Riley watched, the door to the stairwell opened and Winston ambled out. He engaged in chat with the spotter, and by his gestures towards the edge of the roof, coupled with occasional head shakes, Riley deduced that Winston was describing recent events. He pulled away from that side of the building, not wanting to be dragged into a cross-alley discussion about what happened.

Air-conditioning technicians scaled ladders on the roof of

the Colonial Hotel, edging their way across the corrugated roofing to where the units were installed. Riley watched their perilous journey for a while. What if they slipped? If they did, he didn't want to witness that. Jonathan, the manager from the hotel should have been supervising. One splatter for the week was enough.

He took the mug back inside and ran a comb through his hair, or what there was of it. In his teens, he had sported a mullet, but had trimmed the length at the back since then. It still reached his collar in a nod to his individual style. His pronounced widow's peak, showed more forehead than he liked. He took after his father on that score, but at least he had his mother's fine bone structure. He called to Ginge, and the two of them pattered down the stairs to the level below, where Riley pressed the button for the elevator. Time for breakfast.

The front steps were clean for a change. He picked up the bundle of newspapers and dumped them inside the door, before he and Ginge made their way to the Daily Bean. Bruno was busy behind the coffee machine, but a couple of the regulars nodded to him as he made his way to his usual table. They all knew not to sit there. He grabbed a copy of the morning paper from the rack as he passed and dropped it on his table before catching Bruno's eye with a raised eyebrow and a nod of his head.

"Riley, my friend. Are you having your usual or are you surprising me today?"

"Perhaps I'll have lobster tails, lightly braised in truffle oil, and with French beans sauteed with almond flakes on the side."

"What a pity, we're fresh out of truffle oil. Poached eggs

39

and toast coming up. And what about your furry mate? I suppose he wants lobster tails as well?"

"He's not fussy. He'll happily eat whatever you care to give him, as long as it isn't a vegetable."

Bruno snickered. "I'd better not give him soy milk then. Full fat dairy on its way."

Riley opened the paper and smoothed out the creases. He hated crinkled pages. The paper didn't contain a lot of news. Many people got their information online, but a few, like Riley, still looked for the print version. He skimmed the front page. More political mouthing off. Boring. He flipped past the latest accident statistics and wondered if there would be any mention of the jumper. There wasn't.

A headline caught his eye. '*City Soars to New Heights.*' What did that mean? He picked up the paper to read the fine print more clearly. According to the article, zoning changes were proposed for the sector of the CBD in which Blenheim House was located. Density allowances would be increased, permitting taller buildings to be built.

He lay the paper on the table and squinted out the window at as much of the city skyline as he could see. Increased density would result in pressure to demolish existing buildings, making way for new skyscrapers. That could be the death knell for older buildings like Blenheim House. It would be a disaster. His grandfather, if he were still alive, would be devastated.

Bruno appeared at his elbow with the plate of eggs and a mug of coffee. "Anything of interest in the paper? I never have time to read it myself."

"The usual. I haven't got far into it today. Nothing about

the incident yesterday."

"There wouldn't be. They don't usually report things like that. They might get a spate of copycat jumpers."

Riley looked at him askance. "That's a bizarre concept. Somebody jumped off a building today, so I might do it tomorrow?"

"It happens," Bruno insisted. "You're just not in that frame of mind. Anyway, I don't need to read about it. I already know."

Riley raised his eyebrows in silent question. Bruno glanced around the café to see who else was in hearing distance. He wiped his hands down the front of his apron, and then placed them on the table, leaning closer and speaking in a softer voice.

"It was David Barton… you know, the Financial Officer from Excellerate next door."

Riley did know that much, because Winston had mentioned his name the night before.

"He came in here sometimes. Nice bloke. I thought so, anyway. The way I heard it, he was having an affair and his wife found out. They had a big row, and she told her family, and they were going to sort him out. No-one messes with that lot. I reckon he jumped before he was pushed. They're a tight-knit mob. You don't cross them and expect to walk away. Barton must have been mad."

Riley wondered about the woman who inspired the man to take such a risk, assuming the rumour was true. The café door opened and several customers came in and stood expectantly by the coffee machine. Bruno edged away from the table. "People do strange things under pressure. Work calls."

He left Riley trying to digest this information as well as his eggs. It sounded a sad story. David Barton… He tried to put a face to the name. He must have seen him around… perhaps in the café? The thought sobered him.

"Oh, what a handsome cat. I didn't realise this was a cat café!"

Riley looked up to see a woman squatting beside Ginge, giving him a head rub. Ginge sniffed her hand inquiringly. Food was the cat's greater priority in the café. Probably there were laws about cats in hospitality establishments, so Riley just smiled. Easier than inviting controversy.

The woman rose and wandered over to the counter, leaving Riley free to return to the paper. He read the article about the zoning changes in greater detail while eating his breakfast. The reporter mentioned that a public meeting had been called, giving interested parties the opportunity to learn more and to register their comments. He recorded the time and date of the meeting on his phone, and folded the paper. He wanted to attend that meeting.

The street was busier when he and Ginge left the café. The morning buses disgorged city workers at the stops, and foot traffic had increased. That meant Diane would be at work soon. He'd spent too long with the paper. As he swiped his key fob over the electronic pad to open the front door, a voice hailed him from behind.

"Hear you had a bit of excitement the other night, mate."

He turned, and recognised the safety spotter for the window washers, currently working on the Institute.

"Not me. There's never much excitement in my life." The

door slid shut again, leaving him on the outside with the inquisitor.

"Winston says you saw the bloke who jumped off the roof, and have a different version of events."

Winston's got a mouth like a torn pocket. Everything falls out. He tried not to sound as annoyed as he felt. "You know how Winston likes to impress with his wild stories. Take everything he says with a grain of salt."

"What *did* you see then?"

Riley sighed. The man's persistence bordered on ghoulish. He caught a movement out of the corner of his eye and saw that the Ferals stood to one side, listening to the conversation. The intensity of their focus made him uncomfortable and he angled his back towards them.

"I saw nothing, alright? It was dark… wet and stormy. Imagination runs riot when shadows are dancing around like that. I spent the night huddled inside, out of the rain and watching the telly."

The man shrugged. "Okay, if that's what you say."

Time to end the conversation. "I've got work to do, even if you haven't." Riley swiped his key fob again and he and Ginger Puss stepped inside when the door slid wide. He didn't look back.

Phoebe's curtains were open when he took Ginge back up to the roof. He couldn't see her, but no doubt she was fine. As he watched, the flag at Government house made a steady ascent up the pole. That meant Bruce had started work for the day. Time they caught up again, and the others too. He would do something about that.

Riley didn't exaggerate when he said there wasn't much excitement in his life. Routine mapped each day. Diane still managed to find fault or to remind him of things he either should or should not be doing, but he acknowledged her politely—when he had no other choice—and kept out of her way at other times. Her pursed lips when she looked at him gave him the impression that he didn't measure up, though to what, he was never sure.

Two mornings after the barbecue, Phoebe was up early, and waved to him from her balcony when he and Ginge wandered out to check the day. Fortunately, he saw her first, so was able to duck back inside and pull on a pair of shorts. His jocks weren't fit for public viewing.

"Morning, Riley," she called across the chasm. "You'll be pleased to know I haven't killed your herbs yet."

"It's only been a couple of days, Phoebe. Give it time." He knew she took pride in her balcony garden. The herbs were safe. "You're up early today."

"Absolutely. I need to start practising. I've been approached by Tray Thornton and asked to perform a piano recital at a charity event. Nobody outside of the family has asked me to perform in years. I'll be so rusty." The excitement in her voice was evident, even at a distance.

"That's fantastic news. Could be the start of a whole new career coming up."

"At my age and with my arthritic fingers? I don't think so."

Finn Thornton, Luci's new boyfriend, must have told his father about Phoebe. He had seemed a pleasant young man.

44

Perhaps he would follow in his father's footsteps in engaging in philanthropy. Whatever, Phoebe's news impressed Riley. It would give her renewed zest for life.

Her comment about gardens reminded Riley about his. His plants didn't suffer the ravages of slugs and snails, but the wind could cause some havoc. He had to keep up with the watering before the pots dried out. He dragged the hose out and watered the lime tree in its large pot, and then his potted herbs and vegetables in a series of troughs. Tomatoes weren't wildly successful but zucchinis grew well, as did some capsicums.

Lugging the pots and bags of dirt up the final flight of stairs had been a pain, but he still derived satisfaction from having some fresh produce. He planned to try strawberries next. He grew potted geraniums near the back door, and they could always be relied on for some colour.

He scanned the horizon once more. He couldn't see any signals. The Skywalkers should all be up and about at this time, but if not, they would soon see his. Opening the door of his storage shed, he selected the blue flag and ran it up the flag pole standing on a corner of the rooftop. It flapped happily in the mild breeze, making its presence felt. He would check on reactions later in the day.

When he slipped back upstairs mid-morning, there were some replies. Winston had hoisted his green flag, and so had Colin, building manager from the Royal Adelaide Hospital. Bruce couldn't interfere with the official flag at Government House, but he had lowered the flag slightly from the top of his pole, which was an acknowledgement that the message was received. The same response came from Mark at Parliament

House.

When he slipped back upstairs later for his afternoon tea, he saw that Jonathan had hoisted a green flag above the Colonial Hotel. As he managed the pub, he didn't have the same restrictions as Colin and Bruce. No red flags anywhere that he could see. The message was out there. Others may still turn up, but those who had replied would be enough.

That evening, Riley sauntered down the street and around the corner to the Colonial Hotel. The Skywalkers used it as their local watering hole—good for a pub meal, a game of darts and local gossip. Not that any of them called it gossip. They caught up with the news instead. Jonathan had slapped a reserved sign on their table, and Bruce already sat in his usual seat when Riley pushed his way through the evening crowd.

"G'day, mate. How's that cat of yours? I thought you would put him on a leash and bring him with you." Bruce snorted at his own humour.

"Nah. Ginge keeps to himself at night. He comes out for breakfast only. How's yourself?"

Bruce proceeded to tell him in intricate detail, covering his latest ailments, and the trials and tribulations of being caretaker at Government House. His listeners always enjoyed his descriptions of official guests and their foibles. It could have been jumping from the pot into the fire, but Winston's arrival changed the direction of conversation.

By half-past their usual meeting time, six people sat around the table. It was parmie night, meaning the chef's special for the evening was a chicken or veal parmigiana, with a choice of sauces. Throw in a happy-hour drink, and everyone was happy. They placed their orders at the bar and sat down with their drinks to catch up.

"It's a while since you blokes were last here," Jonathan said. "I thought you'd given up on these social evenings."

"Never", declared Colin. "Life just gets busy, and then there's always some emergency that gets in the way. I half expected something to stop me coming tonight." The skinny man exuded a nervous energy, always fidgeting or jiggling his feet under the table. The hospital job kept him running, but he probably would have run anyway, regardless of the job.

Winston looked around at everyone seated at the table. "Did ya hear about the bloke who jumped from my building?"

His tone was almost gleeful. Riley tried not to roll his eyes, irritated by the fact that Winston still got mileage out of the story. Much of the detail he related was supposed rather than actual. His listeners were suitably enthralled, which only encouraged him more.

"And Riley here saw him do it."

"For Chrissake, Winston, I've already told you. I saw nothing of the sort. It was dark, anyway. Nobody could have seen a friggin' thing on a night like that."

The more time passed, the less confidant he was of what he'd seen but whatever, Riley wasn't going to discuss it in the pub. Winston should shut up about the matter. He needed to change the topic of conversation. Where were those meals? Food always kept Winston distracted.

On cue, the waitress appeared carrying a couple of plates, following up with the rest. Conversation stalled in favour of the food. Riley eventually broke the silence.

"Did you read in the paper that changes are proposed in

the city? If the new planning regulations are passed, taller buildings can be built and the pressure will be on for some of our buildings to be demolished. They'll make way for new skyscrapers."

"They wouldn't do that!" Bruce was emphatic. "Some of these buildings are heritage listed. There are laws protecting them."

"Ah, but money talks," Colin said. "Some big developer with a shit-load of cash is likely to get his own way."

"That's what concerns me," said Riley. "My grandfather was the architect on Blenheim House, and I'd hate to see it bulldozed for some monstrosity of glass and steel. Anyway, it's not heritage protected. Someone could knock it down tomorrow if they wanted."

Winston's eyes widened. "You'd lose your job, Riley. We all would if they knocked down our buildings."

"They're unlikely to knock down Government House." Bruce snorted at the ridiculous idea.

"Probably not," Riley agreed, "but our way of life would disappear. We'd be replaced by facilities management companies. There wouldn't be any live-in caretaking positions, and Skywalkers would disappear. We'd become an anachronism, a thing of the past."

Silence greeted this news. Colin cleared his throat. "But it's only under discussion, right? It might never happen."

Riley wiped the sauce from his mouth and folded up the paper napkin and placed it back on the table. "Who knows? There's a public meeting tomorrow night and I'm going. I'll let you know what happens."

"Good idea. You're the one who always has a better

handle on these things." Winston was noticeably relieved that he wasn't expected to go, and the conversation moved onto other things before they adjourned to the dart board for a game.

Riley didn't mean to stay so long, but a glance at his watch indicated eleven o'clock as he drained the dregs from his glass and headed for the door. He knew he would regret the late night in the morning. Colin, Bruce and Mark had already left, and Winston and Riley walked a short distance together before Winston peeled off at Hindmarsh St, leading to the Institute and Riley continued down the street to Blenheim House.

The prickling feeling of unease didn't hit him until he reached the corner of his building. Was there a faint noise behind him? Riley wasn't sure but had a weird feeling of being watched. That was ridiculous.

He stopped and looked over his shoulder. A faint breeze touched the back of his neck with wispy fingers. No-one there. He must have had one glass of ale too many. He breathed out and kept walking.

He noticed the smell first. It was putrid, enough to make him gag. He hesitated at the bottom of the stairs leading up to Blenheim house. There was a dark shape on the top step.

What the fuck?

It was a large rat—a rat in two parts because its head was separated from its body. The little eyes were open, and appeared to be looking right at him. The painted words on the bottom step were not quite dry. "This is what happens to rats."

5 Early Morning Walk

SLEEP DIDN'T COME easily. The stench of dead rat lingered in his nostrils, and his stomach churned just thinking of it. Who would have left it there, and why? The Ferals? He couldn't imagine Jodie killing a rat—Alex perhaps, but it didn't make sense. Someone's idea of a sick joke? A satanic ritual?

At five, he gave up on sleep. Ginge glared at him as Riley threw back the covers and slid his feet over the edge of the bed, bumping the cat in the process.

"Sorry Ginge. If you did your job properly and kept the rats at bay, that rodent wouldn't have been there."

After a moment, the cat lowered its head again and closed its eyes. In truth, Riley knew that living in the building as he did, Ginge probably didn't see many rats, not at their level, anyway. There were bound to be some lurking behind the rubbish bins in the laneway, but not on the rooftop.

He opened the outside door and peered at the horizon. He could see a faint stain of light towards the east. Dawn wouldn't be far off, but for now, the city slumbered. Grittily tired as he was, Riley loved this time of day. The world hadn't quite begun, except for stray cruising taxis, street sweepers, and early delivery vans.

On impulse, he pulled on a t-shirt and pair of jeans. Ginge lifted his head again to regard him with mild curiosity.

"Stay there. I'll be back soon."

He opened the front door at street level and peered into the street, half expecting another unwelcome surprise. The steps were clear. He looked left and right before stepping down onto the footpath, and headed east towards King William Street. A left-hand turn at the intersection led him down towards the river.

He found the crisp morning air invigorating. Riley strode purposefully, relishing the opportunity for an early morning walk. Although the river lay at the edge of the city, it meandered far from the hustle and bustle. Park lands edged the banks, with some areas covered in manicured lawns, but by walking away from the city centre, the river path led through tracts of native vegetation. Riley could almost believe he had left the city altogether.

As he walked, the sky softened into a half-light, revealing shadowy shapes and figures. Already, walkers and early commuters made their way into the city, and bike riders skimmed the path. The bike lights cast a ribbon of light ahead of the front wheel, and bells tinkled on their approach.

Some walkers strode with earphones clamped to their heads and oblivious to everything around them. They emerged silently out of the gloom, and looked straight ahead, passing him without acknowledgement. Eye contact was non-existent, as though it would contravene an unspoken rule to engage with someone else in the dark. In daylight, people would sometimes smile or nod in passing, perhaps even extend a cheery greeting, but not in the absence of light. It compounded Riley's impression of wandering in a loosely defined bubble.

He preferred to be in the present, to listen to the sounds of the river and enjoy the experience. The path wasn't entirely dark. Security lighting cast pools of light at intervals, but sometimes trees and foliage restricted visibility. Frogs croaked in the rushes at the water's edge, and an occasional plop meant that some water creature had breached the surface. Ripples spread across the water, but he couldn't tell if something had jumped into it or out of it.

The air had a damp, earthy smell; a mixture of stagnant water trapped in the reeds at the water's edge, and probably duck poo. He found it preferable to dead rat. The ducks slept with heads tucked under a wing. Occasionally one stirred, causing a response from elsewhere on the river, but mostly they huddled quietly.

He walked steadily until reaching the point where the river snaked into an inner suburb. Daylight had cracked. Riley knew he needed to return to Blenheim House in time to finish the morning chores, but dropped onto a park bench to sit for a while.

The peacefulness of the early morning replenished his soul. Staying a while longer put off the inevitable tedium of the day. The job was hardly challenging, but it suited him. He enjoyed the city buzz; it came with the flat, and there was a camaraderie with the other Skywalkers. He and Ginge had a cushy existence, if you discounted Diane and dead rats.

The pace of life was adequate. It might not have met his mother's expectations, but he managed to resist her cajoling.

Sometimes he thought about travelling or living the van life. There were heaps of twenty-somethings doing it these days, but that would mean stepping out of his comfort zone. Soon he would be a thirty-something, as she frequently reminded him.

Not that he needed telling. Today was one of those rare days when he questioned whether life was passing him by, to the extent that when he looked back in years to come, it would be with regret. He had no answers to that question. Life was simpler for the ducks. They swam, they quacked a bit and marched up and down the river bank and aside from the odd fox that might follow the river, life was sweet. They weren't bothered with existential questions.

The day couldn't be put off any longer. Riley stood and on checking further along the path in case any cyclists were barrelling towards him, noticed a figure standing further up the river bank. The man was in silhouette, but stood with hands in coat pockets and looking in his direction. A shiver of unease washed over Riley. Time to move.

The return journey didn't take as long. Noise of early morning traffic penetrated the river environs. Soft morning light filled the sky, and more people occupied the path on their way to work. They moved at a brisk pace; places to go, places to be. Riley ran through a mental checklist of tasks for the day as he strode behind them. Amongst other things, the meeting about the zoning changes was scheduled for that evening.

He still ruminated on the day ahead, when he paused at the first pedestrian crossing. A woman behind him was engaged in a loud phone conversation.

"But I already told you that… honestly, do I have to do everything myself?... Listen…"

Riley glanced around in annoyance. Surely, she could keep it down? He locked eyes with a man standing to the rear of the group, a man with his hands in the pockets of his coat and who appeared to be looking right at him. It was an 'I got you' stare.

He jerked his eyes away in confusion. Strange coincidence, but it almost looked like the man on the river bank. Riley eased his shoulders into a shrug, aware of the tension they held. The man made him uncomfortable, but without any logical reason. Probably not the same person. When the lights turned green, Riley was the first to step off the pavement.

The morning papers lay on the steps of Blenheim House, and as he stooped to pick them up, Riley glanced back along the street. There, some twenty metres back, was the man in the coat. He stood, looking in the window of an insurance agency. As Riley watched, the man turned his head and looked directly at him. This time, Riley could have sworn he saw the man's lips stretch into a thin but humourless smile. He swiped the door fob and fled inside.

People clustered at the rear of the meeting room, not wanting to take a seat in the front row. Riley signed an attendance sheet at the registration desk, and looked around to see if he could spot anyone he knew. Council staff in suits sat at a long table fronting the room. One of them kept looking at his watch, and Riley couldn't decide if the man was checking how long before the meeting could start, or how long before he could finish the meeting and go home.

The audience seemed to comprise town planning students and their lecturers, some city residents, and then non-descript people in suits who he assumed were owners and developers in the city. There was a woman he thought he recognised, but couldn't remember from where. Perhaps she was a patron of the Daily Bean. Other than that, none of the locals he knew were in attendance, and certainly none of the other Skywalkers.

A man, who had been standing at the front with folded arms watching the room slowly fill, moved to the lectern. He tapped the microphone in front of him, cleared his throat, and introduced himself as the Planning Manager. After requesting everyone to be seated, he began talking his way through a PowerPoint presentation.

Riley seated himself at the end of a row, in case he wanted to leave early. Meetings made him uncomfortable. The gist of the information provided was that according to the Property Industry Council, who had been in discussion with the Minister for Planning, there was an unmet demand for prime office space in the city.

"Why doesn't the government encourage development in suburban centres?" a woman called from the floor. "Decentralisation has benefits for everyone."

"I'll answer questions at the end of the presentation."

The Planning Manager's tone was dismissive, and the woman hissed and muttered to her companion. The Manager continued to speak. He touched on economic incentives, and the need to ensure the city retained its vitality and commercial significance. Existing planning legislation restricted commercial development to strongly defined precincts in the city proper. To cater for unmet demand, if development couldn't spread out, it would have to spread up.

The second speaker was a heritage consultant engaged by the City Council. She gave an overview of heritage restrictions in the city, and advised that regulations would be broadened and strengthened for some buildings and precincts. This would ensure that the desired character of the city was maintained. Guidelines would be put in place to ensure that new development didn't detract from the visual amenity provided by the existing stone nineteenth and early twentieth century architecture.

A mumble swept through the room at these words. Riley couldn't help himself. He jumped up from his seat.

"What about protecting buildings of character and architectural interest in the streets earmarked for re-development? Are they going to be sacrificed for the benefit of some developer's bottom line? Some existing buildings could be refurbished to provide current standard office accommodation."

Someone wearing a suit jumped up on the other side of the room. "You can't make a silk purse out of a sow's ear. Those buildings have too many limitations. You'd never bring them up to the standards tenants expect today."

Members of the audience began arguing between themselves, with some standing and calling across the room. The heritage consultant looked aghast, and gripped the lectern with both hands as she leaned into the microphone and tried to bring the meeting to order.

The audience was roughly divided, with some supporting and some opposed to the proposed planning changes. The woman who had asked the first question said she was forming a committee to rally against the proposal and invited people to leave contact details with her.

"Quiet!" The Planning Manager bellowed into the microphone, and the audience fell into startled silence. "If you have questions, kindly direct them through me, and one at a time. I repeat that these changes are proposed only at this point. You are invited to submit any comments via the website or on the form that can be collected from the desk at the back of the room."

Riley had heard enough. After swiping a form from the desk, he pushed his way out into the foyer through the people standing at the back of the room. The woman he'd seen earlier stood there with her phone clamped to her ear. She had her back turned towards him initially, but swung around as she spoke and he caught snippets of conversation.

"Just wait... be patient. I'm telling you, it's under control."

He brushed past her and at that moment, she glanced up and saw him. He didn't think she recognised him; she wouldn't know him from a bar of soap, but she took a couple of steps towards the edge of the room to continue her conversation in privacy.

Tiredness swamped him as he walked home. The early start to the day caught up with him and he had a slight headache. Probably tension. He never coped well with stress, and the thought that his comfortable existence might be disturbed was enough to upset anyone.

He found himself outside the door of Blenheim House without consciously having walked, although obviously he had. The other Skywalkers might have some ideas on opposing the changes to the city, but he doubted it. They weren't activists, or the type of people to stand up against authority. He was on his own.

He looked up at the façade, tilting his head right back so he could see the stone and brickwork reaching for the sky. He loved the simplicity of the vertical lines, and the patterns created with the brickwork. The stained glass beside the front door and in the fanlight had been specially commissioned, and the turret rooms on either side of the building had always seemed magical when he was a child.

Years before, his mother had pointed the building out to him, explaining that his grandfather had designed it. He half expected Rapunzel to let down her hair from a turret window, and perhaps a drugged princess to be sleeping in the other. His father thought he was too much of an introspective child, and should be playing more sport… cricket at the very least.

Blenheim Pastoral owned the building. When the caretaker position was advertised, Riley was positive the job was meant for him. Prior to that, he'd completed a year of architectural studies, but decided he didn't have his grandfather's talent. Odd jobs followed, but his connection to the building was enough to get him a foot in the door, and swift talking did the rest. On settling into his rooftop flat, he decided he'd come home at last.

Ginge waited by the back door when Riley emerged from the stairwell. The cat had been snoozing in the base of a pot plant when Riley had left, but was now wide awake and expressing displeasure at being abandoned. He wound himself around Riley's legs, making indignant chirruping noises. The cat had a water bowl and dry biscuits available outside, so hadn't starved. Evidently, that wasn't the point.

Riley bent and scratched the cat on the head between his ears. "Sorry Ginge, but I wasn't far away. I'll water the plants and then feed you inside."

He unwound the hose from its reel and dragged it to the far reaches of the rooftop before pressing the trigger and directing a shower of water towards the plants. The trough of spinach looked ready to harvest.

The sliding door was open to Phoebe's apartment across the way and light spilled out onto the balcony. He saw she had a guest. A stranger stood in her living room, a man in a suit. That surprised him, because Phoebe didn't have many visitors outside of her family and the Skywalkers. As he watched, she crossed the room and slid the door shut. The curtains were still open, allowing him a limited view of the figures inside.

He knew Phoebe and her visitor could also see him on his balcony, so made a point of not staring. Keeping an eye on her was one thing; intruding was another. He saw Phoebe shake her head at one stage, but she didn't seem agitated or perturbed. None of his business anyway. When the plants were sufficiently soaked, he wound up the hose and then let Ginger Puss inside. He shut the door behind them, knowing they were both safe in their haven.

6   Heritage Review

PHOEBE'S CURTAINS WERE already open when Riley and Ginger stepped outside the following morning. He would have known she was awake without the obvious sign. She was playing the piano, and the chords bounced and echoed off the surrounding buildings. The piece was far removed from the pretty piece she had played for Finn Thornton. Riley had limited musical knowledge, having never progressed beyond the recorder at school, but made a wild stab at it being something composed by Wagner.

The music paused as they completed their rounds of the rooftop, taking the temperature of the city and seeing who or what was around.

"Morning, Phoebe. You're up early today." He knew his voice would carry across the gap.

"That bloody woman! She can't get rid of me like that. I won't go." Phoebe burst through the sliding doors and strode to the edge of her balcony. She gripped the side-rail and glared, as though the fault were all Riley's.

"What bloody woman? Go where?"

"Harrison's wife. She's trying to get me out of here."

"That sounds serious, but under the terms of your tenancy, I thought she couldn't do that. I'll shout you breakfast in the Daily Bean in thirty minutes, and you can tell me about it. I need to attend to a couple of things here first."

She stood and stared for a while, with eyebrows lowered before giving a huge sigh. "Okay… if you're buying breakfast. It's more than that son of mine ever does."

Riley ignored that comment. Charles did a lot for his mother. They were chalk and cheese, but he still cared for her. She never accepted the fact that her son had turned down the suggestion of a music career and become a dentist instead. Phoebe had thought Charles would receive the acclaim and recognition that had been denied to her, but confidentially Charles had said he had greater success in dentistry.

Riley gave his neighbour a wave and hurried back inside. He threw some cat biscuits in a bowl to appease Ginge and had a shower in record time. He managed to bring in the papers, polish the brass at the front entrance and sweep leaf litter off the front steps within twenty-five minutes. He wasn't sure if a bad smell really hung around of if it was in his imagination, but he liberally sprayed the steps with disinfectant 'just-in-case'.

By the time he slipped upstairs again and fetched Ginge, thirty-five minutes had passed. Phoebe sat at his table, studying the menu, even though it never changed and she probably knew it by heart.

"You're late." She looked up with a small frown. "I never could abide lateness in a man."

"And good morning to you too, Phoebe."

Riley caught Bruno's eye, miming drinking from a cup, with his little finger stuck in the air. Bruno rolled his eyes in response and nodded. Phoebe already had a pot of tea in front of her. She must have arrived early. Ginge commenced his tour of the floor beneath the tables in case any tasty morsels had been dropped.

Phoebe took a deep breath and breathed out heavily. "I hardly slept a wink last night; I was so upset."

"I saw you had a late-night visitor. I thought your luck might have changed. It seems I was wrong?"

Phoebe gave him a withering glare. "That man was a solicitor engaged by Cornelia Mortimer, Harrison's wife. She wants to sell Mortimer House and has asked me to agree to that."

"I thought she couldn't sell. Don't you have a lifetime tenancy with restrictive clauses?"

"It's complicated. Harrison set it up like that for my protection. She can't sell the building unless I agree to leave. Someone has made her an offer too good to refuse, so now she's trying to persuade me move out with an offer I can't refuse. But I have."

Bruno brought Riley's coffee to the table, plus a bowl of milk, which he placed on the floor. "Careful where you put your feet. I don't want that milk kicked over my clean floor." He looked at them, eyebrows raised. "Have you decided what you're having to eat?"

"Smashed avocado on sour dough, with smoked salmon and pickled red cabbage."

Bruno's eyebrows hit the roof. "What happened to the poached eggs on toast?"

"I felt like a change."

Phoebe shunted the menu card across the table. "Riley's paying, so I'll have eggs benedict with smoked salmon. Don't make the eggs too runny, but not hard either."

"I'll tell Maria." His tone rolled his eyes for him. He yelled towards the kitchen door. "Maria... two hipster breakfasts coming up."

Phoebe closed her eyes briefly and shook her head, muttering, "I don't know why I still come here."

"Course you do, darlin'. Where else would you get such good food, with everything cooked just as you like. The barista's pretty good too," he added with a wink.

Customers waited at the counter and he scurried back, denying Phoebe the chance of further comment. She watched him with an air of distraction. Riley brought her attention back to their earlier discussion.

"As I understand it, there's nothing she can do to force you to leave."

"Not legally. She has offered a substantial sum of money if I agree to vacate, with the suggestion being that I buy into a retirement village." Her voice rose to an indignant pitch. "Can you imagine me in one of those places?"

Riley couldn't. "And illegally?"

"He talked in a round-about way, but indicated that if it could be demonstrated I was no longer mentally competent, my intention to live my remaining days at Mortimer House could be challenged. He mentioned a guardianship order being put in place."

"That's bullshit! Have you spoken to Charles about this?"

"Not yet, but I will. I didn't want to ring him last night and ruin his night as well as my own."

"I reckon it's all bluff and bluster. Charles won't let them turf you out. He might not be a lawyer, but he's got contacts in this city. You're one of us, Phoebe. They can't make you go."

"They'll have a fight on their hands if they try."

They paused their discussion as Winston sauntered in. Without being invited, he grabbed a chair from an adjoining table and plonked himself down at theirs.

"Is this a private party, or can anyone join in? Don't often see you here at this time, Phoebe. Watch out that cat doesn't steal your breakfast."

"Good morning, Winston," Phoebe replied in her iciest tone. "Do sit down."

He looked at her in surprise. "I already have."

Bruno arrived with their food and placed it in front of them with a flourish. "And what's your exotic order this morning, Winston?"

"Tea, with toast and vegemite."

"A man after my own heart. Coming up."

"Couldn't you have made that at home?" Riley asked.

"I could, but it never tastes the same. Anyway, then I would have missed out on your company."

"What's news, Winston?" Riley asked, knowing if there was any juicy gossip available, the other man would know of it.

Winston scratched his head and screwed up his face as he thought. "The autopsy results for David Barton were made available, if that's of any interest. Don't know why an autopsy was required. The long drop killed him. The report showed he had a lot of alcohol in his system."

Phoebe pursed her lips. "It wasn't very sensible to wander around the roof at night with a belly full of booze. He might not have done it if he was sober."

"Maybe he didn't intend to do what he did, but the result was the same. Maybe he over-balanced. Who knows?" Winston gave a shrug, and his jowly face dropped into a hangdog expression.

They maintained a respectful silence for a few moments until Riley changed the subject.

"I attended a council meeting last night about rezoning this sector of the city. If the proposed changes go through, higher density development will be permitted. That means taller buildings will be built."

"These streets are fully developed, so I don't know what benefit that will be." Phoebe sounded confused.

"Some of these buildings have passed their use-by date. They don't meet current environmental standards and are classified as secondary accommodation. Tenants want modern buildings with lots of natural light and green-star ratings. Existing buildings will be bowled over and replaced with new structures."

Her face reflected horror. "Do you think that's why Cornelia Mortimer wants to sell Mortimer House? Does someone want to demolish it? Harrison would turn over in his grave."

"It's possible, but these changes are only proposed. There's no guarantee they'll be passed."

"They will be, you know that." Winston was gloomily positive. "The big end of town always gets its way, particularly when there's money involved. A couple of brown paper bags will slide under the table before the decision is made and that will seal the deal."

"You're stuck in the past. Council doesn't operate like that anymore," Riley said. "An effective lobbying campaign is needed, and some woman's organising it. I've signed up to help."

Winston snorted. "Good luck with that."

Riley shrugged and turned back to Phoebe. "So, tell us about this recital you're giving. I've heard you practising."

Phoebe sat up straighter. "Young Finn must have spoken to his father about me, and incredibly he knew of my reputation. That's surprising, because it's years since I played professionally."

She visibly flushed, and lifted a hand to smooth an imaginary strand of hair back into place. She always looked immaculate. "It's not for a while, so I've plenty of time in which to practice. It's a fund-raising dinner for children with heart disease. When I heard of the cause, I couldn't say no."

"That's fantastic. Luci will be so proud of you."

"Good on yer, Phoebe," Winston said. He drained the last of his tea and picked up his remaining slice of toast. "I can't stay nattering to you two all day. I've got work to do. See ya later."

He ambled out of the café, slinging Bruno a wave as he went. Riley looked at his watch. Time he went as well. He scooped up Ginge from his customary window seat and bidding Phoebe goodbye, paid for their breakfasts and pulled open the door, stepping onto the footpath. The drone of morning traffic met him. In the brief time he'd been in the café, the city had sprung into action.

He had to make up for lost time that morning. He'd stayed longer at the Daily Bean than usual. A toilet was blocked on level nine, the hot water wasn't working in the kitchen on level five and he had to organise quotes for new carpets in the lifts.

The surprise of the day came mid-morning, when Diane messaged him requesting that he come down to reception. That could only mean bad news. To his surprise, she had brought in a cake for morning tea. Instead of her usual skirt, blouse and cardigan, she wore a smart suit, with a marquisette brooch pinned on one shoulder. The penny only dropped when he was onto his second slice that it was her birthday. He never remembered dates like that. Even his own would slide by if it weren't for his mother. Life wouldn't be worth living if he didn't acknowledge this event in some way.

"Fabulous cake, Diane. You're such a good cook. Even Ginge would like this and he's a culinary connoisseur."

"I didn't bake a cake for that cat. He's overweight anyway. You spoil him."

"Not me. Bruno does." He brushed the crumbs from his hands on the seat of his jeans. "I have to slip out briefly. I've got the mobile if there are any messages."

"But the toilet on level nine..."

"Fixed. Be back soon."

He slipped out the front door before she could raise any other objections. A florist in the next street over did a roaring trade in office arrangements, and would most likely have a suitable bouquet. The challenge was to get something not too ostentatious, as that would give the wrong message, plus give his wallet a hammering, but not too stingy either.

Twenty minutes later, he dodged around other pedestrians on his way back to Blenheim House clutching a bunch of mixed pink, white and purple lisianthus blooms. He ran into Jonathan from the Colonial, only fifty metres from the front door.

"Ma…a…ate… are they for me? You shouldn't have. I didn't know you cared."

"Piss off, Jonathan. No, they're not for you. Who let you out without a minder?"

"Don't be like that. When're you coming down to the pub for a drink?"

"I was there a couple of days ago. You must think I'm some sort of desperado."

"Might be right there, but no harm in dropping by for a quick one after work, is there?"

Riley couldn't think of a reasonable excuse not to go. He didn't have any other plans. "I might see you later, but no promises."

"Story of my life," Jonathan muttered. "See you if you turn up."

He sauntered off and Riley turned back towards Blenheim House. In his haste, he nearly bumped into a woman who stood on the footpath, looking up at the building. She had her phone out and was taking photos of the façade. For a moment, he couldn't recollect where he had seen her before, but in a spasm of fear, it came back to him. She was the heritage consultant who had addressed the meeting the previous night.

"What are you doing?" It came out more stridently than he intended.

The woman stepped back, clearly surprised. She held up a hand as though warding him off.

"My job, actually. What's it to you?"

"This is my building and if you're recording any information about it, I should know."

"*Your* building?" She sounded sceptical. "And you are…?" She raised one eyebrow.

Riley flushed at her appraising stare. "I'm the building manager, and have a connection to the building beyond that. I saw you at the Council meeting. If you think Blenheim House is ready for demolition, you've got a fight on your hands."

"I'm a heritage consultant, not a developer. I'm undertaking an assessment of the streetscape, and recording details of buildings and structures of interest."

"Wouldn't that information be held by Council already?"

"There's a certain amount of technical information, but I still need to inspect properties to support my research. That includes taking photos. You don't object to my taking photos?"

"So, you're pushing ahead with the re-zoning as outlined last night?"

"It's not up to me. I'm engaged to conduct a heritage survey and to make recommendations according to my findings. I'll write up a report, but the final decision is up to Council and the Minister for Planning. That could be months away."

He looked up at the building façade, trying to see it with fresh eyes. "It's typical of the time in which it was built, and as you can see, it features some noteworthy detail."

He didn't want to tell her that his grandfather was the original architect. She might assume he wasn't objective enough. That was probably true, but he tried to cover it up. He pointed out other buildings in the street, talking up their unique qualities, until she interrupted him.

"I can do my job, you know."

At that point, he really looked at her. She seemed too young to be a consultant. She wore jeans and a black jacket over a white t-shirt. Her hair was pulled back into a pony tail, and she wasn't wearing any makeup from what he could see. Not that he knew much about that stuff. She looked more like a uni student working on an assignment. In his brief stint in the halls of Adelaide University, he'd also walked the streets collating data for student projects.

"I never said you couldn't."

Besides taking photos, she had been scribbling in a notebook. He really wanted to know what she had written, but squinting over her shoulder would be obvious. If he played nice with her, perhaps he could get a look at it.

"I know this city. We watch over it. We have a unique vantage point. To increase the density over this precinct would destroy a part of our history and destroy the culture."

"We? Who's this we?"

"Some friends… mates… other city workers." He didn't use the term *Skywalkers*. They kept that between themselves. "I'll show you."

He regretted his words as soon as he spoke. He never took people to the rooftop. It was his domain. From there, he could overlook his kingdom. Even Diane had never been up there.

Diane! Fuck! He still held the flowers. He needed to get them to her.

"Okay… show me."

He hesitated, thinking rapidly. If he could make her understand what he meant, it would be worth making this exception. He glanced at his watch. Almost lunchtime. He'd have to be quick.

"Follow me."

As the front door slid open for them, he half turned back to her. He nodded in the direction of the lift bank. "I won't be a moment. Wait by the elevators and I'll join you shortly."

She flicked him a slight look of surprise, but made her way through reception to wait by the elevator doors. Diane looked up but before she could say anything, Riley thrust the flowers in her direction.

"Diane… happy birthday. If it hadn't been such a busy morning, I would have picked them up earlier." If she thought he'd ordered them in advance, she wouldn't think he'd forgotten.

"Oh, they're lovely. My favourite colours. I'll fetch a vase for them." She squinted at the woman standing by the elevators. "Who's that?" she asked in a whisper, loud enough that her voice carried anyway.

Riley backed away from the reception desk. "A heritage consultant doing a survey on behalf of the City Council. I'm giving her a brief tour." He managed to stride to the elevator foyer and hit the up button without further questions, which was unusual.

"I do have a name," she said as they waited. "I'm Sophie Robinson. Where are you taking me?" Her voice rose slightly indicating a level of concern.

"Riley... Riley Monroe." He offered his hand hesitantly. What was protocol in these situations? She placed her hand in his, and her skin felt smooth and soft against his palm. He gripped it lightly before releasing it.

"We're heading for the rooftop. It's quite safe. From there, you have a good view over the city."

The door pinged open at the level below the roof, and after allowing her to exit first, Riley led the way to the stairwell rising to the rooftop area.

"Just one flight of stairs. The lift doesn't go all the way up."

They emerged into full sunshine, blinking after the dim light of the stairwell.

"Wow! Someone lives up here." Sophie stood initially and looked around, before wandering to the low brick wall at the roof's edge. "What a fabulous view."

Too late, Riley realised a load of washing hung on the line, including his jocks. He wouldn't have left them on display if he knew he was having a visitor. Fortunately, her attention was focussed elsewhere. He followed her and gave a commentary on the various buildings in the vicinity, not just their current use, but also their history. She listened carefully, asking occasional questions and taking photos with her phone.

"You can see, can't you, why it would be criminal to over-develop this sector of the city. So many historic or significant buildings would be over-shadowed, or worse, demolished. It would destroy the character of the city. It would lose its soul."

"You don't have to convince me. I've never said I'm in favour of the proposal. Someone has to complete this assessment though and it might as well be me. I'm not going to turn down any work that comes my way. The Government pays promptly, so even better."

A soft *brrr-ow* sounded behind them. Ginge uncurled himself from the base of a pot plant where he'd been snoozing, and wandered in their direction, pausing along the way to stretch first his back paws and then the front.

"My God, there's a cat up here. Does he live here too?" She bent down to pet him between the ears.

"Ginge does live here—we both do. There are a lot of people who live above the city. Phoebe Eilish lives in the penthouse on top of Mortimer House, and there are various others who have similar building manager roles in other buildings around us. Even at Government and Parliament House. They are all live-in positions."

Sophie peered in the direction of Parliament House, leaning against the wall as though she could see more in doing that. "I'd never thought of anyone living in those places. It's a community stratum I didn't know existed."

"Not many people do, and we like it that way. When everyone goes home for the day, the city's ours. I'd appreciate it if you didn't talk about us in your report, or to anyone else in fact."

"Well… sure. It's a heritage report, not a sociological analysis. It helps me to understand the precinct more though."

She closed up her notebook and held out her hand. "I shan't keep you any longer. I'm sure you've lots to do. Thanks for bringing me up here."

Too late, he realised he hadn't got a look at her notebook. He accepted her hand and she gave it a firm shake. He almost thought she winked at him, but it was probably a blink. Harsh sunlight did that to people. As she opened the door leading down to the next level, she turned and smiled.

"Nice cat."

7 The pressure ramps up

RILEY TOSSED UP whether to go to the Colonial or not, but after some one-sided deliberation, because Ginge refused to participate in the discussion, decided he would drop in for a drink. Just one, and then he would come home.

He looked both ways on leaving the building before stepping down onto the footpath. He told himself he was checking for oncoming pedestrians, not looking for strange men, and he certainly wasn't paranoid, but no strange men lurked in the vicinity.

The usual crowd were in the bar, some people dropping in after a hard day in the office, and others who lived locally. Some of those residents were part of the new wave occupying recently-constructed apartment buildings. Others lived in the row cottages and workman's houses, built in side streets of the city at least a century ago, probably more. Substantial villas had been built in the south-east corner of the city, but the Colonial was not the sort of watering hole they were likely to frequent. The cultural divide was very real.

Just as real was the silent division between the Skywalkers and the flat-earthers. It was so silent, the flat-earthers didn't know it existed. As Winston often remarked with a hint of superiority, "That lot don't know the city like we do."

The pub dated from the late nineteenth century, and retained many of its original features, with wood-panelled wainscoting, and stained glass in the windows. It no longer smelled of nicotine, with smokers having been banished by legislation, but there was still a recognizable smell of beer, old leather, and something else akin to a whiff of the past. Pub meals consisted of the usual favourites; schnitzels, chicken, or beef parmigiana, salt and pepper squid, and bangers and mash. Minimal vegetarian options were on offer. Not much ever changed, and the locals liked it that way.

A couple of men played darts, and other groups propped up the bar. Riley recognised one woman as being Celeste, a local street worker. They were on nodding terms, but he had never exchanged more than a greeting with her. She sat on her own on a bar stool, alternately staring into her drink and staring at the screen of her phone.

Her skirt barely covered her bum, and the neckline of her top displayed a generous cleavage and a tattoo of a rose on one breast. She looked up hopefully as he entered, and then gave him a small nod of recognition, before resuming her scrolling. Riley wasn't sure whether to be relieved that he wasn't considered an option, or insulted. Either way, he wasn't interested.

He ordered a schooner, and moved down to an unoccupied end of the bar before texting Jonathan to say he had arrived.

The man himself appeared a few minutes later, and propped his backside onto an adjacent stool before ordering a drink of his own. An apron of belly fat, contained within his hotel-monogramed polo shirt, hung over the top of his trousers. Too much pub food, Riley surmised.

"Busy day?" Jonathan asked.

"This and that. Caught up with Phoebe this morning. Cornelia Mortimer wants to get Phoebe out of her apartment."

"She can't do that, can she? I thought she had a life tenancy."

"She has, but that doesn't mean she can't choose to go, or alternatively be persuaded to go."

"I imagine there's no love lost between those two. Harrison setting Phoebe up in the penthouse must have really rubbed Cornelia's nose in it."

"Probably. Cornelia hasn't missed out. Harrison left her well-heeled and she has that swanky apartment on the Gold Coast. I'm sure there are enough investments to keep her in gold-plated comfort for the rest of her days. I think over the years, the two women have learned to live with each other's existence. They probably don't like each other, but living in different states allows each to ignore the other."

"Until now."

"Until now," Riley agreed.

The barman plonked Jonathan's drink on a beer coaster and swiped at sticky patches on the bar surface with a damp cloth before idling down the other end in search of a new customer.

"It's a funny world we live in." Jonathan took a mouthful of his beer and wiped his mouth on the back of his hand.

"Bruce from Government House was asking me about Winston the other day, but I know little about him except that he's caretaker of the Institute. He seems to know everything about everyone else though."

"Yep. He probably knows what you had for dinner last night and when you last took a shit. He refers to himself as the building manager, by the way, not the caretaker."

Jonathan rolled his eyes. "Pardon me. He'll be handing out business cards next."

"Probably. He's cagey about his past. Got the impression there was a wife and kids in earlier days, but if so, they're no longer on the scene—or he's no longer on theirs. I've never asked."

"Is that so? He was chatting to a woman in here the other day, so he doesn't ignore women entirely. One thing I do know," Jonathan said with a note of puzzlement in his voice, "is that Winston doesn't drive. Bit strange for a bloke of his age, don't you think?"

"Nor do I, if it's relevant. He probably doesn't need to. I mean, where's he going to drive to in the city? Everything's in walking distance, or he can easily take public transport or an uber."

"I suppose so. It just seems strange that such a chatty chap, who has his nose in everyone else's business, is so mysterious about his own." Jonathan looked over his shoulder before lowering his voice to a confidential level. "Bruce also reckoned Winston's got a secret past."

Riley shrugged, spinning a beer coaster on one edge on the bar. He had no intention of asking Winston about his past. It might invite a more detailed conversation than he wanted, and anyway, why would he want to know? He didn't talk about his past either, or wouldn't if he had one. Other people were more interesting.

"I saw a woman doing a heritage assessment outside Blenheim House today. She's engaged by the council to provide a report on the streetscape and features of interest. They'll probably use it when they make their re-zoning recommendations. Next thing, there'll be developers walking all over us."

"Not here," Jonathan said confidently. "They wouldn't touch an old pub like this."

"Don't you believe it. It may be heritage listed, but heaps of old pubs get re-purposed, with just the façade or front portion retained, and then a skyscraper stuck on the back."

"Bugga." Jonathan took a gulp of his drink and then burped. "I hope that doesn't happen here. Where would I live then?"

Riley jerked back as the beer-laden fumes reached him. The problem was wider than somewhere to live, but Riley knew that people focused on personal impacts before considering the wider ramifications. If he wanted to get Jonathan onside with any protest about the rezoning, he would have to frame his arguments in that context.

He glanced around the room as he gathered his thoughts, seeking clarity and inspiration before he spoke. The figure in the corner caught his eye. It looked like the man. Could it be? Why here? He turned back to face the bar, clutching his beer, and then tried to pick out the man in the mirror behind shelves of spirits on the wall of the bar. The reflection didn't reach far enough.

"Who's that bloke... the one in the corner?" He spoke softly into his beer as though holding a microphone.

"What bloke? Where?"

"Keep your voice down. The one in the back corner by himself. Don't make it obvious."

Jonathan swivelled around and stared, peering around Riley before turning back and leaning towards him to speak conspiratorially. "That, my son, is Lenny. Keep on the right side of him and better still, keep out of his way. Humourless bugger. Has a quick temper. He's usually in here with his mate, Simmo. He's the nasty one. Bit thick though."

Riley couldn't be sure it was the man who had followed him earlier in the week. He didn't want to draw attention to himself by staring. He drained the rest of his beer. To stay any longer was too risky.

"I gotta go. Things to do, early start tomorrow. I'll see you 'round." He slid off his stool.

"But you only just got here."

"Have an early night, Jonathan. You'll thank me later."

He didn't look back, but walked quickly to the door leading out onto the street. He was bursting for a pee, but to use the toilet in the pub would mean walking past the man in the corner. He would have to wait until he got home. The sooner he was there, the better. Opening the door, he slithered through, trying to be unobtrusive. Normally, he would have turned and waved from the doorway, but not tonight.

The pub veranda straddled a wide footpath. With council permission, the hotel owners had installed concrete planter boxes, and tables and bench seats that were bolted to the pavement.

Sad looking plants sat in the boxes, struggling for survival against the onslaught of carbon fumes and cigarette butts. This was where the smokers sat, and as Riley slipped outside, he noticed the Ferals sitting at one of the tables. As he walked past, he could have sworn he heard Alex hiss.

To look in their direction would only encourage them, and he didn't have time for that. He set off at a brisk walk, hoping to cover the short distance in record time. It only took him five minutes, but with each of those minutes, the pressure on his bladder increased. At one point he stopped and looked back the way he had come. Nobody followed him.

He took his fob-key out of his pocket and had it ready when he approached the front door of Blenheim House. The door slammed behind him as he ran for the lift and then thumped the up button. Thank God the cabin waited at the ground floor, but it creaked and groaned as it made its laborious journey up to the top floor.

He ran up the last flight of stairs, but knew he had reached the end of the road. There was no way he could unlock the door of the flat, get inside and unzip before the unthinkable happened. He ran to the potted lime tree in the corner of the roof, unzipping as he ran. He emptied his bladder in the base of the pot with a heartfelt sigh of relief.

"Riley? What are you doing over there?"

He could just make out the figure of Winston on the roof of the Institute. "I'm watering the garden."

"At this time of night?"

Riley hurriedly zipped up, thankful for the parapet that obscured the lower half of his body. "More to the point, what are you doing wandering around on the roof at night. Isn't that

81

a little dangerous? You know what happened to the last bloke who did that."

"I wanted some air. I needed to clear my head."

"Problems?" Riley mentally kicked himself as he asked the question. Getting involved in Winston's problems was not an attractive proposition. He remembered Jonathan's comments about Winston's past. Some topics were best avoided. He hated that those questions about Winston had now been put in his head. He'd always thought of him as a benign character. He heard Winston's sigh clearly from across the intervening alley.

"You could say that. Phoebe's not the only one. I learned tonight that an offer has been made to purchase this building. It's only a rumour at this stage—Andy Nguyen told me, but if it's true, what will happen to me and my job? Where will I live?"

Andy Nguyen, real name Anh Dung Nguyen, was the Chairman of Excellerate, the primary tenant of the Institute. He and Winston were on casual speaking terms.

"You too! It's started then. Who wants to buy it?"

"I've no idea. An approach was made through Harper Real Estate. They're acting on behalf of someone, but the identity is confidential."

"You seem to know a lot when it's just a rumour."

"I keep my ear to the ground, you know that. The word I have is that this is a valuable corner site, and so its potential is higher than it might otherwise be."

Winston had the reputation of a scaremonger, but this news confirmed Riley's fears. Combatting the rezoning would be even more important. "We can talk about it later, but if the worst happens, there are always other buildings to manage."

"Yeah, but they won't be around here, and they probably won't come with live-in accommodation. Times are changing. These days, you need a flaming degree in facilities management, or some crap like that. What would young kids like that know about maintenance? They don't even get their hands dirty."

While Riley fully agreed with Winston, debating the challenges of the industry on a rooftop and across a void at this time of night was not his idea of fun. A slight noise behind him alerting him to Ginger's presence. The cat made a chirping noise as he padded across the roof surface to wind himself around Riley's legs. It was a feline version of *Where have you been? Do you know what time it is?*

"It might be no more than a rumour, and even if it is for real, there's no guarantee that the owner will sell. We can discuss it in daylight hours. I'm going to bed."

"Okay. Night Riley."

As Riley followed by Ginge went inside, he saw that Winston hadn't moved. He was only visible as a shadowy outline at the edge of his building, looking out over the cityscape. Riley hoped there would be no repeats of the previous exodus from that rooftop.

8   Winston has a new friend

HIS SATURDAYS WEREN'T entirely free, although he didn't have official duties. Riley checked for rubbish on the front step, as usual, cleaned anything that needed cleaning and maintained a security presence in the building. Other than that, his time was his own. The Daily Bean was closed, so he and Ginge shared breakfast at home. Sometimes he ate at the Central Market. If he did, Ginge had to remain behind.

He wandered over to the Market for a coffee at Lucia's late morning and bought the weekend paper. It was the one day of the week when he actually purchased it. He picked up some fruit and vegetables while there, plus a sultana croissant to take home. It was the sort of lazy Saturday that reminded him life was good.

He sat at his outdoor table to read his paper and slowly eat his croissant, unrolling it from the outer edges until finally reaching the sticky centre. Ginge promptly gobbled up the pieces that Riley dropped on the floor. He didn't usually check the death notices, but out of curiosity, turned to the personal columns in the back section of the paper.

He found several entries, for Barton, David Michael, dearly beloved husband of Judith, father of Michael and Emma, result of an accident. Funeral arrangements to be advised. Besides his immediate family, there were notices from his parents and other relatives, plus Andy Nguyen at Excellerate Training Academy. Andy Nguyen stated that Barton was a valued employee who would be sadly missed. The comment left by Mr. and Mrs. Barton senior was that 'someday, we will understand'.

That last comment suggested death by suicide, but his wife's entry referred to an accident. Clearly, the jury was out on the cause. Probably no one would ever really know. He was glad he hadn't made any official comments about what he might have seen. No point in sticking your head above the parapet for no good cause.

Sunday was bike-ride day, not every Sunday but occasionally he met up with Harry, caretaker of the KFG Insurance Building. Riley kept his bike in the basement carpark of Blenheim House, and enjoyed getting out of the city for some fresh air and exercise. Harry was the only one who seemed happy to accompany him.

They varied the route for each ride, depending on what events were happening in and around the city. Their stand-by ride was along the riverside linear park down to the beach. They checked out the local cafes for lunch, and then rode back again. This was their chosen route today.

They weren't the only ones on the path. Sunday joggers, parents with prams, and other cyclists travelled the path in both directions. Ringing the bicycle bell alerted others that bikes were approaching. The route wasn't onerously long, but his calf muscles let Riley know that they'd had a work-out.

They chained their bikes to a rack, and sat sprawled at an outside table at one of the cafes at Henley Beach, competing with the screeching seagulls for their lunch. If you gave in and threw them a chip, the whole flock descended around you demanding their share.

"Just eff off, why don'cha?" Harry bellowed in irritation. He waved an arm at one bird that got too close, resulting in a few of them becoming airborne, only to settle back in the original place almost immediately.

"I hear you had a bit of excitement through the week," he said through a mouthful of sandwich. "Watched a bloke top himself."

"I did no bloody such thing. I suppose Winston told you that."

"Nup. Colin did. I ran into him in the Mall yesterday. He said you and a few others had a drink in the Colonial the other night."

"I ran up the flag… you could have come too."

"Nah, I had something else on. Anyway, Colin said you were a witness. Who was it? He didn't tell me that bit."

"For the umpteenth time, I didn't see anything. I only thought I might have and there's a big difference. The bloke, as you refer to him, was David Barton. He worked with Excellerate, the major tenant in the Institute."

"Barton… what did he look like?"

"I've no idea. All I saw was pink water running down the gutter the next morning as a council worker washed off the stains."

"Ugh. I knew a David Barton once. He was a junior accountant and I was a lowly admin officer in a company we worked for after leaving uni. I didn't have much to do with him. He was the quiet responsible type, while I was cutting loose with my mates. We found him boring."

"Can't be the same person. This one had more of a reputation for wine, women, and song, with a bit of financial embezzlement thrown in."

"Doesn't sound like him. There must be two of them running around. Both working in finance though... funny, that."

"Must be. It's not an uncommon name. Finished? Time to head back."

Winston already sat at the regular table in the Daily Bean when Riley and Ginge arrived the following morning. That was a first. He looked as though he hadn't slept. A long black coffee sat in front of him. Bruno gave Riley a nod of acknowledgement, then pulled a concerned face in Winston's direction before shrugging his shoulders in an 'I don't know what's the matter with him' action.

"Eggs on toast, plus coffee?" he asked.

"Thanks, Bruno."

"Glad to see some things are normal." The comment was delivered to no-one in particular.

Riley pulled out a chair opposite Winston and sat down. He knew Ginge would take care of himself. "Let me guess... you sat up fretting all night."

"It's all right for you. Your life isn't about to be uprooted. You're younger than me, so it's easier for you to move on."

"You don't know for sure that your building is under threat. Who owns it, anyway?"

"Nico Stavros, a tuna fisherman from over Eyre Peninsula. He made his money on the boats and then invested in the city. I see him a couple of times a year, and sometimes he gives me some Coffin Bay Oysters or something like that."

"I wouldn't object if Blenheim Pastoral sometimes slung a few steaks in my direction, but I won't hold my breath. If you're on speaking terms with him, why don't you ask him what's going on?"

"Because what I was told is confidential. I'm not supposed to know."

"Tricky. Best thing you can do is check the source of your information, and then look at your employment contract. If the building is sold, the new owner will still need a caretaker. Your employment might be guaranteed under the conditional clauses."

Winston noticeably brightened as he considered this prospect, but then his shoulders slumped again. "I don't have a contract. There was nothing so fancy when I was employed, but still… the new owners would need someone, wouldn't they… unless they demolish of course."

"The next option I'd recommend is to throw your weight behind the campaign against the re-zoning of this sector of the city. You've got nothing to lose and everything to gain."

Winston sighed, and his face slipped into his customary hangdog look. Bruno appeared at the table and plonked the plate of eggs in front of Riley, followed by the coffee.

"Help yourself to salt and pepper. That's on the house." The comment had been repeated so often it had become stale. Neither Riley nor Winston reacted, and Bruno rolled his eyes before heading back behind his counter.

"I hear you chatted up a woman at the Colonial," Riley said by way of changing the topic of conversation.

"Who told you? Jonathan, I suppose. Nothing's private around here. For your information, we simply got talking, that's all. Interesting woman; we have some shared interests."

"Oh?"

"We both collect vinyl, mostly of the sixties and seventies. If you have any in mint condition, it's a collector's item these days. Not that I want to sell any of mine."

"That's a coincidence. Are you going to see her again?"

"Sure. Just as friends… you know how it is. She's coming to see my collection on Saturday."

"Sounds like a version of 'Come up and see my etchings'", Riley teased.

"Be nice. It's nothing like that."

"Does this vinyl collector live in the city? What's her name? You don't often see women on their own in the Colonial, unless they're mates of Celeste."

Winston rolled his eyes theatrically. "You're so last century, Riley. Women can go anywhere on their own these days. Her name's Katrina—Katrina Dale. She lives somewhere in the city, I think. I didn't like to pry."

Riley wiped the dregs of yolk from his plate with a piece of toast. "Make sure you have some coffee on hand and fresh milk; not that stale tin of brown powder that masqueraded as coffee last time I visited your place. Get some biscuits too. Chocolate ones preferably."

"When I want your advice, I'll ask for it. I don't see you entertaining many women, so you're hardly an expert."

He had a point there, but Riley wasn't going to admit it. He opted not to comment further, instead checking on Ginger. The cat had finished his milk and was engaged in his washing routine, sitting where the early morning sun hit the front window. Winston gave a doleful sigh and pushed his chair back from the table.

"I've got work to do. I'll see you later."

"Sure. Don't forget what I said about throwing some weight behind the protest group." Winston was at the door when another thought occurred to Riley.

"Winston—do you know a bloke who drinks at the Colonial called Lenny?"

Winston stopped and looked around with an odd expression on his face. "Why do you want to know?"

"No reason. I've seen him around a bit lately, that's all. I wondered where he was from."

"If you know what's good for you, you'll keep away from him… and his mate."

With that, Winston pulled the door closed behind him and disappeared. Riley sat for a while, mulling over what Winston had just said. It wasn't like the man to be close-lipped. He must be still stressing over the potential sale of the Institute, but even so, Riley had the impression he wasn't telling everything he knew. That was most unlike Winston.

He scooped up Ginger and headed for the door himself. As the man said, there was work to be done.

9   Drinks with Phoebe

"YOUR GIRLFRIEND DROPPED in. She left you this." Diane held out the envelope, not bothering to hide the smirk on her face.

"Girlfriend? Who are you talking about?"

"I'm not your private secretary. I didn't ask her for details. She was here the other day."

She eyed him expectantly, as though hoping he would open the envelope in front of her. Riley took it, turning it over a couple of times before taking it with him down to his workshop in the basement where he could open it in privacy. He found a scribbled note inside, plus some printouts.

I thought you might like to have a copy of these. If you give me your email address, I can send electronic copies. Sophie.

The attachments consisted of photos of the façade of Blenheim House, plus other shots she'd taken from the roof. To his surprise, he found himself in one of those, standing off to one side and looking out over the cityscape. He hadn't noticed her taking that. He appreciated her providing the photos though.

Her business card advised that she was Sophie Robinson, Heritage Consultant, and gave her mobile number and email address. He thought about calling her but felt stupidly shy. Perhaps he could just text or email her. His interactions with women always left him feeling gauche. He knew that was stupid but that was him. Phone calls were confronting.

For fucks sake Riley, put on your big boy pants. She's someone you've met in a professional context, not a social contact. Just pick up the phone.

He spread the photos out on the workbench where he could see them all, and then took his phone from his pocket before he could talk himself out of it.

"Hi Sophie? It's Riley... Riley Monroe. Thanks for the photos... No really, that's most thoughtful of you... yes, I'd love electronic copies. I'll email my address to you and then you can just hit reply... sure, get back to me if you have any queries."

He felt pleased with himself after he disconnected the call. It could be useful having a contact on the inside of the rezoning process. He should have invited her for coffee or something. That would have been the smart response. The trouble was, he'd never invited a female anywhere before, not since the end-of-year formal in the final year of high school, and that was an experience he preferred not to think about.

He needed a good reason for extending the invitation. He thought of his grandfather's albums. They were full of early photographs of the city. On graduating high school, he had enrolled in a Bachelor of Architecture, and his mother had given him guardianship of the albums. Riley hadn't inherited the architecture gene, and had dropped out of studies after a year, but had kept the albums. His mother had forgotten they were still in his possession. He could offer to show Sophie the photos.

When he slipped upstairs for morning tea, he fired up his laptop and sent off an email, repeating how much he appreciated the images. She might like to see some family photos relating to the early twentieth century in the city, this sector in particular. He could meet her at the Daily Bean for coffee at her convenience.

The sub-text was of course that he wanted to learn more about her findings and what might be included in her report. He reviewed his message twice for typos and coherence before pressing <SEND> and felt both strategic and clever. That done, he made a coffee in an eco-cup, grabbed a biscuit, and headed outside. A new tenant was moving into level eight, and he needed to shut off an elevator cabin to general use and install the wall protector sheets.

A throbbing noise passed overhead as he reached the stairwell, followed by a fast-moving shadow. He paused, looking skywards. A helicopter flew in the direction of the helipad at the Royal Adelaide Hospital. Sometimes they flew so close he could almost wave to the pilots. He hoped whoever it carried would be fine.

The noise drowned out the sound of Phoebe practicing, but not for long. As the chopper sank towards its destination, the sounds of the piano took its place. That reminded Riley that he needed to check on her to see how she was withstanding the pressure from Harrison's wife. Really, if

93

Harrison Mortimer had not been able to keep it in his pants, he should have looked after his long-term lover better than he had. Phoebe gave up a promising career for him. The least he could have done was give her clear title to the apartment. He could have afforded that. Tight bastard. Not that he would voice that opinion to Phoebe. He would contact her later.

"Did you hear about that man who jumped?" Diane asked. "He had a gambling problem with a bit of fraud on the side." She sounded pleased with herself, being the one to impart gossip for a change. She rarely did so with him, which told him how keen she was to pass on this juicy piece of information.

"Bit of fraud?" Riley paused on his way to his workroom.

"Yes, he fiddled the books at Excellerate to fund his gambling problem. The accounts were being audited and he knew he was about to be found out. That's why he did what he did."

"And you know this because?"

"I have lunch with Stella occasionally. She's the receptionist with Excellerate, and she told me. They haven't proved it yet, but something funny was going on. It must have been him. Why else did he jump?"

"And what about the affair he was having?"

"Affair? I don't know anything about that."

Her phone rang. She pushed her glasses up her nose, then reached for the handset with one hand and tapped a key on her keyboard with the other. Her screen sprang to life. He was dismissed, her attention now on her incoming call. Riley continued on down to the basement, turning over what she'd said. Bruno suggested Barton's wife's family had intimidated him into jumping because of an affair, and Diane said that he was about to be sprung for embezzlement. Either way, the stories suggested a man who walked on the wild side and paid the price. They also suggested that he jumped rather than he was pushed. Why wasn't he convinced?

That evening, after he had eaten his stir-fry, fed Ginge and washed their dishes, Riley wandered back outside to check if the lights were on in Phoebe's apartment. They were, and the sliding door was open, letting in the evening breeze. Golden coral colours streaked the sky, bathing the hills bordering the suburbs to the east with a blend of muted colours. Riley always found this to be a magical time of night; day hadn't quite ended but night hadn't begun.

He put the whistle he kept for signalling Phoebe to his lips, giving three sharp blasts. She appeared at the gap in the sliding door and waved. Riley cupped his hands around his mouth and called over the divide. "Are you home to visitors this evening?"

She nodded and beckoned to him to come over. "Come and have a drink"

I see. Like that, is it? "Sure. See you in five."

He slipped back inside and grabbed a jacket in case the temperature dropped before he came home, and also grabbed a bottle of merlot. He didn't like to go empty handed. As the doors of the lift pinged open on the ground floor, he realized Ginger had sneakily entered the lift as well.

95

"Hey, I'm heading out. You need to stay here."

The cat regarded him with a slight tail swish and a look that said, "I'm coming too."

Riley debated what he should do. Taking the cat back upstairs again would be a hassle. "Okay. It's only next door so you can come with me. Just this once."

The cat trotted behind him, occasionally giving a small miaow. It occurred to Riley that he ought to get a leash if Ginger was going to accompany him on the street. He moderated his pace for the cat's benefit. Ducking into the Daily Bean was one thing, but going further afield was another. He scooped up the cat when crossing the laneway between Blenheim and Mortimer House. Couldn't be too careful.

"Here's the man and his cat. Do you reckon he thinks it's a dog?"

Of all people! Alex and Jodie sat on the steps of the main entrance to Mortimer House. Didn't those two have a home to go to? Silly question; of course, they didn't. Alex smirked at Jodie and they both laughed.

"Looks more like a rat to me," Jodie snickered. "You wanna be careful. Anything can happen to an animal on the streets."

This last comment was directed towards Riley. With her spiky, green hair and dark-rimmed eyes, Jodie could have resembled something from Jurassic Park. He was tempted to respond that they ought to know from personal experience, but he didn't want to engage. Instead, he kept a firm grip on the squirming feline and hurried around the corner into Hindmarsh Street.

The Ferals had un-nerved him. He looked over his shoulder before punching the code in the box on the wall that gave him access to the private entrance and Phoebe's lift. He saw a homeless man setting up for the night on the steps of the Institute further down the street. Sadly, the number of homeless people in the city was increasing, and often they slept in the doorways of Skywalker buildings. Sometimes, they slept in the adjoining alley, but that put them at risk of being run over by the garbage removal trucks. It was up to Winston to move the man on, if he felt so inclined. Riley was torn between sympathy for their plight, and annoyance at having to clean up rubbish and puddles of urine in the mornings.

He only put Ginge down when they were inside the building. The ride to the top was swift. The elevator had been upgraded recently and was regularly maintained. At least Harrison had made that financial provision in relation to Phoebe. The cabin opened into her foyer area, and the door to her apartment was already open, presumably in anticipation of his arrival.

"Come in, and shut the door behind you." Phoebe sat out on the balcony, with a platter of cheese and biscuits on the table, and two wine glasses. An open book sat face down on her lap, indicating how she had been spending her time. She peered over the top of her glasses. "Good lord. I didn't expect you to bring that animal with you. Does it eat cheese? I suppose it will expect some milk."

She rose and presented her cheek for Riley to kiss. He never felt gauche or awkward with Phoebe. She had certain standards and expected everyone to fall into line.

"You brought a bottle. How lovely of you, dear. Perhaps you could open it and pour us each a glass while I get a saucer of milk."

Ginger stalked around the balcony, sniffing in the corners and at the pot plants while Riley and Phoebe sat at the table. Phoebe always had an excellent selection of cheeses, and Riley happily helped himself to a small plateful before broaching the subjects that had brought him over.

"Firstly, how's the preparation going for your recital? From what I hear at odd times through the day, it's perfect."

She flexed her fingers. "Not up to my standard when I was in my prime, but still good for an old dame."

"Not so much of the old," Riley said gallantly. "Your fingers are as nimble as ever."

"Tray Thornton seems to think so. I have no idea if he'd heard of me before Luci met his son, Finn. It was such a surprise when he rang me. I thought it was a scam at first, and wasn't going to let him in."

"So, he's been up here?"

"Oh, yes. He brought me a beautiful bunch of yellow roses. No-one's done that since Harrison died."

"That's nice," Riley said, looking around to keep an eye on Ginger. "He knew the way to sweet-talk you then."

"Yes, but he didn't have to. I was doubtful that anyone would want to hear me play, but when he told me about the cause he was supporting, I had to agree."

"You might get your picture in the social pages. It could be the start of a new phase of your career."

"Don't be ridiculous. I'm much too old for that."

Riley noticed that her eyes sparkled as she fingered the pearls that hung around her neck. He sincerely hoped some recognition came her way. She deserved an audience wider than him after all this time.

"What news about the request from Cornelia Mortimer?"

Phoebe's expression darkened. "That bloody woman! Who does she think she is, trying to get me out of my home. Harrison meant me to have this for life, and that's what will happen. If he hadn't died in that crash, he'd still be looking after me."

"Have you spoken to Charles?"

"Yes. He's approached one of his mates from the legal fraternity. I've given Charles power of attorney, so that if I should ever be declared incapacitated, or unable to make rational decisions, he can step in for me. That means Cornelia's lawyer can't claim I'm mentally incompetent and try to force me out. He would have to deal with Charles."

"So, the pressure is off?"

"Not quite. Now there is a fresh challenge to Harrison's will, saying he was of unsound mind when he added that clause granting me the tenancy. Supposedly, I exerted undue influence over him."

Unexpectedly, she grinned. "You've no idea what a boost it's given me to be regarded as a femme fatale at my age."

Riley raised his glass. "Here's to the sauciest femme fatale I know. May you seduce many more."

She swiped at him as though to say, "Riley, you're awful", but was clearly delighted at the suggestion.

"Enough about me," she said. "You're not the only one who keeps an eye on events across the divide. I saw you on the roof with a young woman the other day. Who was that? Is your luck looking up?"

"Nothing like that. She's a heritage consultant with the council. I ran into her in the street when she was taking photos of the buildings and got talking to her. I brought her up to the roof level so I could show her a bit about the history and development of the area."

"She looked quite nice, and about your age too. Are you seeing her again?"

"Phoebe, she's not a social contact. It's purely business."

"It's about time you found yourself a partner. You can't rely on a cat forever." She paused uncertainly. "You're not into men, are you?"

"Definitely not. Women only, but I don't know any."

"Now you do. Listen to me, Riley... you can't simply let life pass you by. You have to seize happiness when it presents itself. Harrison was the love of my life. I had to choose between him or my career, and I chose him. Imagine if I'd never done that. I wouldn't have had that deep and lasting connection, and I wouldn't have my Charlie."

It was the first time Riley had heard her speak so affectionately about her son. Not that he doubted their relationship. As for women, he'd never actively looked for a partner, much to the dismay of his mother, who considered it to be a major failing. He found online dating intimidating, and didn't have the confidence in other face-to-face interactions.

"There's unlikely to be someone of the calibre of Harrison to come and sweep me off my feet. It doesn't happen that way for men. I don't have beauty and talent to offer."

"There are other attributes a woman values, like kindness and empathy. Who knows, you may be a stallion in bed."

"Phoebe! I didn't come here to discuss my sex life."

"That's because you don't have one. Would you mind topping up my drink?"

Riley reached for the bottle and obliged, filling his own as well. He needed a drink after the turn the conversation was taking.

"If I had a sex life, I still wouldn't discuss it. Some things are private."

"I like a man with ethics," Phoebe said. "That's one of the reasons why I like you. Tray Thornton is a man with ethics as well. He's made a lot of money but he came from humble origins as the child of post-war migrants. He hasn't forgotten that, and gives back to the community where he can."

"Does he have some connection with the Children's Heart Foundation?"

"Not personally as far as I know. He just wants to help."

"That's very commendable. His son, Finn seemed a pleasant young man when we met him at your birthday bash. He must take after his father. Are he and Luci attending this function? You will have to ask them to take some photos and forward them to the Skywalkers."

"I think they'll be there. I'll relax more knowing my granddaughter is in the audience."

"You'll slay them, I'm sure."

They polished off the bottle before Riley decided that he and Ginger should wander back home. After prowling around both the balcony and accessible areas of the apartment, Ginger had curled up on a lounge chair and gone to sleep. Phoebe declared him to be a very polite guest, and said he could visit at any time. Riley dropped the empty wine bottle into the kitchen waste bin before scooping up the sleepy cat.

"I'm glad Charles has things under control. I'd be devastated if you weren't here. Who else would serenade me like you do?"

"I'd miss you too. Thank you for coming. I'm so lucky having people like you watching out for me."

Phoebe accompanied them to the elevator lobby, and waved as the doors slid closed between them. Riley stepped out cautiously onto the street after emerging at ground level. He paused in the cool night air, with one hand on the wall for balance. He'd drunk more than he realised. The Ferals were nowhere in sight, and nor were any other obvious threats. He kept a firm grip on the wriggling cat. They only had to walk a short distance around the corner, but after the earlier interaction, he didn't want to take any chances.

The steps were clear, with no unwanted presents waiting for him. He looked around once more when groping in his pocket for the fob key, unable to shake off the weird feeling he was being watched. Alcohol-induced paranoia probably, as nobody was in sight. Once inside, he dumped the cat on the floor, resolving to look for a cat leash in the next day or so, assuming of course that Ginge would cooperate.

Back on the roof, he saw Phoebe at her open doorway. She waved when she saw him and blew him a kiss before sliding the door shut and closing her curtains. Sweet. She was watching out for him as well. Her comments about finding a partner struck home. Having someone who had your back would be unbelievable. That was it. Unbelievable.

As he turned to go inside, he spotted a couple of bright red lights on the skyline. They hung from the end of the jib arm of cranes perched on top of high-rise buildings under construction. Low-flying aircraft were unlikely to be at that level, but the lights marked the position of the cranes at night. Development was occurring in some parts of the city. Hopefully, it wasn't a sign of things to come.

10 The Detectives

TAP WASHERS WERE the bane of his life. Every couple of days Riley received a complaint about a leaking tap on one of the floors and if not that, a toilet cistern wouldn't stop running. He could fix those problems without calling a plumber, but their frequency irritated him. Sometimes, the tap required re-seating and when it got really bad, he would have to replace the tap. Then he had to replace two so that they matched, unless the sink had a mixer tap.

He had his plumbing kit always packed and ready to pick up and go, and this morning he'd had to tackle the tap in the kitchen on level seven. It took several goes at replacing the washer and applying the tape to the threads before he was satisfied that the problem was fixed. Different washers suited different taps. He had just summoned the tenant who had lodged the complaint to make sure they were happy with the dripless tap, when his phone buzzed in his pocked. Diane.

"Riley, there are a couple of policemen here who would like to speak to you."

"What about?"

"I've no idea. As I've said before, I'm not your secretary. You had better come to reception."

"I'll pack up here and be down in a jiffy."

He jammed his tools back into his bag, more haphazardly than they usually went in. The tenant appeared in the doorway to the kitchen.

"Test it for yourself, mate. I've been called downstairs."

He heard an exasperated sigh behind him as he headed along the passage to the elevators and pressed the down button. The doors pinged open downstairs to two men standing with hands on hips under their suit jackets and watching the elevator door expectantly.

"Riley Monroe?" one of them said.

"Yep."

"Detectives James Mullin and Steve Ryan." They held out business cards proclaiming them to be who he said they were. "Is there somewhere we can talk? We want to ask you about what you saw when David Barton fell from the roof of the Institute."

Diane's head jerked up, and she didn't make any pretence of not listening. He knew she would tackle him about it later.

"Sure, but there's not much to tell."

"Can we go up to the roof level?" the other man asked. "You can show us from up there."

Riley shrugged. It wouldn't make any difference if they were on the roof or not. He still couldn't tell them much. They stood looking at him with expressions that said they weren't going anywhere except up to the roof. He turned and led the way to the elevators. Once in the cabin, the two men stood on one side and Riley on the other. He knew it was stupid, but they made him feel as though he had done something wrong. Police always made him feel guilty. They murmured to each other as the lift groaned and rose, but still kept an eye on him.

When they emerged from the stairwell onto the roof, the two men moved to the parapet around the roof edge and looked out over the city. His visitors always did that. No matter what their purpose in coming up to that level, they couldn't resist taking in the view. Finally, they turned towards the Institute and murmured to each other once again.

While this occurred, Riley stood back and petted Ginge. He had understood that the case was closed in relation to David Barton. Suicide. Everyone said so. Why were these two asking questions now? They must be across some new information.

"Where were you standing that evening?"

Riley looked up from Ginge to find that the detectives had now focussed their attention back on him.

"I don't know what you've been told, but I'm not sure that I saw anything relevant."

"Just tell us what you did see." Steve Ryan was the shorter of the two, and Riley noticed that the bottom button of his shirt strained against the pressure imposed by his belly. The man ought to go on a diet. His manner was abrupt, as though talking to someone about to defy him.

"It was overcast, dark with not much moonlight… the storm was coming in, so wet and windy. I was inside, but remembered I had washing on the line and opened the door, thinking I would grab it and bring it inside. The clothes were already too wet, so I didn't bother."

"We're not interested in your washing. What did you see across the way?"

Detective Mullin touched his colleague on the arm, as though to stop him interrupting. "So, it was raining."

"Heavily. As I stood there deciding what to do, I thought I glimpsed movement in the corner of my eye over on the roof of the Institute Building. When I peered more closely, it looked like there were a couple of people there... moving around sort of... dancing like."

"Dancing?"

"It was only a glimpse in a band of light. Then the clouds covered over again and I couldn't see anything. I can't even be sure of what I saw."

Detective Ryan sounded exasperated. "Why didn't you tell us about this?"

"What was there to tell? I might have imagined it. Anyway, everyone said it was suicide. Guilty conscience or something."

"That's a matter for the police and the coroner to decide. You were at the doorway, you say? Where were these moving figures?"

Riley walked over to his doorway. "I didn't get any further than here. The weather was too bad. Whatever it was I saw was around that section of the roof." He pointed over at the Institute rooftop, trying to remember what the vague shapes looked like and exactly where they were. This was a pointless exercise. "Who told you I saw anything, anyway?"

"We've been making enquiries. A few people have mentioned it."

Winston and his big mouth. First, he tells me not to say anything, and then he tells every man and his dog.

On cue, Winston appeared on his rooftop, and he wasn't alone. A short, stoutish woman accompanied him. Riley assumed it was the fellow vinyl enthusiast. Winston spotted them and waved to Riley, almost as though he wanted to draw attention to himself being in the company of a woman. It wasn't a charitable thought, but Riley wasn't feeling charitable towards Winston at that moment. He saw Winston lean towards the woman in conversation, and then nod towards him. No doubt Winston was relaying the story to yet another person.

The detectives watched the couple on the other rooftop, muttering to each other that it gave an indication on what people might look like from that distance.

"We've seen enough," Detective Ryan said. "Thank you for your time. Here's my card. If you remember anything else, give me a call."

They didn't wait for him but headed for the stairwell leading to the lower floor. Riley let them go. He didn't want to take the ride down to the ground floor in their company, nor did he want to be grilled by Diane if he did. As he watched them open the door to the stairwell and disappear, his eyes fell on the leather gloves, still sitting on top of an upturned bucket where he'd left them to dry. He gathered them up and put them away in his outdoor storage cupboard.

Time for a cup of tea. While the kettle boiled, he rifled the biscuit tin for some shortbread biscuits, and then sat down with the phone to scroll through any emails or messages. He thumbed over the usual spammy posts, and advertising emails from companies he'd never heard of.

One email in the in-box stood out from the rest. The sender was Sophie Robinson. The kettle turned itself off with a resonating click. Riley dropped a teabag into his mug and poured over the water. He really wanted to know what she wrote, but forced himself to fetch the milk from the fridge and finish making his tea before opening it and sitting down to read. The message was brief and to the point.

<Hi Riley, thanks for the invite. Would be interested in the photos. They may assist in completing my report. I can meet you at the Daily Bean tomorrow afternoon at 2:00. Sophie.>

Great. If she thought the photos contributed to the report, she might mention what she intended to write. He glanced at his watch. Diane should be at lunch. He still had his plumbing kit with him but it would be safe now to take it back downstairs to his workroom. He could avoid the confrontation.

"Who were those blokes on your roof yesterday?" Winston sauntered into the Daily Bean the next morning, just as Riley and Ginge were about to leave.

"They were a couple of detectives. You could have warned me you'd set the cops on me."

"Cops? Not me. I wouldn't do something like that."

"They seemed to think I saw something the night David Barton jumped. If you didn't tell them, who did?"

Winston's eyes slid sideways, and Riley could have sworn the other man lost colour. "Anyone could have said something... Phoebe or Charles for instance."

"Yes, but they didn't. You told the window washers, because they asked me about it the next day. Who did they tell? You might as well have stood up on your rooftop and yelled out to the entire city."

"I didn't directly say anything to them. I told Andy Nguyen, because he was concerned, being Barton's boss. He had a right to know. The window washers overheard me. I didn't realise they were so close. The door was open to the balcony on that floor."

Riley stood up. "Just to clarify, I didn't see anything definite. It might have been shadows. It might have been my imagination. It might have been nothing at all." He spoke slowly and deliberately so there could be no misunderstanding. He knew Bruno listened as well. "Why would other people have been on the roof if he jumped?"

Winston gave him an unblinking stare. "That's the big question, isn't it?"

Time to change the subject. He didn't need conspiracy theories in his life. "So, who was the woman with you yesterday? Was that your fellow vinyl enthusiast?"

Winston's mood flipped up a notch. "Yeah. That was Katrina. Nice woman. It's good to meet someone of her age with similar interests. We even like the same music."

Riley mimed playing the violin. "You'll be buying her roses next."

"It's not that sort of relationship. We have shared tastes, that's all." He looked meaningfully at Ginger. "It's better than only having a cat for a friend."

"On that note, my friend and I need to get on with our day. Enjoy your tea and toast."

Riley paid for his breakfast and whistled to Ginger. The cat ignored him initially, but lifted his head slightly, which Riley knew meant the cat had heard. He opened the door. "Up to you, Ginger. You can come with me now, or you stay here." The cat stalled for a tense moment before rising and following him to the door. The distance between the door of the Daily Bean and the front door of Blenheim House was only a handful of metres, but the cat still managed to find interesting detritus to sniff at on the footpath.

"Ginger, you are not a dog. Leave that alone." Riley scooped up the cat and carried him into the building. He didn't want to be caught by Diane and so hurried back upstairs in case she came in early. If he could avoid her long enough, he might escape the interrogation over the police visit. He made sure he was in his workshop at her arrival time and found a host of repair jobs requiring his attention but waiting for a spare moment.

His luck ran out mid-morning. A furniture delivery arrived for one of the tenancies, and he had to supervise the elevator access. He felt Diane's eyes on him as he gave the delivery man instructions, sending him down to the basement carpark, to use the goods elevator. With that process under control, he tried to slip upstairs.

"Riley!"

"Can't stop. I've got to check they don't bash into any walls with their trolley."

She acted as though she hadn't heard him. "Why were those detectives asking you about David Barton? Did you see something?"

He paused, and closed his eye momentarily with a brief sigh before opening them again and turning to face her. Might as well get it over with. "No, I didn't see anything. Everyone thinks I did, but I didn't."

"Why didn't you tell me about this the other day? Why would they think that if you didn't?"

This was a perfectly reasonable question. Nobody would have thought anything if Winston hadn't blabbed. "I glimpsed what I initially thought were some people fighting on top of the Institute Building at the height of the storm, but it was only shadows, moving shadows cast by the clouds or something like that."

"Would you recognise them again? How many were there? They were men, I assume."

"I can't recognise people I didn't see in the first place, and I don't know how many I thought I saw... two or three."

"So, you did see them!" She was triumphantly gleeful.

"Whatever." It was useless to argue. He jumped in the elevator and retreated to the corner as the doors slid shut. He hadn't stopped to think about what he really saw that night. When he'd heard the verdict of suicide, he'd accepted that he'd only seen shadows, but the detectives turning up like that made him question himself. If it wasn't suicide, then it was either an accident, or... or it was murder? That was ridiculous, but the question remained; if it wasn't suicide, what was David Barton doing on the roof, especially in that weather? He didn't have any answers.

Riley still ruminated on the questions about David Barton when he noticed the time. Ten minutes to two. He raced up to the roof level, running up the last flight of stairs, and washed his hands before grabbing the photo album. He'd left it out on the kitchen table that morning, after having flipped through it again while having his first cup of tea for the day.

He wasn't answerable to Diane, but on the way past reception, mentioned he would be in the Daily Bean, and he had his phone on him if there were any queries.

"I've told you before," she said, "I'm not your secretary."

"Thanks Diane."

He let the front door slam behind him. It was already three minutes past two. Bruno looked surprised to see him as he slid through the door behind the last of the midday crowd with the intention of grabbing his usual table. Other people sat there and he had to take another without a window view. Sophie hadn't arrived, which unsettled him. He hoped he had the right day, the right time… the right venue even. His anxiety level rose.

"Where is that hairy feline of yours?" Bruno called.

"He doesn't come with me in the middle of the day. I don't like him on the street with all the traffic."

"So, are you having coffee, or you just decided to come here and sit at one of my best tables?"

Best table? He has to be joking. "I'm waiting for someone. I'll order when she get here."

"She?" She was said with an amazed tone and appropriate eyebrow action. "Things are changing around here. First, Winston is in here with a woman, and now you are waiting for one. Have you both been swiping on dating apps?"

"Bruno, I think your customers need you. This is a business meeting, not a social event."

Sophie burst through the door, looking around until she spied him waving from where he sat. "Sorry, I got caught up! I came as quickly as I could."

"That's okay. I was a bit late myself. Can I get you a coffee?"

She sat down and rummaged in her bag for a notebook and pen. "Coffee would be lovely, and a glass of water if possible?"

Bruno had been watching this exchange with undisguised interest, and placed a bottle of water and a couple of glasses on the counter without being asked. When Riley approached to give him their orders Bruno gave him a surreptitious wink. Riley ignored it, fearing that to react otherwise would just encourage the man.

Returning to the table, he slid the album towards Sophie. "I should have thought of this when you visited the other day, but forgot momentarily that it may be of interest. My grandfather was an architect, and worked on many of the buildings in the city. It was undergoing significant development in those years, and he took lots of photos of the streetscape."

He didn't actually say that his grandfather designed Blenheim House, although she might deduce that from the photos. She opened the album and began looking at the pictures, examining each with care.

"This is amazing. It's a real treasure trove."

"I thought you'd find it interesting."

Her enthusiasm was affirming. Showing the album to her was the right thing to do. Bruno delivered their coffees, and they worked their way through the pages, discussing the various scenes.

"I don't know this building… where was the photo taken?"

"It was demolished some years ago, but it used to be on Goyder Terrace."

"That's a pity. I recognise this building though. It's hardly changed, except for the cars that are parked out the front."

She came to the last page and closed the book. "Do you think I could get copies of some of these photos? They will be useful in my report, but I'd also like copies of others for future reference. The state archives would be thrilled to see some of these as well."

"Sure. I can organize copies for you." He wasn't keen to let the album out of his possession. "I can get high-resolution scans." He paused to sip his coffee. "How is your report progressing?"

"I've finished the draft, but it needs review and final polishing."

"Are you able to tell me what your recommendations will be?"

"I shouldn't really until it is tabled, but—"

The door flew open to disclose Winston clutching Ginger Puss. "Riley… the cat… I found him in the street. Something's wrong. I think he's dying."

11   Ginger Puss

RILEY LEAPT FROM his seat. Ginger lay floppily in Winston's arms. His eyes were glazed and he breathed in quick, shallow pants. Drool at the corner of his mouth indicated he may have vomited.

"What happened? Where did you find him?" He took the cat in his arms, willing the animal to survive.

Winston gestured vaguely behind him. "He was in the laneway between Mortimer House and my building. It's a wonder he wasn't runover. I thought he was dead at first, and then heard a faint meow."

"Where's the nearest vet?" Sophie asked. "You'll have to get there quickly if you're to have any chance of saving him.

"It's in Kent Town. Oh fuck… it will take ages to get a taxi. This is shift change-over time."

"Don't you have a car?"

"I don't drive."

She looked astonished, but turned to Winston. "What about you? Do you have a car nearby?"

"I don't have a license," he said. Anguish was written on his face.

"My car is in the carpark opposite Trinity Church. Meet me outside in ten minutes. I'll drive you there." She ran out the door and was gone before they had time to respond.

Bruno had been making coffees, but now with a gap in customers, he hurried over. "What's happened? Was he hit by a car?"

"I don't think so. He must have eaten something bad... rat poison perhaps?"

"My food wouldn't have made him sick. This is a clean establishment. It's inspected regularly."

"He could have picked it up anywhere. He's a cat. He's got a wide territory." Riley looked anxiously out the doorway. It was too soon for Sophie to be back with the car, but he had to do something. He felt helpless. He stroked the animal's head, willing him to survive. More customers entered the café, and Bruno disappeared behind the counter to serve them.

The album still lay on the table at which Riley and Sophie had been sitting. "Winston, can you drop that into Diane, and ask her to look after it for me? Tell her I've got to go. I won't be back this afternoon."

"Sure... Riley, I'm sorry I couldn't drive you. I don't have a license anymore."

"I can hardly criticise you for that. I've never learned to drive... I hope she's quick."

"I'm sure she will be." Winston picked up the album. "I'll drop this into Diane and be right back." He cast a worried look at Ginger before heading for the door.

Riley dropped onto the nearest seat, cuddling the animal. He'd always thought he was happy living alone, and he was, but the arrival of Ginger had subtly changed his life. Riley had never had a pet before, and the cat's presence had been a relaxing influence. Everyone liked Ginger, well except for Diane. He was known throughout the building having acquired mascot status, and by neighbours, like Bruno and Winston for instance.

A hard lump threatened to choke his throat. He shook the cat. "Stay awake. Don't you die on me, don't you dare die." A beep outside alerted him to Sophie's arrival at the same time as Winston burst back through the door.

"She's here."

Bruno followed them out to the car with a towel. "Wrap him in this. Keep him warm. Don't let him be sick in the car. Good luck."

Riley slid into the passenger seat and buckled up.

"You'd better tell me the way," Sophie said.

"Rundle Street, Kent Town—opposite the Bunnings store."

"Got it." She flicked on the indicator and accelerated away from the kerb. As she did, Riley noticed Jodie standing on the footpath and watching. He'd never seen her on her own before. She and Alex appeared joined at the hip.

"How is he?" Sophie asked.

"Not good. He's barely holding on. He might be paralysed." He kept up a stream of muttered encouragement to the cat. If Ginger got through this, there would have to be changes to his routine. No more roaming. He was to stay in the building from now on.

The journey only took around seven minutes, but in that time, Ginger had a seizure. Sophie pulled up out the front of the building, and Riley jumped out, leaving her to park the car and follow him inside. A couple of dogs, and cats in pet carriers were already in the waiting room with their owners. People regarded him with a mixture of curiosity and concern as he approached the reception counter, calling, "I need a vet."

The receptionist glanced up from the client she was assisting as though to tell him to wait his turn. As soon as she saw Ginger, she jumped up from her seat and led Riley into a consulting room.

"Wait here. Someone will be with you shortly."

The door opened again a few seconds later, and a young man entered, took Ginger from Riley, and laid him on the examination table. "What happened? What are his symptoms?"

"He was found like this. I don't think he's been hit. He's been vomiting, just had a seizure, and is almost comatose. I think he must have been poisoned."

"Any idea what with?"

"No. Could be something he picked up while roaming. *Or something someone gave to him.*

"That makes it hard." The man applied his stethoscope to the cat's torso. "I'll insert an IV drip and give him an emetic and anti-seizure medication. He'll have to stay here." He looked directly at Riley. "There are no guarantees. He's a very sick cat. If he gets through this, he'll be lucky. Leave your details at the front desk. I'll call you tonight with an update."

"Thank you. Please do all you can."

When Riley emerged into the reception area, he found Sophie waiting on one of the chairs.

"How is he?"

"Not good. The vet will call me tonight with an update. It's touch and go."

He left his details with the receptionist as requested, then stood uncertainly on the footpath.

"God, I hate the smell of those places," Riley said. "It's so clinical and well… antiseptic."

"That goes with the territory," Sophie said. "Come on, I'll drop you back in the city."

"I didn't thank you before for driving us out here. Ginger wouldn't have had much of a chance without you. I really appreciate it."

"Happy to help. He looks a tough dude. I hope he pulls through." She drove back through the city streets and pulled up in front of Blenheim House. "I'll call you tomorrow to see how he is."

Riley unbuckled his seat belt. "I haven't forgotten the photos. I'll scan those that you thought were interesting and make a copy. Thank you again. I'm in your debt."

She brushed him off with a sympathetic smile. "Only too pleased to help."

As he watched her drive off, he decided it was about time he learned to drive. He'd never felt the need before. He rode a push bike everywhere in his teens and early twenties, and on occasions used public transport or hired a taxi or an uber. He figured he was miles ahead financially. Now that he lived and worked in the city, he had even less need of a car and so hadn't bothered with the license.

He would never admit it to anyone, but the longer he left learning to drive, the more impossible it seemed. He began to doubt his ability, and his anxiety took over. It was easier to convince himself he didn't need a license. It was also kinder to the planet if one less person drove.

Diane appeared anxious as he walked through the door. "How is he? Will he be okay? I was so upset when Winston told me what had happened."

That *was* a surprise. Diane always gave the impression of not having any time for Ginger. Riley rubbed his forehead, aware now of the beginnings of a tension headache. "The vet will ring me this evening with a progress report. It didn't look good when I left him."

"I'm so sorry to hear that. I'll be praying for him."

She handed over the album. Strictly speaking, his working day hadn't finished, but he didn't feel like returning to work. There was nothing urgent on the agenda, and nothing that couldn't wait until tomorrow. He thanked Diane for her concern and took the album when she produced it from beneath the front counter. He might as well start scanning the photos. It would give him something to do instead of fretting about Ginger.

The task took him longer than he expected. Some of the photos needed manipulating to improve the clarity and focus. There was a limit to his skills, but he was able to make some enhancements. He saved them on a couple of USB sticks: one for Sophie and another for himself.

Sitting hunched over his laptop for so long tired him. He made a cup of coffee and took it outside, needing fresh air and to stretch his legs. The city looked the same, yet was never the same. The familiar features were all around him, but each day presented variations in colour, activity, and atmosphere. Today, stressed as he was about Ginger, he cared little for the scene. He heard Phoebe playing, and on another occasion might have stood at the point closest to her building and listened, but for once, didn't have the patience.

As he watched, looking but not seeing, one action did permeate his consciousness. Colin had run up the purple flag above the hospital. That was an invitation to meet in China Town for a meal. They did that every so often. China Town was close to the Central Market, and was their preferred location for a plate of dumplings, or perhaps a bowl of phô. Not tonight. He wasn't in the mood.

Green flags of acceptance fluttered from a couple of poles. Not government and parliament house, of course, but as he watched, Mark lowered the flag at parliament house a smidgen. He noticed Winston hadn't responded. He probably hadn't seen the invitation. Riley glanced at his watch before returning inside. Surely the vet should have called him by now. He hoped that no news was good news.

To give himself some diversionary activity, he travelled down to the ground floor and checked that all doors were locked and that there were no messages for him on Diane's desk. He knew if anything urgent had arisen, she would have rung or texted him. He started with the basement carpark, and then checked each level, ensuring doors were locked and no people wandered the corridors who had no right to do so. He finished up at the roof level, and then didn't know what to do with himself. He looked out at the flags. It was too late to bother raising an acknowledgement himself, but he might as well join the others for a quick bowl of soup. If he had his phone with him, he would hear the vet when he called.

Chinatown was only a couple of streets away. Two stone dragons marked the entrance to the precinct, and the relevant streets and alleyways were distinguished by roast ducks hanging in the windows, queues of people spilling into the street outside popular venues, and families cruising past, checking menus and options. Employees stood outside some restaurants, encouraging pedestrians to enter, proclaiming their specials for the evening.

Riley knew where he was going and ignored all entreaties to try the restaurants and cafes he passed. The other Skywalkers were already seated when he pushed his way through the waiting diners to the large round table that they always booked.

"Riley... I thought you weren't coming!" Mark shunted his chair sideways to make room at the table for another chair. The waiter hurried over and set his place with a rice bowl and chopsticks, and poured him a cup of jasmine tea.

"I wasn't going to—it's been a bad day, but in the end, I decided I still needed to eat. I won't stay long, but wasn't in the mood to cook for myself." He looked around to see who else sat at the table. "Winston's not here?"

"No, he had a better offer. Can you believe it... he's gone to the Colonial with some woman. What's the world coming to?" Jonathan didn't try to hide his amazement.

"What's your problem, Riley? Why has it been a bad day?" Bruce put on his most caring voice.

"It's Ginger Puss. He's been poisoned. I'm waiting to hear from the vet if they've can save him."

123

There was a moment's stunned silence before the questions started. They all knew Ginger, having met him on social occasions in Riley's apartment. They had card nights occasionally. He gave them a summary as best he knew. No, he didn't know what the poison was, or where the cat picked it up. Winston found him. A heritage consultant with the council was with him when Ginge was found and she drove him to the vet clinic.

Riley reached for his tea. He had not had much to drink through the day, with all the drama going on.

"That was convenient, because I don't drive, and it meant I could hold Ginger in the car. Winston doesn't have a license, so he couldn't drive me."

"Two of you who don't drive! That's unusual." Mark screwed up his face with a puzzled expression.

Riley tensed at the questions he knew always followed his admission. "I never needed to drive. I've always walked everywhere or ridden my bike. What's the point when I don't have a car? It must be something similar for Winston. I've never asked him."

"He doesn't drive, because he chooses not to," Bruce interjected flatly. "He was involved in an accident years ago… his fault. Two little kiddies died. He did time for dangerous driving and to the best of my knowledge, has never driven since."

"Did time? Are you saying Winston has been in jail? I thought he used to live in a boarding house." Winston had never talked much about his past, and Riley had never asked him. It was an unspoken rule with the Skywalkers. You didn't ask questions about things that didn't concern you.

"It was the big house, not a boarding house, though he may have lived in one when he came out."

"How do you know this?"

Bruce leaned closer across the table and dropped his voice. "My sister's best friend used to go out with a cop. We got talking at a birthday function, and he told me about it. I didn't say anything before, because it wasn't any of my business. He did the crime and did the time."

They all stared at Bruce, digesting this news. Riley wished Bruce had kept this information to himself. Knowing this about Winston didn't sit comfortably with him. The waiter turned up to take their orders, and conversation moved on to other topics. Riley kept checking his phone in case there was a message for him, or perhaps it had rung and he hadn't heard it over the babble in the restaurant. When it finally rang, he grabbed the phone and pushed his way around the tables to the street outside where he had a better chance of hearing. Also, he didn't want to receive bad news while everyone else watched.

"Hello?"

"Riley, it's the Kent Town Veterinary Clinic. Ginger is holding his own. He's not any worse, but he's not better either. We're doing the best for him that we can. Check in with us in the morning."

Riley leaned against the window of the restaurant. He wanted a moment to himself before going back inside. Ginger was still alive. He had a chance. If he could just hang in overnight, perhaps he would be okay. People paused outside the restaurant to peer at the menu stuck to the window. Riley moved sideways so as not to obstruct their view. They were probably tourists. Locals knew where to go, where to get the best food.

People were doing the same thing on the other side of the street. As he watched, he saw two men enter a restaurant opposite. One of them looked like Lenny, the man who popped up everywhere he was, except this time, Lenny paid him no attention.

Acting on impulse, Riley darted across the road, dodging between the cars slowly cruising past. He slid along the window of the restaurant they'd entered, approaching the door from the side. Peering inside, he could see them talking to a waiter, presumably asking for a table. He slid his phone from his pocket and clicked on camera mode. Before he could chicken out, he stepped in front of the open doorway and snapped their photo. At the same time, Lenny turned around and looked directly at him. Sprung!

12   Winston's Past?

RILEY SPUN AROUND and dashed up the street, putting pedestrians between himself and the restaurant door. If he ran across the road to where the others waited, he risked leading Lenny and his mate straight there. He slipped down a side alley leading to a rear carpark. With his city-living experience, he knew which alleys led somewhere, and which were a dead-end.

Via a circuitous route, he ended up back at the restaurant, having approached from the opposite direction to the one from which he'd originally arrived. He paused ten metres from the entrance to observe. The coast appeared clear, but he kept his face turned to the window and away from the road as he slid through the doorway.

Meals were on the table and the others were tucking in. They looked up expectantly.

"You were a long time," Mark said. "What news of our furry friend?"

"He's hanging in there, but still not good. I have to call back in the morning."

"You okay?" Jonathan asked. "You were gone so long we feared the worst."

"Bit of a long story." He fished out his phone and pulled up the photos. "Jonno… is this that character called Lenny? Who's his mate?"

Jonathon peered at the screen, fumbling in his top pocket for his glasses. Riley took pity on him and passed the phone over. Jonathan enlarged the screen before responding.

"Yep… that's Lenny and the other bloke is his sidekick, Simmo." He passed the phone back. "What's going on, Riley? Why the photo?"

He wasn't sure how much to tell them. They would think he was being paranoid. They all kept eating, but still waited for his response. A bit of drama was always welcome. Riley spooned rice and a serve of beef in black bean sauce into his bowl while he thought. He picked up his chopsticks and captured a piece of beef.

"You're going to think I'm silly, but I think Lenny's been following me."

"Nothing's silly regarding Lenny, but why would you think that?"

Riley described his morning walk and the times he had come across Lenny, with the impression he had that it was not accidental. "His intention seems to be intimidation, rather than actual harm."

"Why would he do that?" Colin asked. "Have you been walking on the wild side? That's not smart with people like Lenny around. Best to keep your nose clean."

"I've done nothing wrong. I'm only guessing, mind, but it might have something to do with David Barton's death."

"Who?"

"The bloke who jumped off Winston's building. I might, and I stress *might* have seen people on the roof that night but it was stormy and I can't be sure. The police still have an open book on whether he jumped or was pushed. Word seems to have got around that I possibly saw something."

Bruce frowned as he picked up the teapot and topped up everyone's cup, managing to dribble tea over the white tablecloth in the process. "If it was on Winston's building, why didn't he see something? Surely, he would know if people were on his roof."

"He says he was inside with the door shut. It was a shitful night. He wouldn't have heard much. He's the one who let the word drop that I might have seen something, after telling me to keep it quiet, I might add."

"Don't you think that's a bit suss? Bruce asked. "After all, he would have made all sorts of contacts in prison. Of course, he's going to deflect any focus from himself. Have the police checked him out?"

Winston? The man had his faults, but he wouldn't do that to a mate. Riley shook his head. It wasn't feasible. "I wouldn't think so."

"You never know who called in a favour from him." Mark stabbed the air with a chopstick. "The code on the inside is strong. You don't contravene that, not if you know what's good for you… or your family."

"Winston doesn't have a family." Riley was sure about that.

"Yes, he has. Just because he doesn't see them anymore doesn't mean they don't exist."

Riley hated the thought that occurred to him, and didn't dare voice it. That would make it a possibility and he didn't want the others to take an assumption as being gospel. How come Winston was the one who found Ginger? Did he know more about the incident than he let on? That was ridiculous. Winston would never hurt an animal. Riley had difficulty imagining him hurting anyone, let alone pushing someone off the roof. Would he turn a blind eye while someone else did? He didn't have an answer to that question.

He needed to go home before the conversation got any worse. Winston had already admitted knowing Lenny. He threw enough cash for his share of the bill on the table, and pushed his chair back.

"I'm calling it a day. I'm not the best of company tonight."

"See ya, Riley," Bruce said. "Let us know about the cat. Hope you get good news tomorrow."

Mark puffed out his chest. "Yeah, and if Lenny and Simmo give you any trouble, they'll have us to deal with. We've got enough contacts in the city, including some of the local cops."

The others murmured their agreement. He nodded to them all and left. He appreciated their support. He was glad now he'd told them about Lenny. He'd learned a bit more because of it, and if need be, they would have his back. He wasn't sure how exactly, but just the fact that they offered him their support made him feel less anxious. Probably the whole thing was coincidence, and his imagination was running away with him.

He looked both ways up the street as he approached Blenheim House, but beyond the stray pedestrian, there was no one around that looked remotely suspicious, not even the Ferals. He let himself into the building and noticed a slip of paper on the floor, looking as though it had been pushed under the door. He picked it up and unfolded it.

First, it's the cat, then ...? Guess who.

Riley lay in bed, listening to noises outside. He knew he was safe. Nobody could reach him on the roof unless they scaled the side of the building and that was unlikely. He kept turning the questions over and over in his mind. Who left the message and why? Did they poison Ginger, and if so, why? He hadn't told the police anything, so why try to intimidate him? Sleep was elusive. He tried slow breathing, counting backwards, and imagining himself walking along a beach and listening to the waves. Nothing worked.

At around midnight, he gave up. He got out of bed and heated a mug of milk in the hope that would help. Braving the night air, he carried the mug outside. The city was a slumbering beast, but it never totally slept. It always kept one eye open.

Until now, he'd always felt the city was his at night. From his perch on high, he'd felt the heartbeat of the scene below, loved the vibe and felt a strong connection to the community that he related to and depended on. He never felt nervous or apprehensive in the city, no matter what time of day or night. This was his home.

Now he was aware of a level of menace that hadn't existed before. Probably it had, but had not impacted him personally. A plane tracked overhead in the direction of the airport. He followed the wing lights with his eyes, wondering what the pilot thought as he flew over the city on his or her descent. Probably how attractive the night lights looked, particularly those lighting up the River Torrens as it snaked around the edge of the CBD. Looks can be deceiving.

He peered through the dim light towards the rooftop of the Institute Building. Did he really see people that night? The comparison was as similar as apples and oranges. Right now, he could see the rooftop clearly. He might not be able to identify strangers, but he could recognise people he already knew, like Winston, for instance. That night was overcast and veiled with torrential rain. He wouldn't have recognised his own father. He wouldn't like to swear to anything in a witness box.

Looking at the Institute rooftop reminded him about what Bruce had told them at the restaurant. Judging by Winston's reaction when he'd asked the other morning if he knew of Lenny, there was more to his past than any of them knew. What was the connection? It couldn't be good.

The hot milk had cooled to lukewarm. He drank the rest of it and returned inside. Time to go back to bed.

He got some sleep, but it was disjointed and disturbed with weird dreams. He forgot the content on waking, but the feeling of unease he'd experienced remained with him. The veterinary clinic didn't open to the public until eight thirty, so he had to fill in time until then.

Bruno looked up expectantly when he entered the Daily Bean, his eyes asking a silent question. Riley shook his head. "I had to leave him overnight. I'll call the clinic as soon as they're open. I'm hoping that the fact they haven't called me means he's holding his own."

"He's a tough cat, that one. He won't give in easily. He gets an extra bowl of milk when he's here next, and perhaps a bit of smoked salmon. That'll perk him up."

Even Phoebe dropped in. Riley hadn't told her that Ginger was ill, but someone else had. Skywalkers were like that. What startled Riley the most was that she wore her slippers. Phoebe never emerged from her apartment unless she was immaculately dressed and made up. Even her hair was a bit straggly this morning. She must have come down in a hurry.

"Riley, what happened to your beautiful cat? I heard he is very sick. Is there any news?"

"Not yet, Phoebe. I'll call shortly. The clinic isn't open for another forty-five minutes."

She patted him reassuringly on the shoulder. "He won't desert you. I'd feel it if he was gone. Let me know when you hear some news." She shook her head at Bruno. "I'm not staying this morning. I just wanted to slip down to check on Riley and his cat."

She looked around at the customers, mostly regulars, who sat at their tables or waited at the counter. "Look after your pets, and they'll look after you," she pronounced, with a finger wagging action to accentuate her words. She then left, with the door banging behind her.

Bruno and Riley exchanged puzzled looks. It was most un-Phoebe-like behaviour. Either her concern for Ginger had over-ridden her usual demeanour or she was under stress of some sort. Bruno shrugged and brought over Riley's coffee, followed by Maria with the eggs. Riley hadn't ordered breakfast, given the interruptions, but Bruno had made assumptions. Maria usually left the eggs to Bruno to deliver, so the fact that she emerged from the kitchen today was noteworthy.

He bolted his breakfast and didn't bother with reading the paper. He wanted to rush through his morning chores in case he had to get to the clinic. At eight thirty on the dot, he made the call. The receptionist put him on hold for two long, agonizing minutes before the vet who had admitted Ginger, came to the phone.

"I wasn't sure last night, but this morning he has perked up and has had a small breakfast. He's unsteady on his legs, and is still on a drip. He's just had a top up of anti-seizure medication. I'm confident now of saying he'll survive, but I'd like to keep him under observation a while longer. Unless you hear otherwise, you can pick him up this afternoon around four."

Riley folded onto the chair in his workroom. He had psyched himself up for bad news. He hadn't expected to be so emotional over a cat, but then Ginger was no ordinary cat. "Thank you... thank you for saving him." The rest of the call related to ongoing care, and potential substances Ginge might have ingested.

"It could be one of any number of things," the vet said. "Rat poison is a biggy... rats eat the poison and cats eat the rats. They can also lick insecticides. Otherwise, tulips or lilies can be lethal for cats, and probably a few other plants."

Tulips and lilies were a rarity in the city, but not impossible to find. Perhaps he had visited the florist in the street one over. On the other hand, there was bound to be rat poison around. Any of the local restaurants probably had baits set around their outside bins. This was something he would investigate later. For now, the news was a relief.

He slipped into the Daily Bean to tell Bruno, and rang Phoebe and Winston, rather than yell across the rooftops. Neither would have heard him. He could hear Phoebe practicing her concert piece, and Winston could be anywhere in his building. Both were relieved to learn of the cat's progress.

Sophie called him late morning. "Sorry I didn't call earlier. Work stuff. How is he?"

"Doing better than expected, given his condition last night. He has responded to treatment, and the clinic said I can pick him up late this afternoon"

"That's terrific news. Do you want me to drive you to the clinic again to pick him up?"

Riley had been pondering that problem. He'd thought he would have to catch an uber, but the driver might object to an animal riding in the car. He hated to impose, but Sophie's offer would be a more practical solution.

"It it's not too much trouble…"

"If it was, I wouldn't have offered. What time?"

"Leaving here about three forty-five?"

"I'll be there."

She disconnected the call abruptly, saying she had work to finish. Riley remembered that he still hadn't found out what she was intending to say in her report. More important issues had interrupted their conversation. He would tackle that question later.

When Sophie pulled up in front of Blenheim House, Riley was waiting on the footpath with a pet carrier. He didn't own one but the word had gone out in the Skywalkers community, and Harry, caretaker from KFG Insurance Building, had turned up with one. Riley promised to return it at the earliest possibility. He had also been offered a possum trap, but politely declined. Ginger Puss was not a possum.

Sophie stopped in a loading zone. She kept the engine running while Riley deposited the pet carrier on the back seat and then slid into the front alongside her. He fished the memory stick out of his pocked and dropped it into the console between the front seats.

"I didn't want to forget this. I've scanned all the photos at high resolution, and made them as good as I can with my limited skills. It would help if I had the negatives, but I've no idea if they still exist. I'll have to ask my mother."

Sophie focused on her wing mirror, waiting for a break in the traffic before pulling away from the kerb. "Thanks. It's a real treasure trove for someone like me. Getting hold of photos that no other consultant has ever seen before will add credibility to my work. I need biographical details of your grandfather. He should be credited whenever they are used."

She pulled out behind a delivery van and in front of a motorbike at a speed which impressed him. It occurred to Riley belatedly that perhaps he should have checked with his mother before handing the images over, but too late now. "Are you thinking of using them in your report to Council?" he asked, as a way to bring that subject into the conversation.

"Probably. It's useful to be able to demonstrate the intentions of our city fathers when making planning decisions about the development of the city. Other cities around the world just evolved, but Adelaide is a rare example of a city that was planned before the first sod was turned."

"So, you like the city the way it is?" He knew it was a leading question. She didn't answer immediately.

"Thought went into where and how people would live and work in the city and that has been built on over the years. The original plan has been modified, and that is as it should be. A lot has changed since the first surveyor drew lines on paper. The city has to adapt to changing needs."

His heart sank. It sounded as though she was indicating support for changes to the zoning in their precinct, with the possibility of higher density development.

"However, in this instance, I think it's important to preserve aspects of the city profile. I understand the need for growth, and better commercial accommodation, but I believe there are precincts currently better suited to the type of rezoning that is proposed."

Riley turned over the significance of her words. "So, you're going to oppose the council rezoning?"

They were approaching the clinic, so had to wind up their conversation. "I don't make the decisions, Riley. Council may support the proposal, but it will still go to the State Planning Authority and the Minister for Planning will also be involved."

She pulled into the carpark. "I will make my recommendations in relation to the re-zoning supported by a raft of arguments supporting my case. What the Council does with my recommendations is up to them."

He hoped that meant she was going to oppose the re-zoning. Realistically, this was the best he could hope for. The rest was up to the protest group. They would have to maintain their pressure against the council and the elected members. That would wait for another time. Ginger Puss waited.

The cat appeared subdued, but gave a small meow of recognition. When Riley picked him up, the cat began a rumbling purr, indicating relief at his person showing up. This relaxed attitude lasted until he was placed in the pet carrier. That mode of transport was probably a first for him and he voiced his displeasure loudly while carried from the clinic to the car and then throughout the ride back to Blenheim House.

Sophie didn't get out of the car, but left it idling while Riley extracted the carrier from the rear seat. She held up the memory stick. "Thanks for the images. I hope you find out what the cat ate so it doesn't happen again."

Riley placed the carrier on the ground, and with one hand on the roof of the car, leaned in through the open passenger door. "Thanks again for helping me with Ginger. I really appreciate it. I'll call you later... tomorrow perhaps. I'd like to take you out to dinner to express my appreciation for your help."

He astonished himself at hearing his own words. He never invited women out to dinner, but then it wasn't as if it was a date type of thing. He was just expressing his gratitude. Ginger wailed loudly behind him."

"Sure, but I think you'd better get that cat inside, and I'd better move before a ticket inspector appears. Only too happy to help."

He shut the car door and she merged into the traffic as he and the protesting cat headed inside. Diane had already left for the day, so he was able to proceed up to the roof level without being accosted. The sooner he could let Ginger out of his mobile cage, the better. When he opened the door of the carrier, Ginger shot out and headed for the door of the apartment. His intention was probably to bolt outside, but on his wobbly legs, he didn't make it. He staggered and lurched sideways before collapsing into a confused sitting position.

"Look here, mate, you need to stay inside for a while. I don't know what you ate, and whether you found it for yourself or someone gave it to you, but for now, you're staying here."

Riley petted Ginger, and placed a saucerful of tinned gourmet cat food in front of him. He'd organized a kitty litter tray earlier in the day so that he could keep Ginger inside, for the first night at least. He knew the animal would protest loudly at the confinement but he was following the vet's recommendations. After a belligerent stare at the food, then at Riley and back again at the food, the cat deigned to lick it around the edges and then settled on the couch. The vet had also warned Ginger was likely to be subdued for a day or so.

Riley left him to snooze and made his final rounds of the building, checking doors were locked and no obvious dramas or messages from Diane. That done, he read until time for bed.

As soon as he crawled between the sheets, Ginge came and joined him, kneading the bedcovers until satisfied it was a suitable place to sleep.

The phone ringing woke him with a jolt, dragging him out of a dream. For a moment, he lay in the dark as his confused brain struggled to decipher the sound. The phone! He leapt from the bed, stumbling over a shoe, and stubbing his toe on the leg of the bed before finding the light switch and grabbing the phone. Caller ID said Winston.

"Hello?"

"Riley, come quick. You've got to help me."

13   The Rescue

"**WHERE ARE YOU?** What's happened?" Riley hopped on one foot nursing his toe.

"I'm locked in the Excellerate offices on Level 5. You've got to get me out of here."

"Why are you locked in their offices?"

"Don't worry about that now, just get me out. I can't be found here." Winston sounded desperate.

Riley wandered outside with the phone clamped to his ear and looked over towards the Institute. The lights were on in Winston's flat and more lights were on mid-way down the building. He assumed this was where Winston was. "Don't you have a master key? You should be able to access any floor, or get off it for that matter."

"This is inside their tenancy. They have their own locks internally. The door slammed on me and it's deadlocked."

Riley rubbed his eyes and peered over the parapet at where he assumed Winston to be. "If that's the case, how do you propose I can get you out? How can I access the building, for that matter?"

"I can open the window. If you can help me, I can climb out there."

"Do you think I'm spiderman? Climbing a ladder is challenging enough for me. I can't climb up the outside of buildings, and if you can't climb down, you're stuffed."

"You'll have to use the gantry. It's still on the roof. The window washers have finished, but some external painting needs touching up so it's been left for that use. The painters should start tomorrow. Go around to the carpark entrance. The pedestrian door has a coded lock. I'll give you the code."

"But I've never used a gantry. I've no idea how those things work. Besides, I was asleep."

"Well, you're not now. Riley, don't dick around. The gantry's easy. Come around the back, but don't let anyone see you. The code for the door is 1973."

Don't tell me… it's your year of birth."

"How else am I going to remember it?" You can't take the lift up to the roof, because you won't have the fob to swipe in the lift. You'll have to take the stairs. The doors to each floor from the stairwell aren't locked, but I don't normally tell people that."

"Fuck! You don't ask much!"

Riley! It will be daylight soon if you don't hurry up. You've got to get me out of here."

Riley sighed. "Okay, but you owe me bigtime for this. I'll get dressed and be right over."

The use of the gantry worried him, but he would figure that part out once he was on top of the building. He pulled on a pair of jeans and a t-shirt. He also grabbed his hard hat and orange safety vest. If he was challenged, he would look like a legitimate safety officer, and if he crashed the gantry, he might need the hard hat. He clipped a head torch to the hat and he was ready to go.

The street was quiet when he emerged through the front door, though he checked carefully before stepping down onto the pavement. A taxi cruised past slowly, looking for a late-night fare, but he avoided eye contact with the driver. He walked briskly and with legitimate purpose down Murray Street and around the corner into Hindmarsh Street. He turned up the laneway beside the Institute leading to the roller door for the carpark. This was where Winston had said he'd found Ginger. He needed to know more about that, but probably at another time.

The door Winston mentioned was alongside the roller door. Security lighting meant that he didn't have to turn on his head torch. He hoped there wasn't a night sensor camera in the lane as well. The buttons on the lock clicked as he keyed in the year of Winston's birth and he opened the door. Security lights in the basement carpark allowed him to find his way to the stairwell. He stood at the bottom, looking up. This would not be fun.

By the third floor, his legs began to grumble. He paused to take a couple of breaths and then continued to the fourth level at a more measured pace, pushing himself then to the fifth floor. He rang Winston's number.

"Winston, I'm here on level five. Are you sure I can't let you out from the inside?"

"Positive."

"Why don't I try? It will save time and be much safer. Where are you?"

"In the Finance Officer's office. It's at the end of the passage and on the eastern side. There's a sign on the door."

Cautiously, Riley opened the fire door from the stairwell, wincing as the hinges squealed. He knew nobody should be around, but still trod quietly as he traversed the passage, looking for the door that said Finance Officer. It was almost at the end of the passage. Somebody more important must have the corner office. The door was shut. He tried the handle, but Winston was right. It was locked.

"Winston!" He spoke in a stage whisper. "The door's locked. I have to keep going up to the roof."

He heard indecipherable muttering from the inside, but had a fair idea what Winston was probably saying. He gave the door handle one more jiggle before returning to the stairwell and continuing the climb. At least the break had given his legs a rest. When he emerged at roof level, his chest heaved and he could feel his heart thumping in his rib cage. He leaned against the external wall of the stairwell, catching his breath.

Lights were on in Winston's apartment, but otherwise the rooftop was in darkness. He approached the edge tentatively. After all, a man recently fell from this level. The height of the parapet made him realise that falling accidentally was unlikely. One would have to be leaning out a long way to overbalance and why would anyone do that in a storm? He found the gantry system and the cradle. There were two control pads, one in the cradle and another at roof level. Normally, when the gantry was in operation, a safety officer would remain on the roof, monitoring operations and with the ability to bring the cradle up if necessary. He was on his own and the thought terrified him.

The immediate task was to turn on the motor. He found the power switch on the wall of Winston's apartment, and then an ON/OFF switch on the rooftop control board. He flicked both switches on, and an array of lights and information screens appeared. Up, down, left, right controls appeared logical, but there was nothing logical regarding what he was about to do. What if the controls jammed? He'd be suspended in the cradle with no way of getting out, and Winston not able to rescue him either.

He tentatively pressed the down, the stop, and then the up button. The cradle responded. Next, he tried the left and right controls. He needed to position the cradle above Winston's window, and that was on the adjacent face of the building. He drove the cradle slowly into position, walking around the roof top alongside it. Once in the contraption, he just wanted to go straight down and back up again.

The screen of his phone lit up with a text message. <Where are you?>

For fucks sake, Winston... stop hassling me. <Just working out the controls. If all good, be there soon.>

He stopped the cradle in what he estimated was the right position. All that remained was to climb in and begin the descent. He peered over the edge at one side of the cradle, and his stomach lurched. He didn't look down a lot, in spite of where he lived. Usually, he looked out. A small step ladder leaned against the wall close to where the cradle had first been located, and he assumed this was used for climbing into it.

Those guys also had safety harnesses, but none were lying around on the roof. They would have been locked away with the rest of their protective equipment. He looked around for a piece of rope, or something he could use as a substitute. Nothing. He hoped someone would look after Ginger if he fell out.

He'd run out of excuses. Dragging the ladder over to where it was needed, he climbed it and then sat on the edge of the parapet with one leg in the cradle and the other on the roof side. Swinging the second leg over truly terrified him. With a firm grip of the edge, he swung his leg over and dropped the short distance into the bottom of the cradle. It rocked alarmingly, and dropping to the floor, he crawled to the middle and sat there until the wobbling stopped.

He should have taken a leak before he left his apartment. *Oh fuck, hold on*. Stress compounded the situation. He groped for the control panel, doing his best to maintain the centre of balance and began a jerky descent in a stop-start fashion. It seemed to take forever, but his confidence grew to the point where he was able to glide three metres in one burst. He'd lost count of the floors, figuring when he came to a lit window, that would be where Winston was.

"Oi, you're too far over." Winston leaned out the window, gesturing madly. "Bring it this way." Riley had been staring rigidly to the front, and almost missed seeing the open window. Winston had turned the light off, which, if he didn't want to be seen, was a smart move. It just made him harder to see. Riley inched sideways in jerky movements, and then adjusted the height so that Winston could clamber in.

"Okay, take it away." Winston slid the window shut behind himself and dropped down into the bottom of the cradle, causing it to rock wildly. Riley clung to the support rope, but Winston appeared to be unfazed.

"Fuck, that was close. I thought I was stuck in there all night."

Riley was perilously close to vomiting. "Would you care to tell me what you were doing there in the first place? Isn't a tenancy private property?"

"Yeah, but it's a long story. Just get us out of here before someone sees us."

He had a point. Riley nearly pressed the down lever again, but quickly caught the action and began their ascent. This was much faster than on the way down, smoother too. At the top, Winston pointed out that there was a small gate in the cradle facing the building, enabling them to step out of it more easily than climbing in. Pity he hadn't noticed that earlier. What he did notice was that Winston appeared to have shoved something under his top, an envelope or folder judging by its shape.

Once safely back on the roof, Riley left Winston to move the cradle back into its starting position and turn everything off, while he dashed inside the apartment to the toilet. As he stood in front of the porcelain bowl, he could feel the tremor in his legs. He wasn't sure which relief was greater; emptying his bladder or being back on a firm surface. What he'd just done was fucking crazy, and normally he didn't swear.

Winston hovered near the foyer to the lifts when he emerged from the apartment. "Thanks, Riley. The lift will take you to the basement. You won't need the fob to go down. Press the green button beside it to open the same door you came in."

"Thanks, Riley... that's all you've got to say? You owe me an explanation. I'm going now, because believe it or not, I was asleep in my bed, and that's where I would like to be as soon as possible, but tomorrow, you are going to tell me what this has been about."

Winston's eyes slid sideways. "Yeah, righto… I guess I owe you an explanation. I'll see you tomorrow."

Riley suspected that the story he was going to get might not be the truth, let alone the whole truth. He looked forward to whatever it might be.

Ginger Puss had slept through Riley's absence, thanks to the sedative administered by the clinic before his discharge. Riley rose early and peeked outside at Winston's Building. The gantry wasn't visible from where he stood. Everything looked so normal. Perhaps the night's escapade had been a dream. He shook his head at the memory. The curtains were open to Phoebe's apartment and he could hear her practicing. She was making an early start to the day. The sound of the music echoing off the buildings reassured him that everything was normal.

He checked his emails. There was a slew of messages relating to the proposed re-zoning. He'd attended a couple of meetings and had written a letter of protest to his ward councillor, the mayor, and the Minister for Planning. The woman convening the protest group had drafted a proforma letter and distributed it with the addresses of suggested recipients. She proposed that those sending the letters should personalise them by adding their own perspective.

Riley had thought carefully before sending his letters and had included an argument about the human scale of development, and social and cultural aspects of living and working in the city. He stressed the importance of heritage and retaining buildings of cultural significance in maintaining the unique character of city streets. The precinct in question had examples of late nineteenth century and early twentieth century architecture that warranted preservation.

The morning's emails filled his in-box because those in the group kept hitting <Reply All> instead of directing to specific recipients. The key information to emerge from the deluge related to a protest at the Council offices when reports were tabled and recommendations made. He made a note of the time and date, and headed downstairs to tackle the morning chores.

A couple of coffee cups and an empty chip packet sat on the front step and weird marks on the glass in the door indicated someone had got up close and personal with it during the night. Otherwise, nothing major. He brought the papers inside and grabbed the cleaning rags and brass cleaner from the storeroom behind the lifts to give the required polish to door plates and handles. That done, he slipped into the Daily Bean.

"Where's the cat?"

A regular customer challenged him as he walked through the door. He didn't even know the man's name, but evidently, he was known as the cat man. Bruno also looked up enquiringly.

"Snoozing this morning. He hasn't been well these past two days, so I let him sleep in."

"I wish people would do that for me whenever I felt unwell," the man muttered to no-one in particular.

149

You wouldn't say that if it meant having a gutful of poison first. Riley nodded at the man and after grabbing the paper, headed to his usual seat. "The usual, Bruno—thank you."

Bruno was busy with a customer but he nodded in his direction, and Riley knew his order would be delivered promptly. There wasn't much of interest in the paper. The headlines proclaimed the government's stance on renewable energy, and the impact of a spectacular vehicle accident claimed most of the front page. He flipped over the pages, noting snippets of interest here and there.

The name Tray Thornton jumped out at him. Recommendations for Australia Day honours were being sought, and his was one name put forward. Known for his charitable works, Tray Thornton was described as a man who never forgot his roots, and had pledged to give back to the country that had done so much for his family, first his parents and now for him.

"I like to help where I can. If everyone did just a little, the world would be a better place," he was quoted as saying. There was a photo of him visiting a sick child in hospital, underneath reference to life-saving equipment he had subsidized for the Children's Hospital. Very commendable. He would have Phoebe's vote.

Riley flipped the page and was half-way through the Sudoku by the time his breakfast arrived. When he got up to pay prior to leaving, Bruno handed him a small take-away container. "Some tuna… for the patient. He'll need to build up his strength."

"I'm sure he'll appreciate that. Do I receive get-well treats next time I'm sick?"

"You're big enough to look after yourself," Bruno said in a disdainful tone.

Riley knew he was right, but seriously, would anyone even know if he wasn't well... or care? Probably not. In a world that was increasingly single, people like him could disappear, and nobody would even notice. Probably his mother would, eventually. He didn't see her often, cue guilty feelings, so it would be a while before she missed him. He sighed and braced himself for whatever complaints Diane had that morning.

Diane already sat at her desk when he returned to Blenheim House. Riley glanced at his watch, checking whether he had lost thirty minutes, but no... she had turned up early. She looked up from her monitor screen with concern.

"Ginger isn't with you? I had left before you came back yesterday. I was so worried about him. How is he today?"

"He's going to be fine, but I left him upstairs this morning. He'll be subdued for a while, thanks to his medication. Until I know what he ingested and where he found that, I'm cautious about letting him out."

"Very wise. I brought him a little present. Perhaps it will keep him entertained during his recovery."

Diane bringing gifts? Pinch me, someone. "That's very kind of you. I'm sure he'll appreciate that."

She handed him a wind-up cat toy, a spiderlike creature that scooted around the floor, waving its little legs. Smiling and nodding his bewildered gratitude, Riley headed for the elevators with both gifts. When he emerged from the stairwell at roof level, he could hear Ginger yowling behind the closed door. He sounded both annoyed and unimpressed, which was a good sign. It meant he was in recovery mode.

Ginge tried to bolt outside when he opened the door, and Riley had to block the cat's path with his foot. "Not so fast. I've got treats for you, and I don't want you going outside." The cat glared at him, twitching his tail, but consented to stay a while longer when presented with the tuna. He even took a passing interest in the toy, which Riley took to mean that Ginge was on the mend.

With Ginge being suitably entertained, Riley turned his thoughts to crucial matters of the day. Firstly, he needed to catch up with Winston and find out what he was doing in David Barton's office in the Excellerate tenancy in the middle of the night. Secondly, he needed to research where he could take Sophie Robinson for dinner. Not too expensive, but something that expressed his level of appreciation. He would consider the matter throughout the day. He could ask Phoebe for advice, but then she would jump to conclusions. That only left… Diane.

14 Katrina

DIANE PURSED HER lips and gazed out the window as she pondered the question. "A restaurant. Do you think I have the time and money to dine out in the city?"

Riley waited patiently. He knew a certain level of drama was to be expected before she actually addressed the question. She sniffed and reached for a tissue, swiping at the tip of her nose.

"It depends *why* you're going. Are you taking your mother for her birthday, or going out with your rowdy mates? Horses for courses." She took on a more speculative tone. "Of course, if you're looking for a more intimate setting, you'd choose something different again."

"I just want some suggestions. Nothing too expensive, reliable food, walking distance for me, and good reviews."

"You'll have to check the reviews for yourself, but there are lots of restaurants around the Central Market. You must know most of those. Rundle Street has some good options; there's that Thai place half-way down. You know the one I mean." She clicked her fingers as though that would help her remember the name. "Don't forget Hutt Street. There's a fabulous Italian restaurant at the southern end, though a bit pricey."

Nothing she suggested was really helpful. Riley gave the counter a pat by way of thanks and farewell as he turned to head down to his workshop.

She called after him. "And the cat? Did he like his toy?"

"He's subdued, but annoyed at being confined. Your toy is helping to keep him entertained. Thank you again."

Diane held up a finger. "There's always Louca's on Pulteney Street, if you like seafood."

Louca's… that was it. He'd heard of the restaurant and always wanted to try it. Until now, there hadn't been the right excuse. The Skywalkers usually ended up in Chinatown, or somewhere in the east end. Thanking Diane, he retreated to his workshop to contemplate his next step while sharpening his chisels and drill bits. Winston had to be next. Tackling him would be less confronting that picking up his phone and calling Sophie.

When he judged it time for morning tea, he slipped up to his flat to make a brew and check on Ginger. He looked in his biscuit tin, but his supply was reduced to stale crumbs and broken pieces of his favourites, Chewy Chai Cookies. Time for another baking session.

He wandered outside, munching on the broken pieces that he'd salvaged, with the hope of spotting Winston perhaps doing something similar. He wasn't visible on the rooftop, but should be in the building somewhere. Riley took his phone from his pocket and dialled, listening intently in case he heard the ringtone from across the divide. Nope. The call almost rang out before Winston picked up.

"Yeah?"

"Good morning to you too. You owe me a chat."

"I'm busy."

"It won't take long. I'll be right over. Ginger sends his regards, by the way. I can see you in the Daily Bean or up in your apartment."

"You'd better come up to me. I don't want flapping ears overhearing our conversation." The phone call was immediately disconnected.

He knew Winston would always be busy when he didn't want to have a particular discussion. He had evasion down to a fine art. Riley tickled Ginger under the chin, topped up the water bowl, and travelled down to ground level and out onto the street.

He dodged morning pedestrians as he followed the same path around the corner that he had traipsed in the middle of the night. Before entering the building, this time through the front door, he squinted at the neighbouring facades, searching for cameras. None that he could see and that was a relief. So was being able to ride up to roof level in the lift instead of huffing up the stairs.

Winston wasn't around when the lift doors opened. Riley wandered over to the edge of the roof again while he waited, looking at his own rooftop. He had done that on previous occasions, but now looked more carefully, curious about what others could see. Who was likely to do that though, other than Winston and Phoebe who were the closest Skywalkers?

The gantry sat where they had left it. Presumably, the painters hadn't started work. Tradies and the window-washers would have a view of his rooftop, but that would only be occasionally, and by day, not at night.

The elevator door slid closed and he spun around to see that Winston stood behind him.

"You'd better come inside. There are fewer prying eyes there."

"Who's going to see us up here?"

Winston gave him a side-eye but didn't answer. Paranoia perhaps? Riley followed him inside and pulled up a seat at the kitchen table. This apartment was no bigger than his, with both properties focused on functionality rather than designer comfort. Both were only suitable for single occupancy, or one man and a cat. Winston didn't even have a goldfish.

"Okay… what's the story? What were you doing in the Excellerate offices last night? What were you looking for?"

Winston didn't reply immediately. He screwed up his face as though searching for the right words. Searching for the right lie, more like it.

"I was helping out a friend," he said finally. "David Barton had something of hers in his office and she needed to get it back."

"She? You're talking about the woman you were with the other day?"

"Yeah, Katrina. She is in a spot of bother and I said I'd help her. She's a good woman. She doesn't deserve this shit."

"If she needed something from that office, why didn't she get it herself, preferably by going through the front door and asking someone?"

"It wasn't that easy. You can't tell anyone about this, Riley. I shouldn't even be telling you. I promised her I'd keep it quiet."

"I won't tell a soul... cross my heart and hope to die."

"That David Barton, he was a real bastard." Winston thumped the table to emphasize his point. "He was a liar and a cheat."

"Those are strong words. What did he do?"

"What didn't he do. He gambled, he stole, he cheated on his wife and he was a blackmailer."

Riley had already heard some of those allegations, but the bit about being a blackmailer was new. "Okay, he was rotten, but that doesn't explain what you were doing in his office in the middle of the night."

Winston glanced at his watch. "I don't have much time, so I'll give you a synopsis. Barton was in a relationship with Katrina. She had no idea he was married, nor that he had a gambling problem. When she found out about the marriage, she was devastated and broke it off. She never wanted to see him again."

Winston stared out the window as he spoke. "Thanks to the gambling issue, he was in financial difficulty. From what she said, it was pretty bad. He started blackmailing her. He had photos of them together, you know... intimate stuff. She never even knew he'd taken them. Pervert! He said that unless she coughed up money, he would release the photos on social media and send them to her family. She's going through a messy divorce and this would give the ex some ammunition to use against her."

Riley tried to imagine what those photos would look like and failed dismally. "Why didn't she just tell his wife?"

"That's what I asked. He still would have released the photos, and Barton reckoned they had an open marriage anyway. His wife didn't care what he did, or who with, as long as he kept her in the manner to which she'd become accustomed. She had a flamboyant lifestyle. There was nothing to be gained from telling her."

Riley closed his eyes while he digested this sorry story. It sounded just the sort of thing Winston would get involved in. "That still doesn't explain last night."

Winston gave a heartfelt sigh. "She said the photos were still in Barton's office. She knew where he kept them—in the bottom drawer of his desk. She was petrified that when people went through his desk, the photos would be found. When she told me about that, she was a quivering mess. I promised I'd do what I could to get them back. I couldn't tell Excellerate what I wanted; they would have asked too many questions. That's when I came up with the idea of going through his office at night, only I shut the door, not realizing that it would then be deadlocked. I couldn't get out."

"How did you get in?"

"I have the master key to the floor, but not the keys to individual offices. His office was shut, but the lock was snibbed so I could enter. I didn't want to be disturbed while I hunted for the envelope, so shut the door properly. Then I was stuck."

"That is the craziest story I've ever heard. Did you find the photos?"

"Yes… well I found the envelope with her name scrawled on the front. I didn't look inside. I promised I wouldn't do that. She would be so embarrassed."

"What happens now?"

"I'm catching up with her this evening after work, and I'll give her the envelope then. One of her big fears was that if the envelope was found by the police, or whoever, questions might be asked about Barton's death. They might think she pushed him off, or something ridiculous like that.

That possibility hadn't occurred to Riley, but now that Winston mentioned it, it sounded plausible, especially since she and Winston had some sort of connection. Would he have covered for her, or even helped her to toss Barton over the edge?

"How long have you known Katrina?"

"Only met her recently, but long enough to know she's a good woman, Riley. She doesn't deserve that sort of treatment. Do you know she sponsors a couple of kids through World Vision? She was brought up in foster care, and knows what it's like to grow up with nothing. It broke my heart listening to her story."

Winston looked at his watch again. Riley took the hint and stook up. He also had work to do.

"I hope that's all sorted for her then. I'd hate to see you get into strife on her behalf. You haven't known her long. It's not as if you had some committed relationship."

Winston gave him a half-lidded look, that made him look like a droopy spaniel. "Riley, when you know, you just know."

Riley put off calling Sophie until that afternoon. He told himself he was too busy, and had to get his priorities sorted. He ran into Phoebe in the street while coming back from a small city-based hardware store in the south-west corner of the city. She walked slowly, weighed down with a supermarket brand shopping bag, and didn't see him until he tapped her on the shoulder.

"Can I carry that for you?"

She appeared lost in thought, and jumped slightly at the touch. "Riley, you startled me. It's not far to go, I'm sure I can manage."

"I'm sure you can, but you don't want to strain your hands before the big performance. It won't take me long. I'll walk with you. How's it all going?"

Her sigh as she relinquished the bag gave him some indication. "I've got a fight on my hands. That bloody woman's not going to give up until she's seen me on the streets. You'd think after all this time she would have moved on."

"You mean Cornelia."

"Who else? Yes. I assume she's behind it. That lawyer is now telling me that there is a challenge to my monthly allowance. He's not stupid enough to say it outright, but the inference is that if I move from my apartment, the problem might be easily resolved."

"That's intimidation. You can't be made to leave, can you?"

She snorted. "They'll carry me out in a box. If this shonky solicitor Cornelia's found really can challenge the will and freeze my allowance, I'll be in a right pickle."

"Weren't you getting legal advice of your own? I thought Charles was looking after that."

"Yes, he is, and Tray Thornton has been helpful as well."

"So, you've told him about it?"

"I didn't mean to, but he's been very supportive. When he visited recently, he could see I was upset. He even drove me to see one of his retirement complexes in case I might be interested. He said he could pull strings for me and get me one of the luxury suites on the top floor." She scrunched up her face. "As if I would live in a place like that. Not that I told him that."

"If there's anything I or any of the others can do, let us know. We could always commission a hit-man or send out a posse to take this lawyer down."

She laughed at that, breaking out into giggles like a little girl. "Only if I can come along too. I could do with a good adventure."

Riley walked with her to the foyer of her private lift.

"I can take it from here, dear. Thank you for your help. It's good to know I have friends who care for me."

She reached up and kissed him lightly on his cheek. That surprised him. It gave him a dose of the warm fuzzies. With that in mind, he hurried back to Blenheim House and by-passing Dianne, went straight upstairs to his apartment. Time to call Sophie.

She appeared distracted when she answered the call.

"Who?... oh, Riley, how's Ginger? Sorry I sounded confused. I've got my head stuck in this research."

"I didn't mean to interrupt. I won't take up much of your time. Ginger is doing well, thanks. Chafing at being restricted, but he's much better. I really appreciate your help in getting him to the vet so quickly. I hate to think what might have been the result if you hadn't done that."

"I'm pleased I could help."

An awkward silence followed. Riley wished he'd thought through what he was going to say before picking up the phone. "Umm... I won't keep you when you're busy. I owe you a dinner for what you did. I wanted to suggest Louca's in Pultney Street tomorrow night."

"Dinner? You don't have to do that." She paused, then her tone changed. "You know I can't discuss the content of my report?"

"I wouldn't expect you to." *Liar. He hoped she might let something drop.* "No expectations about that at all, but I did want to express my appreciation. I know you had to take time out of your day. If you're too busy, that's fine..." He trailed off, not sure what else to say. He didn't want to come across as pushy or desperate.

"Okay then... that would be nice. I've been working all hours lately; such is the life of a freelancer, so some down time would be good. Should I pick you up?"

"No!" It came out more forcefully than he intended. "I mean, thanks for the offer, but I can walk. I'll book for seven and meet you there."

He sat for a while after disconnecting the call. Being dependent on her for transport yet again did not sit comfortably. Still, inviting her out had been easier than he expected. Perhaps learning to drive would be the same.

15 Dining Out

OFFICE RELOCATIONS ALWAYS took a bit to organize, and that afternoon, there were two. An IT consultant on the sixth floor moved out, and a psychologist moved in on the seventh. Riley coordinated separate moving trucks, and managed lift access for the furniture moving out, and the furniture moving in. The incoming tenant needed to do an induction for the building, but he decided the sessions could wait until Monday, after the chaos had settled. He left the woman with a sheath of instructional papers, detailing security and emergency issues, and told her they would discuss them in person after the weekend.

With that activity taking up his time, he'd had little opportunity to think about what Winston had told him that morning. He mentally deferred it until after clock-off time. Activity in the building stopped at about four pm. Most of the tenancies worked until five, but on Fridays, the halls were suspiciously quiet. Either people wanted to make an early start on their weekend, or else they took an early mark and headed out for Friday night drinks.

Riley caught the vibe. He still had to attend to building security at the specified time, but he too was in slow-down mode as the afternoon wore on. As he thought about the evening ahead, he decided to get a take-away meal instead of cooking. The deliberations then focused on what. Not pizza... bored with Chinese... Japanese perhaps? There were plenty of options he could grab at the Central Market, even a gourmet pie.

He checked the security cameras and shut down the building in record time. Everyone on the street appeared to be in a hurry to be somewhere else, not in the proximity of the office. He risked being bowled over by the briefcase brigade, but dodged around them, on a mission of his own.

Fifty metres down the street, he saw Winston and the woman he now knew to be Katrina Dale. They walked in his direction, but to his surprise, Winston didn't immediately acknowledge him. Riley waited for the eye-contact that never came, though Winston had to have seen him. Katrina made up for it. As he glanced from Winston to her, he was surprised to see that she looked straight at him. It wasn't a casual glance, but a deliberate look of recognition.

He'd only seen her at a distance before, on the day the detectives stood with him on the roof top, but seeing her up close twigged his memory. She'd been at the council meeting a couple of weeks ago. Made sense if she lived in the city as well. He wondered if she had also signed up to the protest group.

"Hey, Winston... you heading out somewhere special?"

The couple stopped, forcing people behind them to dodge around.

"Oh, Hi Riley. Didn't notice you there. We're on our way to the Colonial."

"For a change," Riley joked. Winston didn't smile and Riley turned his attention to Katrina. "I'm Riley… I live next door, more or less. Looks like Winston's forgotten his manners."

He earned a filthy look for that remark. "Riley, this is my friend, Katrina."

She gave a small nod of acknowledgement, and besides a muttered 'hello', didn't engage in further conversation. Perhaps she was shy with strangers. They made an odd couple. Winston was tall and gangly, with rounded shoulders and no bottom to speak of, so his trousers always had to be held up with a belt. Katrina was on the shorter side, and dumpy. Her age was difficult to pick, and her pale complexion indicated someone who kept out of the sun.

He was about to ask about her interest in the zoning issues, when Winston took her elbow, saying, "We need to keep moving. See you 'round." Next thing, they were gone, leaving him standing in the middle of the footpath until a pedestrian muttered, '*Somebody die here, or what?*' He took the hint and got out of the way.

Korean barbecue won the internal vote, and when he arrived home with the takeaway containers, it soon got Ginger's vote as well. The cat had been snoozing on a mat outside, but woke up instantly when the meaty smell permeated his senses. Riley sat at his outside table, eating straight from the container and dropping occasional morsels in the cat's direction. He had a cold beer to wash it down, and overall, life felt good, for him, anyway.

165

Perhaps it looked good for Winston as well. A relationship would lift the man out of his continual cloud of gloom. Sure, they had the mutual interest in vinyl, but identifying the attraction in the relationship for Katrina wasn't so easy. The story Winston had told him that morning, surprised him more, now that he had seen her close up. She definitely didn't look like some femme fatale, not the type to be fooled by a scumbag taking sneaky photos.

Perhaps she also had a gambling problem, and that's how she became entangled with David Barton. He hoped Winston knew who he was mixing with. Big, boofy Winston would be easy to fool. He had the feeling that Winston hadn't told her about their antics in the middle of the night, involving him also. If she didn't want anyone to know about her association with David Barton and the predicament that left her in, she wouldn't want him to know either. Why would he tell anyone? She could keep her messy little secret to herself... and Winston.

He set the alarm on his phone to indicate when he should shower and get ready. Not that he was likely to forget the time. The next debate focused on aftershave. Should he wear it or not? Was it manly to do so, or the opposite? It wasn't as if she would get that close to him, so he settled for just soap and water.

He never expected to be agonizing over what to wear, but here he was, standing in front of his open wardrobe. His clothing was suitable for work, or riding the bike, and little else. In the end, he pulled on his best pair of jeans, and a shirt he last wore for a job interview. His anxiety level was about the same. He rolled up the sleeves of his shirt a couple of turns and ruffled his hair in what he hoped was an edgy look. He swapped out his work shoes for a pair of RM Williams boots. Not trendy, but not steel-capped safety shoes either.

The restaurant was located about fifteen minutes from Blenheim House, more of a comfortable stroll than a brisk walk, but Riley arrived fifteen minutes early. He paced up and down the footpath outside, unsure whether to wait there or inside. He tried not to keep glancing at his watch, but he did, hating that it made him feel like a desperado.

At five minutes to the hour, he decided to find their table inside the restaurant. At least then he could check that it wasn't too close to the kitchen or perhaps outside the toilets. The table the waiter showed him to was set for two and positioned close to the window, so they could easily watch outside if they wanted. That suited him, because he could still watch for her in comfort.

"Can I get you a drink while you wait?" the waiter asked, offering the wine list.

"Scotch thanks, with a cube of ice. What scotches do you have?"

They discussed the merits of the two options provided by the restaurant, and by the time the drink sat in front of him, it had gone seven o'clock. At five past, the door flew open and Sophie rushed in, looking vaguely disconcerted. Riley raised his hand to attract her attention. She pushed past other tables to reach him, shrugging her jacket off as she came.

"Sorry I'm late. It took me ages to find a park. I should have anticipated this and left home earlier."

Riley stood up politely as Sophie hung the jacket over the back of her chair, then sat down again when she did. "I only just got here myself. Would you like a drink while you catch your breath?"

"That's the best suggestion I've heard all day. I'd love one."

Riley caught the eye of the waiter, who took her order and disappeared again. "Busy day, then?"

"I had a few loose ends to sort out, and then you know… weekend stuff. How's the cat?"

"He's recovered well. Ate a reasonable portion of my chicken last night, so no problems with his appetite. I wish I knew what he'd eaten and where though. I hope nobody deliberately tried to do him in."

"Why would anyone try to do that? There are always strays in the city, but nobody takes action against them. It's mostly in the suburbs that you get the rogue poisoner."

Sophie's drink appeared, and she took an appreciative sip with a small sigh of contentment. "You walked here?"

"Sure did. Saves trying to find a park."

"So, you do drive then?"

"Um, no… I never got around to learning in my teens when most people do, and then I got used to riding my bike or taking public transport. There never seemed to be a need. Recent events have made me re-think that decision. I should take steps to learn. Only catch is, I haven't got a car."

Sophie stared into her drink, twiddling the stem of the glass before looking up "I could give you some lessons if that would help. I taught my younger brother, so I know the process. You'd need regular access to a car though to get your hours up in your log book."

Her offer took him by surprise. She hardly knew him. "My mother has a car. She's been on at me for years to learn to drive, mostly so I could drive her where she wants to go. It was my father's car and he was the main driver, but since he's gone, she's had to fend for herself."

She rolled her eyes. "I don't know how you'll work that relationship out, but the offer's on the table. Up to you; no pressure or expectations. It seemed such a shame you were left in a predicament recently when Ginger was so sick."

Sunday lunch would be with his mother, so he could raise the question of using the car at that time, assuming he took the idea seriously. "Perhaps I'll sit for my Learner's Test and then make a decision after that. Thanks for the offer though. It's very kind of you."

He shuffled the salt and pepper shakers around the table as he considered the next topic of conversation. "Is most of your work in the city?"

"Not at all. Heritage issues arise all over the state. I specialize in the built form, but some of my colleagues focus on other cultural issues associated with place. They are addressed before any development takes place or if a location requires preservation for future generations."

"How do you balance the desires of the development community and the drive to make a profit against the non-quantifiable benefit to the community?"

"Now you're asking the tricky questions and we haven't even ordered main course! I do the research and present my findings. My work needs to speak for itself. I'm not the ultimate decision maker."

The waiter appeared at their side, and they made their selections before continuing their discussion. Riley debated with himself how far he could push the conversation. "So, what happens in relation to this proposed re-zoning depends on the persuasiveness of your report?"

"Not necessarily. There are other contributors to the decision. People with vested interests will be lobbying, like the protest group, for instance. They have a vested interest in keeping things as they are."

"You mean preserving architectural heritage and cultural amenity for the future." Riley tried not to sound defensive.

She raised her glass in acknowledgement with a small nod. "Of course."

He suspected she had been gently stirring him, and if she wanted a reaction, she got it.

"Other interests will argue that the city needs to grow to meet current and future needs, and that future benefits will outweigh other constraints or considerations."

"So, who decides?"

"Various people make recommendations, but the decision for something significant like the city re-zoning goes up to the senior bureaucrats in the Department for Planning, and then the Minister."

Their meals appeared shortly after this, and their focus turned to food and favourite eating experiences.

"You're so lucky living in the city," Sophie said after extolling the virtues of her pan-fried barramundi. "You must get to try all the good eateries around. Have you tried them all?"

"Embarrassingly, I tend to patronize the same cafes most of the time. I'm a creature of habit. I cook for myself most nights of the week. Eating out is reserved for special events or catching up with... with friends who also live in the city." He nearly said Skywalkers.

Sophie leaned across the table towards him. "It's still an interesting life. I didn't realise that people had live-in caretaker roles until meeting you. Are you saying there are other people who have similar roles?"

"Sure. The more recent buildings tend to have nine-to-five facilities managers, but the older buildings, and significant structures like Parliament House have live-in caretakers."

"How did you get the job?"

Nobody had shown such an interest in him and his work before. Expansively, he ordered them another round of drinks and asked to see the dessert menu. Talking with Sophie was easier than he expected, with the time passing quickly. Looking around, he noticed that they were one of the remaining tables, and the wait staff were tidying up and re-setting tables for the following day.

"I get the message they're waiting for us to leave. Would you like to go on somewhere else for a nightcap? There are a few boutique laneway bars that have opened recently."

"Next time, maybe. I wouldn't bring the car if I thought I was going to drink more. That's the down-side of driving."

Next time... that sounded promising. Riley hadn't allowed himself to think beyond the current evening. "Sure. I'll give you advance notice of the options next time." Sophie

171

wanted to visit the bathroom before leaving the restaurant, and Riley made the most of the opportunity to settle the account. On her return, he held her jacket out for her so that she could thread her arms into the sleeves. Just that simple action was an unexpected intimate moment, for him anyway. He had no idea what her reaction might be.

They paused awkwardly on the footpath outside the restaurant door.

"I'll walk you to your car," Riley said. "The city streets aren't unsafe, but sometimes you encounter some unsettling people."

"I don't want to take you out of your way."

He laughed. "I live here, remember? Nowhere in the city is really out of my way. Lead on."

"Don't forget what I said about the driving lessons," she said as they walked. "I'm serious. I'll be happy to give you some lessons to help you build up confidence."

"I'll keep that in mind. It's a generous offer."

Her car was parked in a side street where the street lighting was shaded by street trees. Sophie glanced over her shoulder as they turned into the street. Riley knew the feeling when the hairs on the back of your neck prickled, but he was confident that nobody had followed them. This was generally a safe part of the city. He had checked behind them a couple of times, but not obviously so. Until recently, he wouldn't have bothered to do that, but Lenny had put the wind up him, and he still didn't know why.

They stopped at the car, and Riley waited while she unlocked the door. "Thanks for coming," he said. "I enjoyed your company." Not giving himself time to think about it, he leaned forward and pecked her on the cheek, much the same way that Phoebe had after he'd helped her with the shopping.

The poor lighting probably hid the flush he knew had invaded his face, but he stayed until she pulled away from the kerb, giving a wave before turning and heading back in the direction of Blenheim House. He sauntered home with more confidence than he'd had when he left.

Riley swung his bike into the driveway, having built up a layer of sweat on the ride. His mother hated to be kept waiting, and he'd promised to be there on time. Because he'd dallied that morning, he'd left the city later than he should have. The table was already set for lunch when he walked in the back door, and platters on the table were covered with mesh food covers.

"Hi, Mum," he said, dumping his helmet and backpack in the laundry on the way in. "How's your week been?"

"Better now you're here. The light globe in the bathroom has blown, and the tap there is leaking as well."

"Right. I take it you want me to fix both issues?"

"What do you think? Sit down and have your lunch. You can do it after. Don't forget to wash your hands before coming to the table."

It only took five seconds and she made him feel like a kid again. "Did you know I'm old enough to vote, Mum?"

"What are you talking about? Of course, I do. Hurry up or lunch will get cold."

Consistency provided a sense of normality to their relationship, even if frustration was never far from the surface.

Since his father died, Riley's mother relied on him more, and took a stronger interest in his life… and his failings.

Over lunch, his mother regaled Riley with reports of her interactions with various neighbours, the discussions held at her book club, and the ongoing clash of personalities within her quilting group. None of it was new, or even that different to what she told him the last time he visited. The joys of being an only child.

"Now," his mother said, blotting her mouth with the napkin, "What is happening with your job? Have you had any thoughts about returning to university? You could get a better job if you had qualifications."

"I'm not returning to uni, Mum. We've discussed this before. It's been an interesting couple of weeks, actually. A man jumped off a neighbouring building, Ginger Puss ate something poisonous, and nearly died, and I'm thinking of learning to drive."

She blinked at him, as though his words were more difficult to digest than the lunch had been. "If you lived somewhere else, people wouldn't jump off buildings. On top of a city building isn't a proper place to live."

Riley shrugged. "It comes with the job, and I like living in the city. A lot of people do similar work, and it's a supportive community and Ginger practically has his own fan club."

"It can't be too good if someone has poisoned him. You can't let a cat roam, Riley, it's not right."

He could see that his mother was in one of her moods, but even so, she was probably right about Ginger roaming. He wouldn't have encountered something poisonous if he'd

174

stayed at home. She put a bowl of fruit salad and custard in front of him.

"What's this about learning to drive? It's about time you did. Who's going to teach you?"

A person I met through work and who helped out when I needed to get Ginger to the vet in a hurry. She offered to help."

His mother sat up straighter. "She? You've met a woman? Why haven't you introduced her? You could have invited her to lunch."

He should have anticipated this reaction. Next thing his mother would be asking how old Sophie was, and was she still young enough to have babies. "We're not in a relationship, Mum. She's just a friend—acquaintance really."

'Not many acquaintances would offer to give you driving lessons." Her scepticism was sharper than the knife used to cut the Sunday roast.

Riley pushed back his chair. "Thanks for lunch...I'll get on with those jobs you mentioned." Anything rather than further grilling.

16   The Sack

MONDAY, MONDAY, SO good to me – can't trust that day...

Riley whistled the tune as he swept the steps to the building, fortunately relatively clean for a change. The clear, melodic voice behind him jolted him from his reverie with the next two lines from the song.

He paused mid-sweep and spun around to find Jodie standing behind him sporting a cheeky grin under her spiky emerald-green fringe. She gave him a thumbs-up and sauntered off towards King William Street. Not for the first time, he wondered why she hung out with Alex, and where they usually slept. A squat somewhere probably.

He had the impression that living on the streets was a new experience for her. Perhaps she slipped home periodically to mummy and daddy for a hot shower and a change of clothes. Nice voice though.

On arriving home from visiting his mother the previous day, he had downloaded the road rules that he needed to learn before sitting his written test. He skipped breakfast at the Daily Bean with all its distractions, opting instead to have avocado on toast at home. He studied while he ate. Ginge had to make do with a bowl of cat milk and a handful of crunchy cat biscuits, plus the opportunity to chase some cheeky birds in the bird bath near the lime tree.

The road rules weren't unfamiliar, given he'd been riding his bike on the road for years, but some of the specific detail was new, like how many metres before an intersection he should activate the turn indicator and things like that. He set himself a timetable of three days in which to be confident enough to sit the test. There wouldn't be time to study that evening, because of the yoga session at Torrens House. He hadn't been for a couple of weeks and the stiffness in his muscles reminded him of that.

Carmen and Steve ran a weekly class for Skywalkers on their rooftop, depending on the weather. They were a rare husband and wife team, with the couple not only filling the caretaker role, but having the cleaning contract as well. Mid-morning, he saw Winston sweeping on his rooftop, which was unusual. He wasn't normally so fastidious. Another behavioural change.

Riley cupped his hands around his mouth. "Hey, Winston… are you going to yoga tonight?"

Winston looked up, and for a moment, Riley thought he was about to shake his head, but then he responded with a thumbs-up.

"I'll see you downstairs at seven."

He received another thumbs up; a man of many words. Riley smirked to himself as he took the elevator back downstairs. A less talkative Winston was something to be appreciated.

Diane spoke to a courier in the reception area as he passed through, and another waited impatiently to drop off his parcel. She looked up and flapped a hand in his direction.

"Riley, don't rush off. Help that man while I fill out a delivery docket."

He nearly said, "I'm not your secretary", but thought better of it. From her tone, she was a bit frazzled. Surely, she could handle two couriers at once? He took pity on the waiting man, and scribbled a signature where required and relieved the courier of the package.

"There you go, mate."

The man gave him a half salute and disappeared out the door at a semi-trot. By the time Riley deposited the parcel behind the desk for Diane to record and process, the other courier was also leaving.

"Put it over there." Diane waved her hand in the direction of a table behind her desk. "It would be helpful if you took it up to level 6 after I've recorded the details."

"What did your last slave die of? Don't they come down and collect their own parcels?"

Her head jerked up. "You should be pleased you have a job—if you still do."

What was that snippy comment about? He decided not to engage and made his escape before any other couriers arrived.

Winston waited at the corner when Riley jogged out of Blenheim House after work. Katrina was with him. This was getting to be a habit. Winston must be serious about the woman. He couldn't take her to yoga though; the class was for Skywalkers only.

Surprisingly, given their last encounter, Katrina spoke first. "Hi, Riley. How's your day been?"

"Um, fine, thanks. Nothing out of the ordinary. Days like that are good, especially Mondays."

She laughed. "I know what you mean."

It changed her whole demeanour when she smiled, with cute crinkles around her eyes. Perhaps that's what drew men to her. Riley noticed she clutched a Jethro Tull LP under her arm. She followed his gaze. "Winston is lending me a record from his prized collection. I don't have this one."

"You should feel honoured. Winston doesn't usually let people even touch them, let alone take them to play."

"That's because other people have no respect for vinyl and don't know how to handle it," Winston said.

"Point taken." Riley nodded at Katrina. "I think I saw you at the council meeting the other week discussing the local zoning issues. Have you joined the community group? It needs all the support it can get if we're going to oppose the proposal."

She looked surprised, but quickly recovered. "No, I've never been one for getting involved in that sort of thing, but perhaps in this instance I should."

"It's not too late. I'll give the contact details to Winston and he can pass them onto you."

"Sure. That would be the best." She patted Winston on the arm. "You'd better be going. I think you said your class was at seven."

"Yeah, you're right." Winston hesitated, and it seemed to Riley that he was wondering whether to kiss her goodbye or not. If so, he decided against it. "I'll speak to you tomorrow," was all he said, and Katrina gave them both a brief nod before walking away in the direction of South Terrace.

"She's right, Winston, we'd better hurry. We're running late."

Riley waited for Winston to say something about his association with Katrina, and the fact that they appeared to be growing closer, but the man remained close-lipped, choosing instead to discuss the merits of their record collections and the albums he would still like to collect, if only he could find them for sale at an affordable price. Their arrival at Torrens House was a relief.

Winston was chattier on their walk home after the class. "I feel as though I've been stretched on the rack", he said, easing his shoulders with small backwards rotations. "It's good though."

"Are you doing the exercises regularly between classes? Neither of us have been to one for a couple of weeks. I try to remember to do them at home, but get a bit slack sometimes."

"I remember for a day or so," Winston admitted, "but then slacken off. Moving heavy office furniture around doesn't help."

"Tenants moving in?"

"I wish. They're going and another went today. Marguerite from Hands On. She's the second tenant this month. Where will I get discount massages now?"

There were plenty of massage services available in the city, in fact a practitioner occupied a suite on Level Eight of Blenheim House, but they probably charged Winston more than Marguerite. Riley sometimes wondered at the nature of the services that Marguerite provided, but knew better than to ask.

"Did she say why she was moving?"

"She got a better deal... more modern premises, and allied with other natural health practitioners. She said it would be better for business."

"Can't blame her then but you can still book an appointment with her at the new place."

"I know, but it won't be as convenient and not the same. The financial planners on the floor below went last week. Not that I ever used them... I don't have that sorta dough, but the floor's half empty."

Empty offices were never good for business. It was like a cancer that could spread if the atmosphere in a building changed.

Winston shook his head. "It's never been like this before. It's been a community in this building, with everyone getting on together. It's not the flashiest place in town, but the rents are reasonable. Nico Stravos has always been a fair landlord."

"I'm sure he has, but he'll have to take note of what the opposition are offering. Some buildings now have gyms and swimming pools, or co-working spaces and shared facilities."

"This isn't the place for any of that stuff. The only swimming pool is in the basement carpark when it rains."

"Perhaps he could bring in an operator for a child care centre. Parents always want more child care in the city, preferably close to where they work. They'd love to work in the building then."

"The thing is," Winston said, stabbing his finger in the air for emphasis, "if there aren't any tenants in the building, Nico might think he doesn't need a building manager any more. I could be out on my arse. Excellerate are the major tenant, but they aren't enough on their own."

That was a fate that they all could face. Tenants came and went in Blenheim House. Some tenants stayed forever; it suited them, but others used it as a stepping stone. They were micro-businesses in start-up phase. Either they grew, and then wanted bigger and better premises, or they crashed and burned, and couldn't afford to stay. So far, the occupancy rate had remained steady, with new tenants replacing the outgoing.

Equally as worrying was the possibility that if the buildings became less utilized, that would lend support to the argument that they no longer met the needs of the business community. If that happened, the owners would be more inclined to sell or re-develop. Surely Blenheim Pastoral wouldn't sell his building though. They couldn't afford alternative accommodation. His employment should be secure.

They paused at the corner of Murray and Hindmarsh Streets, where each turned towards their respective buildings.

"I meant to ask… was Katrina happy that you retrieved her photos?" He posed the question nonchalantly, not wanting to sound too intrusive. Some indicated gratitude for the other night's escapade wouldn't go astray though.

"Oh, yeah… she was real happy. Big relief there."

Winston didn't elaborate further before turning with a half-wave and heading towards the Institute.

"Mr Symes would like to see you." Diane caught Riley's eye as he passed through reception.

"What about?"

"How should I know. He said to go up to his office asap."

The fact that she wouldn't meet his eyes and used her most officious tone made him uneasy. He thought over the last week or so. There hadn't been any problems in the building or issues of concern. There was only one way to find out. Diane was just being, well... Diane.

Eric Symes was the General Manager for Blenheim Pastoral, and when he wasn't travelling around the various rural properties owned or managed by the company, he sat in his corner office on the fourth floor. He was Riley's boss, but aside from monthly meetings they rarely crossed paths. Even then, the meetings were sometimes deferred if Symes was unexpectedly out of town or overseas.

The fourth floor was a quiet, carpeted enclave, far removed from the bustle of the city street. The board met here on a monthly basis, and senior executives also occupied the adjoining offices. Pictures of some of the pastoral properties hung on the walls of the reception area, and more were in the board room and in Symes' office.

The personal assistant looked up as he stepped out of the elevator and pointed to a chair. "Take a seat, Riley. I'll let the boss know you're here." She didn't meet his eyes either. Bad sign.

Soft, deep armchairs were positioned around a low table. They were the sort that once you sat in them, an ungainly, arm-waving struggle would be required to get out again. Riley eyed

183

them for a moment before opting to remain standing. The chairs would put him at a disadvantage.

He only had to wait five minutes before the assistant looked up, no doubt notified via an invisible signal, and said, "You can go in now."

Eric Symes sat behind a huge desk, devoid of clutter. The requisite family photo sat in one corner, and his laptop sat to one side of a large desk blotter. He was one of the few people Riley knew who still used a fountain pen. He gestured towards the vacant chair opposite him, slightly lower than his own.

"Park yourself, Riley." He then sat for a while looking out his window, with his elbows on the desk and forming a steeple with his fingers. He pursed his lips and worked them back and forward as though doing exercises. At the point where the silence became weird, he turned to look directly at Riley. The light from the window caught his pale blue eyes, giving them an icy appearance.

"I've learned something which distresses me greatly. You recently broke into a neighbouring building in the early hours of the morning. You accessed the offices of Excellerate after hours. Specifically, you gained access to the Financial Officer's office and rifled through his desk."

Stunned was not an adequate word. Riley's mind raced, tripping over itself as he tried to work out who had seen him and exactly what they had seen. Where was Winston in all this? What should he say?

"That's not correct. I didn't break in anywhere."

He hadn't. Winston had given him the access code. Whatever he said though was going to drop Winston in the shit. Had Winston done that to him?

"Are you denying that you were in the building in the early hours of last Friday morning?"

"No, but I only accessed the stairwell to get to the rooftop. The building manager, who lives onsite was in a spot of bother and asked me to come over and help him."

"You're lying. My advice is that the building manager was not present, as he slept elsewhere that night." Symes took on a sorrowful look. "Riley, I've worked with you for a long time now and I trusted you. To learn that you have been involved something of this nature is devastating. What were you doing in that man's office? Did you have something to do with his death?"

"What! No! How could you even think such a thing. I didn't know the man."

"I hadn't pegged you for a liar, but maybe I'm not such a good judge of character. If you didn't know him, why were you in his office?"

"You've got this wrong. I was never in his office. Winston *was* in the building that evening. He rang and asked me to come over. You can check my phone. It will be in my call log." He patted his pocket, realising belatedly that he had left his phone on the bench in his workroom.

"I heard the police visited you last week to ask what you knew about that poor man's death. They must have been acting on information given to them. In my experience, where there's smoke, there's fire."

"They just wanted to know if I saw anything from the rooftop here, and I didn't. I told them that."

Symes sighed heavily. "You've put me in a very awkward position. I have no reason to doubt the veracity of my information, and you don't deny you were in the building. By rights, I ought to inform the police about this. If it weren't for your track record with us, I would. But Riley, I'll have to let you go."

"Go?"

"I'm terminating your employment as of now. Please hand over your keys. You will need to vacate the apartment you occupy by the end of the week. My assistant will arrange for someone to accompany you while you pack up and vacate."

"But that's unfair dismissal. I'll fight this. You're taking the word of some unknown or un-named person without any proof. I can show you my phone records. You'll see where Winston called me asking for help."

"Help to do what?"

This was getting tricky. It meant breaking a confidence and with his prison record, that might have ramifications for Winston, but the alternative was losing his job. "Winston was in the Excellerate offices and had become locked in. He called me and asked for my help in getting him out. I used the gantry to travel down the outside of the building to where he waited at a window. Then I took him back to the rooftop. I didn't go into that office, I swear."

Symes sat and stared at him. The cogs were whirring, or that's how it appeared to Riley. He didn't dare look away. That would appear shifty and an indication of guilt. Where could he go if he had to leave the apartment? Would his mother let him bring Ginger to live in her house, for a short time at least?

"All right." Symes slapped his hand on the table. "Your employment is suspended without pay until this situation is resolved. Your story borders on the bizarre. Evidence of that phone call proves nothing. That doesn't tell me the nature of that call, nor where the caller was at the time it was made. For all I know, you are both in this together. You can stay in the apartment for now until the facts are reviewed, preferably by the end of the week."

Riley stood up. Someone had dropped him in the shit and he needed to find out who. Winston was first call on his list. Next was a solicitor. He needed support and advice. "I appreciate the reprieve. I need to know who has given you this information. I will be in touch with my solicitor. I am sure they will be asking the same question."

He stalked out of the office with his head held high, conscious of the assistant's eyes following him as he swept past her desk. Let her look. It took a lot to rile him, but this situation had. He was truly, bloody angry. Winston had some answering to do.

17   Making Plans

HE CAUGHT THE look on Diane's face when he stepped out of the elevator on the ground floor. He slapped the top of the counter with the palm of his hand. "You knew, didn't you. Why didn't you warn me?"

She sat back in her seat, wheeling the chair back further as well. "It's nothing to do with me. I hear very little of what happens upstairs."

"Who's the snitch? Who's been telling tales about me?"

She recovered enough to fix him with a frosty glare. "Don't speak to me with that tone. Whatever you've been doing, I know nothing about it."

Little would be gained by badgering her. Riley doubted she knew much except that she had already heard his job was under threat, thanks no doubt to the internal grapevine. The person he needed to find was Winston. Bastard. Of all people to stab him in the back… he had to be behind this. What Riley couldn't understand was why. Why throw a mate under the bus? What would he gain by that? It didn't make sense.

Everything had seemed fine after yoga, except for his concerns about the building occupancy.

His call to Winston went through to voicemail. "Winston, you bastard... you owe me an explanation. Thanks to you and your lady friend, I'm losing my job. What have you done? Call me."

He could hardly think straight. A solicitor, that's what he needed. There weren't any in Blenheim House as tenants, but there might be one in the Institute. That was irony. If he was blacklisted, gaining access might be tricky, but he would try. Bruno... Bruno would know if there was one. Bruno knew everyone locally.

The early-morning rush was over when he pushed open the door of the Daily Bean. Bruno was wiping down the tables, while his niece Lexie, who helped out in the middle of the day, was busy behind the counter. Bruno looked up, wiping his hand on his apron and wearing the relaxed demeanour that came with quieter moments.

"Riley, my friend... twice in one morning... this is an honour."

Riley chewed at his lip and an incipient headache threatened in the face of such jovial bonhomie. Something must have shown on his expression, because Bruno now regarded him with a look of concern.

"Trouble, my friend? What can I get you? Do you need something for the nerves?" Bruno delivered this comment quietly at Riley's shoulder. He kept a small bottle of whiskey in the back room, for medicinal purposes only. He was known to take the odd nip at other times.

Riley remained standing. "Bruno, I need a solicitor. I may need representation in an unfair dismissal claim. I think there's one in the Institute. Do you know his name?"

"Sure, but why don't you ask Winston?"

"He's part of the problem. Anyway, he's not answering his phone."

"There is Tom. Tom Hansel. He's a small operator, just him and a couple of others."

"That will do me fine. He can point me in the right direction if he can't help me personally."

Bruno nodded to Lexie. "Hold the fort for a while, and bring me a macchiato. One for my friend, too... a special," he added with a wink. He put an arm around Riley's shoulder. "Sit, and tell your Uncle Bruno the problem."

Bruno pulled up a chair to a table and Riley sat also. He avoided eye contact. He had no idea where to begin. Should he tell him about Katrina's request of Winston and then how he was dragged into her sorry mess? He'd promised Winston not to say anything, but under the circumstances, all bets were off.

"I've been accused of break and enter... entering the Excellerate offices in the middle of the night and rifling through David Barton's office. I've been suspended without pay. Initially, the General Manager wanted to show me the door, but I pleaded my case. It's up to me now to prove I didn't do it, at least I didn't go in his office."

"This is a confusing story you are telling me. Why don't you start at the beginning?"

Lexie arrived with the macchiatos, and also put a plate of biscotti in front of them. "They are still warm from the oven. Maria thought you might need them with your drinks."

Bruno lifted his cup in salute to his wife, who stood in the kitchen doorway. "Maria is a beautiful woman. She always looks after me." He shook his head. "But Riley, I have always known you to be a cautious and law-abiding man. Tell me what led to this situation and I will see how I can help."

Riley took a sip of his coffee and then choked. It was hot and strong. Bruno had to thump him on his back. When he had recovered enough to talk, he told him the story, how Winston had called him in the middle of the night, how he managed the rescue and then the explanation that Winston gave him the next day.

"Now I have to prove that I didn't enter David Barton's office, and I didn't take anything. I've no idea how to do that, but if I don't, I lose my job. I need Winston to tell the truth. I also want to check out the building to see if there are any security cameras, either inside or out. I had a look the other day and didn't see any security outside the building, nor any on the inside."

"Winston is indeed the key to this puzzle. How did you get up to the roof level?" Bruno asked frowning.

"I climbed those bloody stairs. Do you know how many there are? A lot. My leg muscles were screaming when I got to the top, in spite of having a break half way."

"And when you left the roof after rescuing Winston, did you walk down the stairs?"

"No way. I couldn't access the elevator on the way up, but I could when going down. I bypassed the ground floor reception, which probably does have a camera, and exited in the basement carpark."

Bruno shook his head. "That's where you might have been caught. There are probably cameras in the elevators, and perhaps also in the carpark. You would have been seen on the way out."

He was right. Riley turned the suggestion over in his head. Blenheim Pastoral hadn't upgraded the elevators to that degree, but Nico Stravos had done a major upgrade of the Institute only a year ago. Cameras had probably been installed then. Why didn't Winston erase the tape? Because he's dense, that's why, or else he was using him as a scapegoat. He would have known about any cameras in the elevator and probably walked down the stairs to the fifth floor. There wouldn't have been any evidence of the building manager accessing that level in the middle of the night.

"I'll check if they do have cameras there… if they let me in the building. I might have been blacklisted."

"I'll do that. I am often delivering catering orders there. Back in a tic."

Bruno grabbed a cardboard tray and stuffed a couple of take-away cups in the holders. He walked out of the Daily Bean as though carrying a couple of coffees. Riley dropped his head into his hands. Hopefully, Bruno wouldn't be very long. His mind raced at a million miles per hour as he tried to decipher how he had become embroiled in this mess.

Get a grip, Riley. Put on your big boy pants.

He grabbed the paper off the rack and tried to read, but the words danced senselessly in front of his eyes. He tried not to keep looking at this watch. It wouldn't make Bruno return any faster.

The man in question pushed the café door open, no longer carrying his make-believe coffees. He fell back into the chair he'd recently vacated. "In the elevator. There are cameras in the corner. That will have recorded you when you left the building. I didn't go down to the basement, because there was no point. Besides, I would have shown up on camera where I had no business to be."

"Fuck!" Riley knew he had a battle ahead of him. "Sorry Bruno. Didn't mean to swear in your café."

Bruno shrugged. "I'd probably do the same in your shoes, but don't make a habit of it. What will you do now?".

Riley had been asking himself that question. "Speak to Winston, when he returns my call. Find out who reported me to Eric Symes. Find out what that person knows, or think they know. I'll try to call Winston again in a moment. I can't understand why someone would do this to me. They would have to understand the consequences." He took another cautious sip of his potent coffee, which did little to calm the churning in his guts. He needed lower his stress level, or he'd give himself a migraine.

"You've trodden on someone's toes," Bruno said. "Someone wants you out of the way. When you understand why, you will have a better idea of who."

"Bruno, I'm an open book, a simple man who lives with his cat. What harm could I possibly pose to anyone else?"

The other man looked at him expectantly, as though waiting for him to provide the answer. He didn't have one. It was a total mind-fuck.

"If I lose my job over this, I'll have to move. I couldn't keep living here."

"You can't leave. You and the cat are my best customers."

"I'm still living upstairs for now. Not working will give me time to revise for my learner's test. I might sit for it this afternoon. I'll give the rules one more read through and I should be right."

He downed the last of his coffee. That would give him a turbo boost. "I'll try calling Winston again. I'll slip outside while I do that." He pushed back his chair and made his way outside. Bruno darted back behind the counter to help Lexie who looked to be flat-out as the mid-morning crowd filtered in. Riley leaned against the café window while he dialled.

Pedestrians traipsed past, living their own lives and quite oblivious to the turmoil in his. He suddenly remembered the note he found poked under the door when he returned from the evening in Chinatown.

First it's the cat. Then... Guess who?

It had been a warning, but with everything that had happened since, he had forgotten about it. Until now. As threats go, it was juvenile, and if he had to pin it on anyone, it would be the Ferals, but what did they have against him? It didn't make sense. He didn't have time to think about it. Winston was a more urgent priority. He dialled the number and tapped send. Once more, his call went through to voice mail. He didn't bother leaving another message. Winston already knew he wanted to speak to him.

Bruno looked up expectantly as he re-entered the café. "No answer. He must be ghosting me."

'Maybe he is busy, or perhaps his phone is on silent and he's not aware of your calls."

If Winston was working, his phone wouldn't be on silent, but there was no point in raising that. Riley could see that Bruno needed to focus on the customers lining up at the counter. He mouthed "See you later," and left. As had become his habit, he looked left and right on the street, checking that there was nothing or nobody to cause him harm, and then headed back into Blenheim House.

Diane did not look happy when he walked into the reception area. She glared at him, more than usual, and huffed as she shuffled things around her desk. *Et tu, Brutus?* What did she have to be upset about? It wasn't as if she'd lost her job.

"Bad day?" He knew as he said this that it was likely to inflame her further, but he was in a what-the-hell mood.

"It's all your fault. Now that you've been suspended, someone has to fill in for you. I've been asked to come in early to clean up the steps and the reception area, and then stay later to lock up. I haven't been offered any more pay for this. I have enough to do already without taking on your job as well. I'm a receptionist, not a cleaner or caretaker." She almost spat the last words.

He held up both hands against the onslaught. "Hey, not my fault. I'd like to be able to say, "Nothing to do with me", but clearly it is. I just don't know how. Perhaps you and your admin network can help there."

"What did you mean?" Her frosty tone did not indicate a willingness to help.

195

"You see Stella next door sometimes. I know that the admins in an organization often know what's happening before the rest of the staff do. Can you find out who leaked to Eric Symes about me. It was total bullshit in case you don't know."

"I don't know what you get up to at night in the city."

"So, you have heard something. I didn't tell you anything about the allegations that have been thrown at me. What have you heard?"

"I'm not at liberty to say. You're persona non grata at the moment. I shouldn't even be speaking to you."

"Suit yourself. If you want to keep doing my job, including all the tedious and grotty bits—did I tell you about the vomit on the front steps yesterday morning? If you would prefer not to clean up those messes, perhaps you could put out a little feeler. See what Stella knows, like who spoke to Eric and why."

She glared at him, her lips pursed. She did not look at all happy.

"While you think about this, I'll fetch you morning tea from the Daily Bean. It must be so awful for you not able to leave your desk. To have other tasks on top of that isn't fair."

As he headed for the door, he called over his shoulder. "I should remind you it's bin day. The tenants' bins need to be moved from the carpark to the laneway out the back." He disappeared outside before she could reply.

The café was full of late-morning patrons. Bruno was surprised to see him back so soon, but made up the coffee as per Diane's preferred order, and slipped a Danish pastry into a paper bag. "I'm using this as a bribe," Riley said by way of quick explanation. "I'll tell you later if I learn anything."

When he provided the coffee and Danish, Diane didn't appear to be in a better mood. His words must have had some impact, because she grudgingly said that she would speak to Stella at lunchtime. She did offer up one piece of information. "It was Anh Nguyen... you know... the boss next door. He came to see Eric Symes late yesterday afternoon while you were checking that leaking cistern on level seven."

"Andy? Why would he make allegations against me? I always thought he was a nice guy."

She shrugged before pulling the Danish from the bag and taking a bite. "He probably is. That doesn't change the fact he had a serious complaint to raise."

Someone came up to the reception desk, enquiring about an appointment they had on the fourth floor. Riley left her to it and slipped upstairs. While it was still on his mind, he wanted to call Tom Hansel. It clearly was a small office, for the solicitor answered his own phone. He listened as Riley outlined his problem.

"Look, I'm willing to help where I can, but I specialise in family law. I'm probably not the best person to consult in matters of industrial legislation, but can point you in the right direction if the situation progresses to the point where your employment might be severed. Contact me then, and I'll see what I can do."

Riley thanked him for his taking his call. Hopefully, he wouldn't need a solicitor beyond backing up the bluff he'd made. Something had to go in his favour. He looked over at the Institute rooftop, but still couldn't see Winston. Time to de-stress. He took a couple of deep breaths and breathed out slowly. Rather than fret over things he couldn't control, he needed to focus on things he could. He would make the most of the pleasant day and his free time, by sitting outside with the notes for the driving test. Ginger joined him and sat on an adjoining chair for company.

When his phone rang, he jumped to retrieve it, hoping it might be Winston. It wasn't. Jonathan's name flashed on the screen.

"I hear you're in a spot of bother, mate."

"What have you heard? Who told you?"

"I have my sources. One of my regulars mentioned it to me, though without much detail. His partner works in the Excellerate offices. She told him."

"You mean Stella?"

"I think that's her name. She just said that charges were being laid against you for break and enter. What have you been up to?"

"It's a long story, but I think I've been set up and Winston has something to do with it."

"Drop in tonight, and I'll round up the others. Don't worry, mate… we've got your back."

18   The Stakeout

WHEN HE ARRIVED at the Colonial, Mark already sat at their usual table, nursing a schooner. Riley paused inside the door, checking who else was in the room before crossing the floor to where Mark sat. The amplified voice of the quiz master could be heard in the adjoining lounge bar, punctuated by either cheers or groans from the patrons. He'd forgotten this was quiz night.

"G'day, mate," Mark said with a disgusting chirp to his voice. He had no right to sound so chipper. "I'm the first, but I think Bruce and Colin are coming. Jonathan's changing a keg, but he'll join us shortly. I'm dying to hear your story, but I'll wait for the others to get here."

"Good move. I'll get myself a drink. Keep that seat free. I want to keep my back to the wall."

"You're not getting paranoid in your old age, are you Riley?"

"I am, with bloody good reason." He wanted to keep an eye on anyone else who came into the bar, plus make sure that the path for him to the exit remained clear. By the time he

199

returned to the table, Bruce and Colin had arrived and Jonathon joined them shortly after. There followed a bit of general chat while they all bought their drinks, and Jonathon plonked a large bowl of hot chips on the table for everyone to share.

"Now, Riley, tell us the story. I heard the basics today, but you know... Chinese whispers and all that." Jonathon gestured to the others. "I only told them that you were in a spot of bother and needed some help.

Somehow, other people's problems were more interesting than your own. As Riley looked around at the faces turned in his direction, he derived little satisfaction in being the one providing entertainment on this occasion. He took a breath and began with the phone call in the middle of the night, covered the escapade on the side of the building, and finished with Winston's explanation the following day.

"Then this morning, I was summoned to Eric Symes' presence and informed that there was evidence I had broken into David Barton's office and that this was grounds for dismissal and police involvement. It was further suggested that I might have had something to do with his death. I didn't even know the man!"

"Shit! That's heavy news. What's Winston had to say about this?" Bruce asked.

Riley shook his head. "That's the infuriating part. He hasn't answered any of my calls today, and I haven't seen him on his rooftop either. It's been radio silence. He must know what's happened.

"Initially, I was shown the door but I threated legal action for unfair dismissal. I've been suspended for now, but still have my accommodation. I have until the end of the week to prove I did not enter that office. I don't deny accessing the stairs and using the gantry at Winston's invitation."

His throat felt dry from talking so much. He drank half his cider in one draft, then belched softly before continuing. "I've since learned via the local grapevine that it was Andy Nguyen who complained to the boss, but I don't know why. Andy's the General Manager of Excellerate. Jonathon, have you heard anything else?"

Jonathon rubbed the side of his nose while he thought. "Not really, only what Steve told me and that was based on what his missus told him. He said you'd had the chop because you raided the Excellerate offices in the middle of the night. He said David Barton was fiddling the books, and you were in cahoots with him."

"Anyone else know anything?" Riley wasn't hopeful, but no harm in asking. The grapevine sometimes moved in mysterious ways. They looked at each other, but none of them had anything productive to offer.

"How about I try ringing Winston," Jonathon said. "He might answer if he sees that it's me calling. If I can, I'll get him to come down here, but otherwise I'll try talking to him myself."

"That's as good an idea as any," Colin said. "It would help to have his side of the story."

"Yeah, do that," said Mark. He was not talkative at the best of times, but when he offered an opinion, the others tended to listen. "It seems to me that someone has it in for you, Riley. Agreed?"

He looked around, seeking consensus. "The question is why, and how can we lure them out into the open. There's only one reason I can come up with. Maybe you did see something on the roof that night when Barton took a dive. Maybe that's why they want you out of the way. They're scared of what you might say. You could be in danger if you don't leave the building."

"But I keep telling you, I didn't see anything. It was only shadows and my imagination."

"But was it? You can't say one hundred percent for sure, can you?"

"Well, no, but—"

"But nothing. There's already doubt and innuendo, and if we put it about that you did see something, it might lure these people out from where they've been hiding. You need to say you saw two blokes on the roof that night, and you've kept quiet until now because you were scared of repercussions."

"I *am* scared of repercussions. If someone really did push him off the roof, or persuade him to take a dive, they'll come after me next."

"And we'll be waiting for them."

"You can't be with me every hour of the day. Someone watches what I do, even at night." He told them about the note pushed under the door. He'd forgotten to mention it before.

Jonathon hadn't tried to make the call to Winston, having been drawn into the conversation but now he slipped over to a quieter corner of the room, away from the reaches of the quiz master's voice. They couldn't hear what he was saying, but could see him with the phone pressed to one ear and a hand pressed against the other. He returned in a couple of minutes.

"It went through to voice mail. I left a message. Strange that. Either he doesn't want to or he's not able to answer."

"My bet is that he doesn't want to. He'll know by now what the implications have been for me. Does anyone know how else to contact him?"

They all looked at each other and shrugged. Why would anyone know that?

"Perhaps you should move out of your apartment for now," suggested Colin.

"I'm not going to be forced out of my home. Besides, I have Ginger Puss to think about."

"Well, perhaps we can take turns sleeping over. You're unlikely to strike too much trouble during the day when there are other people in the building. Do you have a spare bed?"

"The apartment's not very big; you've been there. I can put a blow-up mattress on the floor, but honestly, I think you're over-reacting."

"What security do you have? Mark asked. "It won't cost you much, but you could install a camera at the bottom of that last flight of stairs leading up to your roof. You'll get an alert on your phone if there's any movement at night. At least you'll know if the cat is trying to sneak out."

"That's a good idea. I'll try that first and if I have any concerns, that roster can be organized. I don't have much time to put this strategy in place. I was given a deadline of the end of the week to prove that I didn't do what Andy Nguyen reported to the boss."

"Why don't you speak to him?" Mark was still the pragmatist.

"I will. I'll try that in the morning. I might head for home now. Talking to you blokes has put the wind up me so I don't want to be out late, plus I'm sitting the test for my learner's permit in the morning. I need to be refreshed for that."

"About bloody time," said Jonathon. "If you end up having to get another job, a driver's license might be a prerequisite. Good luck with that."

Riley checked out who else was in the room before standing and heading for the door. Anyone could have slipped in while his attention was diverted by the conversation. The coast looked to be clear, so he repeated his farewells, thanking them all for their support and promising to keep them informed. He paused outside the door also, clocking all those who were in the vicinity. Nobody seemed to pay any attention to him, and he set off at a brisk pace, not wanting to linger.

Riley sat the theory test for the learner's permit online, and blitzed it early the next morning. It felt odd not to be downstairs undertaking his usual tasks, but liberating as well. It gave him time to logon to the government website and do the test before slipping downstairs to the Daily Bean. Phoebe's curtains were still closed, but that wasn't unusual for that time of morning.

He took Ginger Puss with him. The cat had been clearly annoyed at the disruption to his regular routine, and raced down the stairs ahead of him and sat expectantly in front of the elevator doors. The pile of daily papers sat on the doorstep, and he took pity on Diane and heaved the bundle inside the front door. They might disappear before she arrived for work.

Following his newly adopted routine, he looked both ways in the street before stepping down onto the footpath. The Ferals sat on a street bench outside the Daily Bean, smoking as usual. Alex flicked his butt into the long-suffering planter pot on the street. That tree would be forever stunted with the treatment it received.

"Hey, dude." Riley had to look twice to realize that Alex was extending his first and only greeting. "Howzit goin'?"

"Um… good thanks." He nodded at them briefly before opening the door to the café and shunting Ginger inside. Perhaps they were about to ask him for money, or something like that. Beyond the sneering, they'd always kept to themselves before."

"Here's my furry mate," Bruno called from behind the counter and Maria peaked out of the kitchen at hearing her husband. She gave a quick nod and a smile before disappearing back inside again.

"The usual? Any news?" Bruno asked.

"Not yet. I hope to find out more later today."

"Keep us posted."

Coffee arrived shortly after, plus the plate of eggs and a saucer of milk with some smoked salmon on the side. Ginge expressed his satisfaction by dragging the fish over the floor as he ate, but eating it all and then licking his whiskers. Riley grabbed the daily paper but skimmed through the pages. The words danced in front of this eyes, being too difficult to read with his current state of mind. He even ignored the sudoku.

Diane was polishing the front brass door plate when he returned to Blenheim House. A fresh vase of flowers sat on the front counter, and the magazines by the guest chairs were neatly arranged.

"Morning, Keep up the good work." The comment earned him a glare. *I'll have to be careful, or she'll be snaffling my job.* He resisted the urge to apply finger prints over the metal surfaces in the elevator, and hurried back to the roof-top level with Ginge. His next task was to ride his bike to the hardware store to pick up a security camera kit and also a set of L-Plates for when he had his lessons. On his return, he would try to speak to Andy Nguyen.

Phoebe's curtains had been opened in his absence, so he knew she was up and about. He would be devastated if she left her apartment, assuming that he would still be living in his flat in future and could notice. He made sure that the water bowl outside was freshened for Ginger and slipped back downstairs to get his bike.

Instead of travelling directly to the basement carpark, he stopped in reception again to speak to Diane.

"Let me know if you need information on where anything is or if anything major needs sorting," he started by saying. No harm in keeping sweet with her. "I know I'm not working officially, but I can still help you out if necessary."

"I appreciate that. It's a bit much expecting me to take it all on. I don't know anything about plumbing and stuff."

"No, of course not. Have you heard anything else from Stella? Any news about Winston?"

She looked over her shoulder as though expecting that someone might overhear her and leaned closer. "Winston has taken two-weeks leave. It's possible he's gone to stay with his daughter. Something about her having a baby."

"You sure about that? Winston has never mentioned a daughter, let alone a baby or the fact that he planned on taking leave."

Diane shrugged. "I only know what I've been told." She focused her attention on her computer screen, signalling that the conversation was over.

Riley pondered the information as he rode his bike to the hardware store. The fact that Winston had taken leave would not prevent him from answering his phone, unless he'd left the charger behind. He'd run away. There was no other reasonable explanation. The big question still remained; why had he run and why had he fabricated the events of that night?

Fixing the security cameras in position was relatively straightforward. He used the drill normally kept in his basement workroom, and nobody stopped him from accessing that. The camera recordings linked to his phone via Wi-Fi, so he would know if anyone attempted to access the roof level at night, or any other time. Nobody ever came up without an invitation.

When the job was complete and tidied to his satisfaction, he made himself a cup of tea before tackling Andy Nguyen. He didn't know the man well, but had often heard Winston speak of him positively and they had met in passing. The man had struck him as a reasonable person to deal with. His parents had escaped Vietnam after the end of the war, and made their way to Australia by boat.

Andy had been a baby at that time, but the family had arrived after a convoluted journey via refugee camps and treacherous seas. That was a time when the refugees arriving by boat were welcomed and given safe haven. He had done well, working his way through the Australian education system, and now running his own company, often providing training to the current refugees who managed to navigate the complex visa system.

He couldn't just barge in there and demand to know what was going on, much as that was his initial reaction. That would not be the right approach in this instance. Andy might have grown up in Australia, but still carried the cultural norms of his parents. Softly, softly would generate a better strategy.

He had to sit in the reception area for nearly half an hour before being escorted to the fifth floor. There appeared to be an internal debate about whether he should be permitted in the building at all, and when he was allowed into the elevator, it was in the company of one of the male senior teachers. What did they think he was going to do? Jump the desk and throttle Andy? He maintained a bland, polite expression, and sat where he was directed.

Andy Nguyen matched him with an impassive expression, and commented without taking his eyes off Riley, "Derek will stay for this conversation."

Riley wondered whether he should have brought a support person as well, just to even up the numbers. "Thank you for agreeing to see me, Mr. Nguyen. I understand that the recent sad loss of one of your senior members and events since that time will have been causing you some distress. My condolences to you and your staff."

Andy Nguyen inclined his head in assent. "I was not expecting you to visit me this morning, nor on any other occasion. But thank you for your kind words. I don't have much time for this meeting. Would you like to tell me why you are here?"

Riley took a deep breath and exhaled. "I was upset yesterday when allegations were expressed to me that I had broken into the premises of Excellerate recently and accessed the personal office of David Barton. I did not know this man, and to my knowledge have never met him. You can understand my distress therefore at the implications behind those allegations, both for my continued employment and my relationship with my employer."

Andy nodded slightly again, but did not speak.

"I should state most emphatically that although I was requested to come to the assistance of the building manager several nights ago, after he had inadvertently locked himself within an internal office of the building, I did not access that office myself, nor obviously did I touch or remove anything in that office. I would like to know what caused you to believe that I did."

Andy and the teacher exchanged a fleeting glance, but Riley caught it. He assumed they were debating what to tell him, if anything.

"You were seen. Late at night. You were seen and identified."

"Who saw me, and how was I identified."

"I am not at liberty to say who saw you, but I have it on very reliable evidence that you and David Barton were associates, in spite of what you have said, and that you entered his office by secretive means at night to retrieve evidence of your relationship with this man."

"We have it on camera," the teacher interrupted. "After being notified that there had been an illegal entry, we saw you exit the building via the elevator. You are known to a few people in this building, and the building manager confirmed it was you. There is no mistake. You broke into this building illegally."

"Winston told you that? Can you bring him in here to confirm that? It's an outright lie."

He knew from what Diane had said that Winston was no longer in the building, but wanted to hear what Andy Nguyen had to say.

"Winston has taken leave. He had family matters requiring his attention."

"That's very convenient. So, I assume he didn't tell you what he was doing in the office himself, nor how I had to come and rescue him."

"There is no evidence of Winston being in that office, nor any reason for him to do so."

That would be right, Winston would have walked down the stairs before riding the gantry up to the roof after his rescue. There wouldn't be any recording capturing him at all.

"And you won't tell me who supposedly saw me and how they came to do that? Were they also in the building late at night? What's their excuse?"

"That is not information we can divulge at this time. I notice you haven't denied you were here."

"Only to rescue Winston, but it appears he has not been entirely honest with you."

"You realize," the teacher said in him most officious tone, "that given the ongoing investigation into David Barton's death, and some of his actions before that event, that we will need to report this to the police."

"By all means, do so." Riley hoped he sounded more confident that he felt. "When they continue their investigations, I will be completely exonerated from having any association with David Barton, and also from doing this break and enter which you're now accusing me of."

He stood up. There was nothing more to be gained from the conversation, except perhaps to drop them a crumb. "The police have already been to see me about what I saw from my roof on the night that David Barton was pushed over the edge. It seems I was the only witness. I'll see myself out."

He turned to leave the office, and the teacher followed him out, clearly agitated. "We hadn't been told that Barton was pushed."

"It seems there are things that happened you haven't been told about, and things you've been told about that haven't happened. I'd think about your sources if I were you."

19 The Baited Hook

THE THOUGHT OF what he'd just said and done left him feeling sick to his stomach. It was all very well for the others to suggest using himself as bait to lure his antagonist out into the open, but they weren't the ones in the cross hairs. Now he could expect another visit from the police as well. He still needed to speak to Winston. If he'd found out where Katrina Dale lived, he could have asked for her help, but there had been no reason to do that. Come to think of it, getting her side of the story about her relationship with David Barton could be useful as well.

He tried calling Winston again, with the same result as before.

<Winston. Now I'm getting really worried. What's the story? Where have you gone and what did you tell Andy Nguyen? Call me.>

He messaged Sophie instead of calling, being conscious that while *he* may not be working, she probably was. He could let her know about getting his learner's permit without disturbing her. She can't have been too busy, because his phone rang shortly after he sent the text.

"You don't waste any time, do you? That's good news. Now I suppose you want those starter lessons I promised. When did you want to begin?"

"Long story, but my time is my own at the moment. I've been suspended from work so I can be available anytime of the day or night. Preferably not in the dark, as yet. I'd like to find my feet in daylight hours. It's up to you and the time you have free."

"Wow… what have you been doing to warrant that response?"

"It's more a case of what I've been accused of doing, rather than what I've done. I'll explain it all when I see you."

"Oh… okay. Don't forget the Council meeting is happening tomorrow evening, so that time is out for me. I could give you a quick lesson this evening, once peak hour is over. We can slip down to the open-air carpark by the Mile End Trade Centre. You'll be able to get the feel of the car there and to practice a few basic manoeuvres without much traffic around."

Now that the prospect of getting behind the wheel of a car was real, he couldn't decide if he felt apprehension or anticipation. He hoped she knew what she was doing and didn't get excitable when under stress. Teaching someone to drive could cause fractions in the best of friendships, and as far as friends went, they hardly knew each other. He tried to sound more confident than he felt.

"Sure. Text me when you're on your way, and I'll wait on the street out the front. I'm still living in the apartment—the job situation hasn't changed that. I'll have the L-plates to attach to the car. And Sophie? Thanks for this."

Riley passed the rest of the day with doing some reading and then baking a fresh batch of Chewy Chai Biscuits. He didn't know what else to do with himself. He fielded a call from Mark in relation to the security cameras, checking that they had been installed. Riley reported on the conversation with Andy Nguyen, and the fact that Winston had disappeared and still wasn't answering his phone. Mark couldn't offer any information about Winston's daughter or where else he might be.

"Can't promise anything, but I'll drop the word with a couple of my copper mates. See if they have any idea on where he might be, given he's got a record and all that. They could keep tabs on him."

"That might not be a good idea. I'm trying to avoid the police at the moment. Andy Nguyen's sidekick said he was going to advise the constabulary that I'd seen more than I let on. I may receive another visit in the immediate future."

"You're probably over-thinking things. The cops I chat to will be different to the detectives who paid you a visit."

"Perhaps. I'm not totally reassured."

All right for Mark. He wasn't the one expecting challenging questions from the boys in blue. He slipped downstairs to ask Diane if she had heard anything on the grapevine. She did not seem pleased to see him.

"This is most awkward. I'm not sure I should be speaking to you."

"What happened to the principle of innocent until proven guilty? I'll expect an apology for unjust thoughts when this situation is resolved."

Diane gave him the side-eye look which she had fine-tuned over the time he'd known her, and tried to focus on her monitor. She spoke out of the side of her mouth.

"I heard that Winston was picked up by his lady friend early Tuesday morning. He hadn't formally applied for leave, but messaged his boss after he left saying that it was a family emergency."

Strange, but not surprising after what he'd already learned. Diane pushed her glasses up her nose to look at him more clearly. She had to tilt her head back to see through the bottom of her multifocal lenses when working, but then had to adjust them when she wanted to talk to someone. This resulted in a continual process of lifting her head backwards and forwards, and sliding the gasses to a more comfortable position.

"Those people keep hanging around. I wish they'd go away. They stare at me whenever I step outside the door and make me feel uneasy. They do it on purpose."

"What people?" A band tightened around his chest. Riley frowned as he moved to the side of the front window, standing in a spot where he hoped he couldn't be seen from outside. The usual stream of pedestrians passed by on the other side of the glass. "Who do you mean? I can't see anyone intimidating."

"Those young ones… always dirty and unkempt. I don't know why they hang around here. They were outside early this morning."

By her description, it had to be the Ferals. Riley opened the front door and peered out, looking left and right. "I can't see them anywhere. They must have disappeared down whichever black hole they live in."

"I wish you'd tell them to move on."

I'm not working… remember?"

The comment earned him another of her disdainful looks.

Riley scanned the oncoming vehicles watching for her approach. Sophie had messaged him with her expected time of arrival, but he waited on the footpath five minutes before in case she was early. It gave him a few moments to check out who else was in the street. He couldn't see the Ferals, which didn't mean they weren't around. He had the unsettling sensation of being watched, which was ridiculous. He hated the thought that he was becoming paranoid.

She pulled up to the kerb in her blue Mazda, deftly slipping out of the stream of traffic to stop in a *No Standing* zone.

"Jump in. I'll drive us down to the carpark and we'll get organized there."

Sophie focused on the traffic and her merging manoeuvres as she pulled back into the flow of vehicles before glancing at him. "How was your day?"

"Confusing, if I'm honest. I'm not sure how I've ended up in this situation, and then being 'at work' but not working was a weird experience. I'll be driven crazy if it continues for too long."

"I'll be interested to hear the story…" She broke off and sniffed. "What can I smell?"

"I baked this morning. I had to do something productive. "Chewy Chai Biscuits. I brought you a container full as part of my thanks for the lessons."

"A man who bakes! I won't say no to that. When we stop, I'll have to try one. It might be a while before dinner."

"Sorry about that. I hope the biscuits make up for it."

The trade centre lay on the western edge of the city, separated from the CBD by a belt of parklands. A parking lot adjoined the main buildings and towards evening, the area was often empty or at least only minimally occupied. This was one of those times. Sophie pulled up, and they both got out. The L-Plates were self-adhesive, and Riley stuck one to the rear of the car and the other to the front windscreen. While he did, Sophie rifled the biscuit box.

"These are yummy! There could be a new career waiting for you if you can bake like this. What else is in your repertoire?"

"You'll have to find out. I don't disclose all my talents in one go."

She raised one eyebrow in amusement. "Is that enticement for future lessons?" She pointed to the front of the car. "Okay. Your turn. Get in."

Sophie slid into the passenger seat and buckled up. He did as instructed, gripping the steering wheel firmly and looking at the array of electronic displays in front of him.

"They'll make more sense when the engine is on and the dashboard comes to life. We'll start slowly. First adjust your seat so that you can reach the pedals comfortably. Then, adjust

217

the interior and side mirrors so that you can see to the rear and the side."

This part was easy, once he understood how the electric mirror control worked. Sophie talked him through the controls, and then told him what they were going to do first. The car was an automatic, so he didn't have to concern himself with manual gear changes, though she recommended that he learn to drive a manual vehicle later. This version was enough. With some trepidation, he flicked on the indicator, released the hand brake, and eased away from the kerb.

For the most part, the lesson entailed becoming familiar with the car handling features, accelerating, turning, slowing down and stopping. They followed a meandering path around the carpark. Few vehicles were around, but Sophie insisted he use the indicator for each turn they made. His confidence grew slowly, to the point where he managed a three-point turn, and tried reversing into a parking bay. He succeeded by moving at about one inch per second.

"You'll soon get the hang of it. That's probably enough for today. We can swap over and I'll drop you back in the city. I won't make you drive through the evening traffic yet."

"Yeah, I'm not at that level of competency. It's more complicated than I expected. It's been good though," he added in case she thought he didn't appreciate the lesson. "I'll feel more confident with the next lesson." He flicked a glance at her judging her reaction. "You will give me another lesson, won't you? I'll bake some more biscuits, something different next time. You can try my full repertoire. I'm not just a one-trick pony."

"With an offer like that, how can I refuse? Of course, I'll give you another lesson. We'd better take the plates off the car and I'll drive you back."

Riley applied the hand brake, and they both climbed out to swap seats. He peeled the L-Plate from the front windscreen, and walked around towards the back to retrieve the second plate. He was level with the rear passenger door when Sophie screamed.

"Watch out!"

He spun around, flattening himself against the side of the car just in time. A black SUV swung past at speed, almost hitting him before zooming off and completing an erratic circuit of the parking area before leaving via the exit.

"Holy shit! That car nearly collected you. They swerved towards you on purpose. I saw them."

Riley clung to the side of the car, not sure if his knees would support him if he stood up straight. "Did you see who was driving?"

"Not really. I was more focused on the car, but I think there were two people in the front. They could have killed you."

"They could have, but they didn't. Either it was a bad driver or he or she wanted to scare me." He took a deep breath, exhaled, and then straightened. "I don't suppose you caught the number plate?"

She shook her head. "It happened too fast. I didn't think…"

"I didn't really expect you to. They were probably just a couple of local hoons who thought it was funny to scare a learner driver. For some reason, an L-Plate brings out the worst in some people. Lucky they didn't hit your car."

She stared at him for a moment without speaking, then peeled off the back L-Plate and handed it to him. "We'd better make a move before more of these local hoons turn up."

Sophie guided the car back onto the main road leading into the city centre before speaking again. "You haven't told me what happened at work. Is there a problem?"

What to tell her? He chose his words carefully. After the incident that had just happened, he didn't want to scare her off. "There has been a mis-understanding and I have been accused of something I didn't do… couldn't have done. I have to prove that but, in the meantime, I've been relieved of my duties. It's a bit complicated."

"Sounds tricky. Anything I can do?"

"Not really, but thanks for asking. I'll have to sort this one out myself."

"She pulled up in front of Blenheim House. "I nearly forgot to ask. How's Ginger Puss?"

"Has his appetite back and the attitude to go with it. He's fine, thanks to you."

She smiled. "That's good news. The council meeting is on tomorrow evening, so I assume I'll see you there. We can arrange another driving lesson then."

He opened the car door and with one foot on the road, swivelled to face her. "That sounds like a plan. I really appreciate this. I'll owe you another dinner at least."

She flapped a dismissive hand at him. "Only too pleased to help. See you tomorrow."

He shut the car door and stood watching as she pulled out and accelerated away. It had fallen dark during the course of the lesson, but overhead lighting illuminated the front of the building and beyond. He looked both ways up and down the street, not seeing anything unusual. His feeling of unease persisted. Maybe they were hoons, but maybe they weren't. Maybe it was someone who thought he'd seen what he shouldn't. Was that a warning? If so, they'd been followed to the Mile End carpark. That put Sophie at risk. Perhaps he should cancel lessons for now. He shivered at the thought of being watched, and quickly swiped at the door fob to get himself safely inside. There at least, he was secure.

20 Bike Ride

THE PHONE EMITTED a soft dinging noise. Riley snatched it from the bedside table. Someone must be on the stairs. He pushed himself into a sitting position, kicking Ginge aside in the process. The cat voiced a protest and gave what Riley assumed was a baleful glare but the room was too dark to tell for sure. He swiped over the phone screen. The notification signalled a message in his In-Box, nothing to do with the cameras at all.

He lay down again, aware of his heart beating an alarmed tattoo in his chest. He'd been in the middle of a weird dream when the phone woke him, and now he felt truly out of sorts. What if the cameras didn't trigger when they should have? Someone who knew what they were doing could probably disable them. He lay and listened for noises. The city slept. He couldn't hear any sirens, let alone traffic noise or anything else.

He hated letting paranoia rule, but the thoughts running rampant in his head left him uneasy. The only option was to get up, check the stairs and the rooftop and then go back to bed. Hopefully, he could then drift back to sleep. He slid out of bed in the dark, not wanting to put on the light in case... in case that might alert someone watching that he was awake. Holding his breath, he padded quietly to the bedroom door, opening it slowly so it didn't squeak.

Soft moonlight filtered through the window to the apartment, allowing him to peer into the darkness on the rooftop. Nothing stirred. Taking heart from that, he opened the external door and stepped out onto the deck. A light, cool breeze made its presence felt, but nothing else moved. He made his way to the stairwell, but that was shrouded in quiet darkness. He stood for a moment at the top, waiting for his eyes to adjust before walking down, one cautious step at a time.

Nothing. Nobody was on the stairs, nor hiding down below when he peered around the corner at the bottom. The concrete stairs were cold beneath his feet, ensuring he was now wide awake. Back at roof level, he wandered over to the edge of the roof to check out his surrounds. The roof of the Institute was shielded in darkness, but an outdoor light shone over Phoebe's balcony. Her curtains were closed, but she must have forgotten to turn the light off before she went to bed. He looked out over the city, towards the hills in the distance and towards the sea. Everything was as it should be. He could go back to bed.

Not surprising after his nighttime drama, Riley slept in. Ginger Puss woke him, impatiently patting his face. After he'd had a restful night, the cat was ready for breakfast. Riley lay there for a while, reviewing the events of the night. He'd panicked. Nobody had come near him and probably nobody would. He'd allowed the others to spook him.

For once, he didn't feel like breakfast in the Daily Bean. He made a light breakfast of toast, fruit, and yoghurt instead, and Ginge had to be satisfied with his usual cat biscuits, a bowl of milk, and a walk around the rooftop. After that, Riley wasn't sure what to do with himself. He still hadn't come up with a practical idea for proving his innocence to Eric Symes and Andy Nguyen. If he didn't do that, perhaps his job loss would be permanent. Not only would he lose his job but his accommodation too. Living with his mother again was not something he wanted to contemplate, even for the short term. Only one more day and it would be the end of the week.

He put a perfunctory call through to Winston's mobile, not really expecting to reach him. As before, the call went through to voicemail. He didn't bother leaving a message. Winston would know he was trying to contact him.

A bike ride might clear his head. He could pack some snacks and his water bottle and ride the linear park trail along the river from the city and towards the hills that framed the suburban areas to the east. He would easily be back in time to attend the council meeting that evening. He packed his backpack with some essentials, checked that his phone was fully charged, and clattered down the stairs to the elevator on the level below.

Being so absorbed in contemplating the route he might take with the bike, he nearly missed it. A cigarette butt lay on the floor not far from the elevator. He didn't smoke. It was a non-smoking building; all the tenants knew that. It hadn't been there during the night when he'd come up to the flat, but on reflection he couldn't be sure. The tenants on the level below his never came near the stairs. They knew the roof level was out of bounds.

He glanced back towards the roof, wondering if the wind could have blown it down at some point when the top door was open, but that was implausible. Someone had been on the stairs, someone who had no right to be there. The app on his phone didn't show any activity, other than himself, but that didn't mean someone wasn't out of camera range.

Diane was already in reception and was untying the bundle of morning papers when he stepped out of the elevator.

"Diane, have you let anyone in this morning? Who's been up on Level Eleven?"

She began shoving papers in pigeon holes. "I haven't let anyone in. Why would I? Any of the tenants could have come in but that's their right. They have their own access fobs."

"But only authorized people should be up on that level."

"And only authorized people would have been up on that level. What's this about anyway?"

Probably nothing. It could have been a tradie, and he just hadn't noticed before. "Someone dropped a cigarette butt on my stairs. I wondered who that might be."

"I've no idea, unless it was that wretched couple outside. He always smokes, flicking his butts around. I thought young people were supposed to care about the environment. They were in the street this morning. They followed me as I walked down from King William Street. They make me feel very uncomfortable."

No guesses who she meant. The Ferals. Diane was right, Alex did smoke, but he couldn't possibly be in the building.

Riley opened the door and checked outside. They sat on the ground outside the Daily Bean with a cap on the ground in front of them, presumably seeking spare change. That wouldn't last long. Bruno would soon move them on.

"Unless they actually cause us harm, or do something to the building, there is little we can do. They look worse than they are. If you're really worried when you're coming to work though, I can always meet you up the road and escort you the rest of the way—provided I still have a job."

She shrugged at that comment, but didn't offer a response. He took that to mean she hadn't heard anything else on her grapevine. "I'm heading out on the bike for a ride, so if any crisis develops, you'll have to deal with it."

That earned an eye-roll, which he ignored in favour of making a hasty exit to the basement carpark where he kept his bike.

Being out on the bike on a weekday bore with it the sensation of an illicit luxury. Riley recalled playing hooky from school, and equated that experience with his elation at zooming along the path by the river. He'd chosen a goldilocks day, not too hot and not too cold. Best of all, getting away from the city meant he was also putting distance between himself and the dramas of the recent weeks.

Although he'd previously followed the bike path adjacent to the river down to the sea, this time he followed it in the opposite direction, via various twists and turns towards the foothills. He pushed the bike at a cracking pace beside the eucalyptus-lined river bed. At times the path opened out into park areas, where people could have a picnic or perhaps a barbecue.

Late morning, he stopped for an iced coffee at a café adjourning the path, and sat for a while, watching the magpies that strutted around the park, proclaiming loudly that the surrounding area was theirs. He admired their insouciance, as they rummaged for tasty titbits in the leaf litter, or warbled to each other in glorious song.

It gave him the opportunity to take stock of his life from a distance. Winston would have to come back to work sooner or later, and then he could support Riley's story. He and Katrina might show up at the Colonial, if that was where they first met and, in that case, Jonathan would call him. The CCTV records from the elevator in the Institute would show that he wasn't carrying anything when he left the building that night, and that should support his claim that he never entered David Barton's office. He'd been getting himself worked up over nothing. Really, it was that simple.

The ride back to the city took less effort, in part because there were more downhill bits, and in part because he took the ride at a slower pace. He cruised along, enjoying the fresh air and the freedom. It almost made him query why he bothered with getting his license, except that he couldn't imagine taking Ginger Puss on the bike.

The path took him back into the heart of the city, through surrounds that became more formal and manicured once he passed the zoo. He diverted from the bike path back onto the road, once he hit King William Rd, which led into the CBD and then became King William Street. He'd never understood the naming difference.

Riley didn't normally ride through the centre of the city on a weekday. Weekends were quieter, but now he had to negotiate the buses, trams, kamikaze pedestrians, and three lanes of traffic in either direction. King William Street provided the quickest route to Murray Street, but he soon regretted he hadn't taken a less direct route. He clenched his teeth as he ducked around a bus pulling into a stop, and then nearly collided with a taxi that pulled away from a rank without indicating.

A horn blared behind him, and he wobbled in fright, almost into the path of an oncoming van.

Fuck – I need danger money for this. What fool would ride a bike through the city? Bike couriers did it all the time, but they had either a death wish or a desperate need for money. Perhaps both.

Noting that the traffic behind him had been held up by a red light, he crossed into a middle lane, ready to make a right-hand turn into Murray St. He looked back over his shoulder to make sure the coast was clear. If he hadn't done that, he wouldn't have seen it. A black SUV appeared to be heading directly for him. There was nowhere to go except sideways onto the tram tracks running down the centre of the road. His front wheel locked into position in the channel of the track, and the bike abruptly stopped. Riley didn't. He flew over the handle bars and smashed face-first onto the pavement.

The car must have swept past, as it didn't hit him. He lay where he had fallen, aware of grating pain on his face, his arms, and his legs. His feet were hooked under the frame of his bike, which was now looking to be an unrideable shape. If he didn't get up soon, a tram might come along and finish the job the SUV started. The ringing in his head made it hard to hear, and when he put his hand up to his face, it felt wet.

"You okay, mate?" A pedestrian had darted across the road to check on him. "Can you stand up? Let's get you off the road"

Riley raised himself onto hands and knees. "I don't think anything's broken. I'm winded, that's all."

"By the look of you, it's more than that. Lean on me."

The man helped him to stand. Grazing ran the length of his forearm, and Riley wasn't sure if the pain he felt was from that plus bruising, or perhaps something was broken. Another good Samaritan picked up his bike and he was helped off the road and to a bench on the footpath.

"I've called an ambulance. They'll be here soon." A woman approached them with the phone still clamped to her ear.

"I don't need an ambulance; I'll be fine." Riley felt dizzy and wobbly, and the grazed side of his face was settling into a stiff mask.

"You might have concussion. I saw you dive head-first onto the roadway. Just as well you were wearing a helmet."

"You saw it? Did you see the car that swerved at me?"

"There was a car that zoomed past," the woman said hesitantly, "but I didn't pay attention to it. I was more concerned with you. I thought you might have broken your neck, or something horrible like that."

Riley put his hand up to the side of his head and gingerly eased it from side to side. There were ominous creaks coming from his neck, but everything seemed to be moving as it should. His bike looked a bit sad. The front wheel had taken on a new shape, one not conducive to further riding. He would need that driver's licence after all.

He was about to insist that he didn't need an ambulance, when the siren further up the street indicated it was on its way. The woman stepped onto the roadway, waving it down.

"They'll look after you now," she said comfortingly. "Do you need me to call anyone for you?"

Who would he call? Not his mother and the drama that would entail. "No, I'm fine. Thank you for your help."

The paramedics were quick and efficient. "You're not a pretty sight, mate," said one reassuringly. "Best you get checked over. Those tram tracks keep us in business. You're not the first to come to grief with a bike wheel stuck in one of those."

Yeah, but I might be the first who was pushed into one by some bastard who was trying to run me over.

"But my bike…"

"Have you got a lock?" asked the man who first came to his aid. "I'll secure it to the back of the bench and you can pick it up later."

Riley fished the lock out of his backpack and handed it over to the Samaritan. One of the paramedics removed his helmet, checking for spinal injuries as he did. They checked his eyes, and ran a series of tests.

"I think you've been lucky in that there probably aren't any major injuries, but we'll drop you off at the Emergency Dept for a more in-depth assessment. That arm looks a bit dodgy."

Much as he didn't want the drama of a hospital visit, it looked as though he would not be given a choice. The ambulance gurney was wheeled to his side and the two paramedics eased him onto it and strapped him in. A small cluster of people watched this process, no doubt finding it more entertaining than whatever else they had planned for the afternoon. As he was wheeled into the back of the ambulance, Riley looked up and noticed that the Ferals were also part of the crowd. His eyes met those of Alex, and the man gave him a thumbs up in acknowledgement. Acknowledging what, Riley wasn't sure.

"You stupid bastard. What did you go and do something like that for? I would have brought you grapes, but I ate them first."

While Riley waited to be seen in the Emergency Department, he sent Colin a message outlining where he was and why. Colin had responded that he was sorting out a sliding door in the north wing that wouldn't shut, but after that he would join him. He turned up after Riley had initially been assessed and while he was waiting to be wheeled down to the x-ray department. As the Building Services Manager, Colin had been unchallenged when he slipped behind the cubicle curtain. He pulled up a chair beside the bed and sat down.

"It wasn't intentional. I was almost home, but I had a little help in the shape of a black SUV that thought I needed a nudge onto the tram tracks."

"It was an accident, right?"

Riley paused while he played the scene back in his head. It looked like the same vehicle that had swerved at him in the carpark, but both times everything happened so quickly, he couldn't be sure. "I think so. I'd never be able to prove if it wasn't."

"Sounds like you've got doubts. What happened?"

Riley outlined the events of the previous evening in which the SUV had appeared out of nowhere, and then again when it seemed the car drove directly at him. Each vehicle had a dark windscreen, so it was impossible to see who was driving, or even how many people were in the car."

"It seems that you're safest at home where you've got the security cameras. Not many people have access to you and your apartment. It's when you leave there that you're in strife."

Riley pulled a face and then regretted it. The grazing had set his face into a scabby mask, and any expression other than one possibly induced by Botox hurt like hell. "I think someone accessed the floor below my level last night. There was a cigarette butt on the ground, just out of range of the camera. Nobody on that level smokes, and I'm sure it wasn't there when I climbed the stairs last night."

"Probably a tradie. He or she wouldn't want to go all the way downstairs and outside for a quick fag. They just snuck in a quickie upstairs and hoped you wouldn't notice."

Colin was right. He was imagining things that weren't there. His head began to throb. Thinking was too much effort.

"Anything I can do for you? What about the cat?"

Ginger! He'd totally forgotten the cat. He definitely wasn't thinking straight. "Yeah—he'll need feeding and if my bike can be picked up, that would be great. It's locked to a seat in King William Street. Some moron might try to take off with it, though they won't get too far with the front wheel bent like it is."

"Give me your keys and tell me what to do. I'll take the work van and shove your bike in the back of that, then I'll feed puss. I'll let the others know what's happened in case anyone's looking for you."

An orderly turned up with a wheel chair to take Riley down to the x-ray department. He quickly handed over the key to open the lock to his bike. "Jonathan's got a spare fob key to the building, with my door key on the chain as well. I'm not supposed to give them out, but I felt happier knowing someone else had a fob in case I lost mine or locked myself out."

"Okay. Leave it to us. Between us, we'll look after the cat and take care of the bike. I'll leave you to it."

With the orderly's help, Riley manoeuvred himself off the bed and into the wheel chair. He was glad he didn't have to walk. In spite of his protests, stiffness had set in and he now felt incredibly sore and his head throbbed. He settled back in the seat. It was good to have people around he could rely on. Belatedly, he remembered the council meeting. That was one commitment he wouldn't be keeping. Right now, he had other things on his mind.

21   What did Phoebe See?

BY THE TIME his wounds had been cleaned and diagnostic tests had indicated bruising and grazing, but no lasting damage, it was almost ten pm. Riley caught a taxi home. After getting himself up to the roof level, he made himself a cup of tea and sat for a while to catch his breath. He messaged Colin and Jonathan to let them both know he was home and in one piece. Ginger Puss had been sleeping on his bed, but jumped up on hearing the door open and rubbed around Riley's legs with a purring rumble.

He'd been given pain killers at the hospital, plus sleeping tablets to get him through the next couple of nights. Normally, Riley preferred to stay drug free, but this evening at least, he decided that both would be a good idea. He'd had enough nights of disturbed sleep before the accident, and the pain and stiffness would inhibit him from getting a solid sleep this night too. He tried to make sense of what had happened, but in the end, deferred the analysis until the morning. He really needed to lie down.

Riley drifted on a cloud of semi-consciousness in the morning, with a foggy brain dragging him backwards towards sleep again. In the end, his bladder forced him to a greater state of alertness, pushing him to stumble out of bed and towards the bathroom. It was an hour past his usual rising time, and for the first time in recent days, he was glad not to be working.

He stood in front of a mirror after emerging from his shower and took stock of his body. He had a huge hematoma where he'd connected with the end of the handle bar on his dive towards the road. His face sported grazes down one side and around his mouth, as did his right arm and both his knees. His wrist ached from where he'd flung out an arm during his fall, and possibly still had bits of road grit embedded in the pad. All in all, it was not a pretty sight. He carefully applied a layer of pawpaw ointment over the grazes, touching the wounds as lightly as he could. He pulled on wide-legged shorts instead of his customary jeans, so that the fabric didn't stick to the ointment.

That done, he made a cup of coffee and slice of vegemite toast and took both outside to sit in the morning sun. He took his phone with him and scrolled through emails and messages. The Skywalkers' grapevine had gone into overdrive and he received a slew of messages asking for updates on his condition.

He also found a message from Sophie. <Didn't see you at the meeting.> He'd meant to call her before falling asleep and had then forgotten. He dialled her number.

"Sophie? Is this an okay time to talk?"

"Sure… missed you last night. I thought you were going to attend."

"I was, but…" He filled her in on the events of the previous afternoon and where he spent the evening instead.

"I'm so sorry to hear that. Not that your presence would have made any difference. Council voted to support the re-zoning proposal."

"What? But I thought your report recommended against it… at least that's the impression I gained from your hints."

Her sigh came down the phone. "It did, but my report wasn't the only one commissioned and some industry bodies made separate submissions. The Property Council for instance strongly supported the proposal."

"I should have anticipated that. Those industry bodies with powerful connections probably have more sway than a group of concerned residents and small business owners."

"And they have deeper pockets."

"What do you mean?"

"They or their lobbyists can wine and dine the councillors, provide tickets to entertainment or sporting events, make beneficial introductions… that sort of thing."

"Isn't that illegal?"

"It's a grey area. Any benefits of that nature should be declared, but that doesn't always happen. Perhaps the benefit is given to a partner or child."

"Did that happen in this case?"

"I don't know, but one of the senior council managers changed his stance from being critical of to in support of the rezoning last week. I know he's been in financial strife since his divorce. I suspect a brown paper bag may have changed hands, but that's a dangerous allegation. I wouldn't suggest it to anyone else."

"That's bribery."

"That's life." Her voice was flat and devoid of emotion, leaving him feeling hopeless about the ability of the individual to make a difference in matters of public interest.

"I guess aside from my current situation, I need to start thinking about future options for work and accommodation."

"Don't be too hasty. The rezoning has a few hoops to jump though before being signed off by the minister. Anything could happen in that time."

"That's some hope, but I won't rely on it. Incidentally, I don't think I'm up for a driving lesson for a few days. Perhaps on Sunday, but I would want to be less stiff than this before I get behind the wheel again."

"That's understandable. I'll give you a call Sunday morning and we can make plans from there, depending on how you're feeling."

The conversation left him feeling deflated. What was the point in debating these planning issues if more powerful interests were always going to get their way? It seemed his future at Blenheim House was limited, regardless of what Eric Symes said. Feeling in need of company, he wandered down to the Daly Bean. Diane shrieked when he emerged from the elevator.

"My God, what happened to you? Is it catching?"

For once, Riley rolled his eyes instead of her. It was the only movement he felt comfortable making with his face as stiff as it was. "It's gravel rash, Diane, not leprosy. I came a cropper off the bike yesterday following an altercation with a tram track." He didn't mention being pushed in that direction.

Her look of horror slowly eased, being replaced with one of maternal concern. "Shouldn't you be lying down? That looks very painful."

"If I stop moving, my face and the rest of my body will probably set rigid. I'm not going to do anything energetic though. If there are any dramas today, I don't want to know."

Her face still reflected a degree of horror as he let himself out and took the few steps into the Daily Bean. When he pushed open the café door, Phoebe and Lucinda, sat at one of the tables having morning tea. Phoebe preferred a cup and saucer to a mug—not very elegant— and Bruno kept a special set just for her. He'd picked it up at an Op Shop, complete with matching side plate. She now sat with a small pot of tea, a jug of milk, her tea cup and a Danish pastry cut into pieces on the plate. Luci also had a special cup.

"Riley," Phoebe exclaimed on seeing him, "you look a mess. Sit down and tell us what happened."

He cleared his throat "I don't want to intrude. It's been one of those weeks. I'm probably not good company right now."

"Don't be silly. Sit down, dear, and tell me what's been going on. Bruno... bring another cup." She addressed her granddaughter. "You don't mind, do you Luci?"

The younger woman shrugged politely and moved her phone to the other side of the table, clearing a space in front of Riley. Bruno noted the interaction and held up a mug with an enquiring look in Riley's direction, his eyebrows rising towards his balding scalp. Riley gave him a thumbs up, and mouthed "coffee" towards the other man.

Luci squinted behind him. "Where's your cat? I still haven't seen this animal, but I heard he visited Gran recently. Doesn't he usually come here with you?"

"Only for breakfast. He's confined to the rooftop at the moment. Long story."

Phoebe patted his hand. "A lot must have happened since we last spoke. Why don't you start at the beginning?"

Somehow, he had thought that news of his escapade with Winston and the repercussions would have seeped back to Phoebe. It soon transpired that nobody had told her. He was impressed that Bruno had not said anything, assuming the café to be a hive of information and gossip, and gave her a precis of his rescue mission with Winston and the subsequent results.

"I wondered what you two were up to."

"What do you mean? Did you see us?" It hadn't occurred to him to ask her. Given the time of night when it all happened, he thought she would have been in bed.

"I couldn't sleep. I was thinking about the recital, and playing my piece over and over in my head. In the end, I got up and made myself a chamomile tea. I wandered out onto the balcony, and that's when I saw you on the roof of Winston's building."

"I didn't see you."

"I didn't put the outside light on. There was no need. There was enough moonlight. Besides, my nightgown is sheer. I wasn't going to highlight that."

Riley kicked himself for not thinking to ask Phoebe if she'd seen anything days before, and suppressed the thoughts her words evoked. "What exactly did you see?"

"I saw you emerge from the stairwell, after fluffing around you got into the gantry and slid down the side of the building. I was incredibly curious as to what was going on at that time of night. I heard your voices before I saw you both emerge over the edge, but you went down alone and came up a short time later with Winston. Then you disappeared again, and Winston went into his flat and shut the door."

"Phoebe, you might be my saviour. Can I cite you as a witness? It means that you may get a couple of phone calls asking you to verify what you've told me. When Winston surfaces again, I need him to back up my side of the story as well."

"What will you do if he doesn't? He seems rather keen on this Katrina woman you've mentioned."

"Winston with a girlfriend! That sounds improbable." Luci snickered but soon stopped when her grandmother gave her a warning look.

"He is keen. He's tried to tell me it's just about their mutual interest in vinyl, but blind Freddie could see it's more than that... from his side anyway."

Phoebe poured herself and Luci another cup of tea from the pot and Bruno delivered Riley's mug of coffee.

"Mate, you're going to scare away all my customers, coming in here looking like that. I'm busy now, but you'll have to fill me in later." He disappeared back to look after his morning trade.

Phoebe shook her head. "I'm so disappointed in Winston. I never thought he would do something like this to you."

"Nor did I. I've learned a few new things about the man recently."

"Oh?"

"He's done time for driving under the influence. There was an accident and two small children were killed. That environment could influence anyone in bad ways."

"Yes, I was aware that was in his background. Very sad. He told me about it one day in a confessional mood. You can't hold a man's past against him though. He's done his time and was devastated about what happened."

"I imagine so." It impressed him that Phoebe had never mentioned this before. Some people couldn't wait to share a secret like that. Riley tried not to frown and aggravate his face. "In the meantime, I need to find a solicitor who can give me advice. Bruno recommended Tom Hansel, but he works in a different area of law."

Phoebe patted his uninjured hand reassuringly. "I can speak to the solicitor that Charles found for me. That might be better than consulting someone who works in that building. There could be a conflict of interest."

She had a point, as long as this bloke didn't cost an arm and a leg. Phoebe rummaged in her bag for her phone, and began scrolling through the screens.

"Here are the contact details. They play golf together, or something like that. I'll tell him he mustn't over-charge you."

"That's very kind of you."

She did what she needed to do on her mobile and Riley's phone pinged as her message arrived. "Hopefully, I won't need him. It's not only the unfair dismissal I want support on. Eric Symes even tried to suggest that perhaps I had something to do with David Barton's death. How would I prove that I didn't? I don't have an alibi for that night. The word of a cat doesn't count for much."

"No-one would seriously think you pushed him off the roof!"

"I hope not. I didn't even know the man. Maybe I'm being paranoid, but now I think someone's either trying to intimidate me or cause me serious harm. After my driving lesson on Wednesday, someone in a black SUV swerved at me and nearly hit me, and then a black SUV veered towards me in King William St yesterday, causing me to crash."

"You're learning to drive?" Phoebe sounded incredulous. "It's about time. Who's teaching you?"

"Sophie, the woman who drove Ginger Puss and me to the vet the other day. After that scare, I decided I need to get my license. Not that it would have helped in that situation, as I don't have a car, but it might be useful in the future."

"You know what I think?" Luci asked, sounding pleased with herself. "I think David Barton was pushed off the roof and if you get killed in a road accident—" She used finger quotes around *road accident,* "—then it's easier to blame you for his death." She sat back and folded her arms.

Phoebe held up a warning finger. "Luci, that is a macabre thought. Nobody is going to kill Riley. We don't need that sort of talk."

Yeah, thanks, Luci. That's just what I need to hear.

Phoebe turned her attention to Riley. "Still, you need to be careful. These incidents you have described are most concerning. Perhaps keep off the roads for a while."

He half smiled, half grimaced, trying to ignore the pain. He wouldn't argue with her on that score. "Enough of my dramas. I don't want to think about them anymore. You haven't updated us on any of your news. When's your recital? I've been listening to you practicing."

"It's Wednesday evening of next week. She's going to blitz it," Luci said. "I'm so proud of her. It's about time more people appreciated her talent and understood that just because you are older, it doesn't mean you can't keep performing. Finn's dad has given her a fantastic opportunity, hasn't he Gran?"

"You're going to attend this event?" Riley asked.

"Absolutely. Tray has booked a table at the fundraiser, and Finn and I will both be there. Gran is lending me her string of pearls to wear that night. It's going to be a dress-up event."

He noticed Phoebe was massaging her fingers. "Break a leg, Phoebe. I look forward to hearing how it goes.

"I'll probably have a small soiree at home afterwards. Hopefully, it's celebratory. You must come over."

"I'd love to. Not sure that I have any pearls to wear, but I can find some clobber to suit the occasion. Changing the subject, what about the challenge to your income?"

"All communication is through Cornelia's solicitor. Charles has taken over management of the negotiation. They are still trying to prove that I, or Charlie and perhaps both of us, used undue influence in persuading Harrison to set up the trust account in my favour." She blotted her lips carefully with a paper serviette. "That's ridiculous. Nobody could manipulate Harrison. If anyone did the manipulating it would have been him. He was a man who knew his own mind and always made sure to get what he wanted."

"Surely, Harrison did this with the assistance of an accountant or trust lawyer? They would have asked the right questions."

"He did, but they were in his employ. The inference is that as they were on his payroll, they did as he wanted, no questions asked."

"Sounds like Cornelia is sinking to desperate levels. I would have thought she had enough income from all the other assets she inherited without worrying about this one." He stood up and pushed his chair back under the table. "Thanks for your support, Phoebe. If I don't see you before your recital, I hope it goes well. I need to speak to Eric Symes. With a bit of luck, your comments will convince him my story is true."

He nodded in Bruno's direction on the way out. He knew he would be grilled on his next visit, assuming the café wasn't so busy at that time. Nobody of note was in the street when he emerged from the café, not even the Ferals. Still, he didn't linger, with the view that today was a day best spent inside.

"Diane, can you call up to Eric Symes' office and ask if he has time to see me?"

"I'm not your secretary."

He fixed her with an unblinking stare. She gave a theatrical sigh and reached for the phone. "Ten minutes," she told him shortly. "He can see you now for ten minutes only."

"Thank you." In a mood buoyed by Phoebe's recent revelation, he attempted to blow Diane a kiss, then winced at the resultant pain. She just looked at him and shook her head, and continued watching with disdain until the doors of the elevator swallowed him.

The PA looked up as he entered the inner sanctum, screwed up her face at his appearance and pointed him towards the office. "He's expecting you. Ten minutes only."

I've got the message.

Eric Symes glanced at his watch as Riley tapped on the door and without waiting for a response, walked in, and sat in the guest chair facing the desk. The other man's eyes widened as he took in Riley's appearance.

"Fighting?"

"Small accident on my bike."

"I'd keep off the bike if I were you."

"I shall for a while, but that wasn't what I wanted to talk to you about. I've just had an interesting conversation with Phoebe Eilish, who lives in the penthouse apartment in Mortimer House. She told me that she witnessed the events of the other evening when I rescued the building manager from the internal office of the Institute. She was standing on her balcony at the time."

He started to fold his arms, then abandoned the action as the pain hit. "She is prepared to confirm that to anyone who asks. She saw me emerge from the stairwell at roof level, effect the rescue using the gantry, and then exit using the elevator a short time later. The cameras in the elevator will confirm that I was not carrying anything. The building manager is on unscheduled leave at the moment, but when he returns, I'm sure he will corroborate my story."

Riley pushed a piece of paper over the desk. "Here are Phoebe's contact details. She knows to expect a call. Her balcony is at a higher level than the Institute rooftop, giving her a clear view over that area."

Symes took the piece of paper, examining the details as though they might reveal something more than just the name and mobile number. "I've heard a bit about this woman, but never met her."

"Now's your opportunity. She's giving a recital next week in support of the Children's Heart Foundation. You can hear her practicing from my apartment."

"It seems you have influential friends. I would like to believe your version of events. You have never given me a reason to doubt your integrity in the past. It's just that the information I received was so specific."

"I know that Andy Nguyen made these allegations based on information given to him, and I intend speaking to him also. I still don't understand why I've ended up in the firing line over this, but until the building manager returns to work, I'm unlikely to find out."

"Hmm." Symes sat back in his chair. "Innocent until proven guilty... on the basis of what you've told me, I'm prepared to lift your work suspension. If information changes in relation to those allegations, we might need to talk again. Start back on Monday." He peered over his glasses. "You look like you need the time off anyway."

22   A Feral in the Bar

WHAT HE REALLY wanted to do was lie down and sleep, but before he succumbed, he needed to chat again to Andy Nguyen. Rather than ring him, Riley decided to front up to the Institute. He was more likely to get a quick audience that way.

He didn't have to wait quite as long this time, and Derek came down to the foyer again to escort him upstairs. The man was no friendlier than before. A wave of hostility emanated from him, filling the elevator with claustrophobic atmosphere. Riley decided against trying to start a conversation with him. Andy Nguyen didn't look pleased to see him either, but at least he remained polite.

Riley remained standing. "I wanted to let you know that there was a witness last Thursday night when I came to the assistance of your building manager. I won't tell you exactly what she told me she saw; I'll let you ask her the question. She will confirm my version of events that night. If you refer to the security camera footage from your elevator, you will see that I was not carrying anything. I didn't remove anything from your private offices."

He slid a piece of paper across the desk on which he had written Phoebe's name and contact details. "This is how you can contact her."

"That doesn't prove anything. This person could be saying whatever you told them to say." Derek didn't hide the sneer.

"You can believe what you want. It doesn't alter the facts. When Winston returns, I'm sure he'll back up what I've told you."

Derek looked as though about to come back with a smart retort, but Andy Nguyen held up his hand, signalling the teacher to be quiet. "I will check the camera footage. We already have received advice from Winston about his version on the series of events." He didn't elaborate on what Winston had said.

"Just so you know, I have also engaged a solicitor and briefed him on the false allegations that have been made about me. I will not hesitate to pursue further action if you persist in making these claims. I would appreciate your advice to Eric Symes indicating you have been mis-informed with written confirmation to myself."

It was a lie, but if necessary, he would brief the solicitor very quickly. If Derek whatever-his-name-was hadn't been so obnoxious, he wouldn't have said that. He looked deliberately at both men. "What you alleged to Eric Symes has caused me significant distress and injured my reputation. That has not been without cost. An apology would also be appreciated."

He didn't wait for a response, which probably wouldn't be given anyway, but turned and left the room, calling over his shoulder, "I'll see myself out."

His phone pinged as he reached his apartment. Phoebe messaged him reporting a conversation with the solicitor Charlie had contacted on her behalf.

<I contacted him and told him to expect your call.>

Lovely, reliable Phoebe. Having these friends around made him feel slightly better. Ginge purred contentedly as Riley joined him on the bed. The cat began an enthusiastic kneading on Riley's leg until he nudged the cat aside.

"Not today, Ginge. Stay in your own lane."

The cat looked momentarily nonplussed, before lifting one leg and beginning an enthusiastic washing regime. Riley closed his eyes, willing sleep to claim him and by the time he opened them again, three hours had passed.

Easing himself off the bed was a slow and painful process. He washed down a couple of painkillers with a cup of tea and wandered outside to check how the world had progressed while he slept. Everything appeared to be in order. A balloon floated past, presumably having escaped from a product display in the Mall. He watched its wavering progress until it shrank to a small dot in the sky and then disappeared from sight.

Tufted cirrus clouds settled over the sky towards the west, promising a spectacular sunset later in the day. The golden, peachy colours at that time were usually reflected in the glass facades of some of the surrounding city buildings, creating an inspiring display. He made a mental note to come out again at sunset to enjoy the scene. Some of his pot plants looked thirsty, so he dragged out the garden hose and gave them all a drink. His patch of greenery bestowed a touch of normality in his living arrangements. Picking his own cucumbers and zucchinis remained a source of pride and satisfaction. If he had to move from his rooftop home, there would be a lot of pots to take with him.

Watching the traffic in the street from hie eyrie perch reminded him he hadn't checked the camera footage in a while. He swiped over his phone screen and clicked on the app which monitored the camera. He saw tenants from the floor below walking along the passage, and saw himself as he accessed the stairs.

My God, that's not a pretty sight. It's enough to frighten animals and small children.

Lucky that Ginger was a resilient and faithful cat, although Ginger knew who fed him. That was an influencing factor. Riley's amused grin at this thought abruptly disappeared when another figure appeared on the screen. It looked like a man, but not someone who had a right to be there. He strolled past the stairwell, and then appeared again as he walked in the opposite direction. On the third pass, the figure stopped and then began to climb the stairs.

He must have been asleep at that time and so hadn't heard any alerts on his phone. Riley couldn't see the action at the top of the stairs, but as of the last week, he had locked the door at roof level. A few moments later, the figure came into the frame again, this time coming down the stairs. At the bottom, the figure looked up. Riley froze the replay and zoomed in on the face. The image was hazy, but he still recognized him. He was staring into the upturned face of Alex, the Feral. How did he get into the building, and why?

Riley broke out into a light sweat, with a surge of adrenaline that made his chest ache. He remembered the cigarette butt he'd found earlier. He hadn't seriously thought it had been dropped by Alex, but now the possibility was real. He checked the time. Diane should still be at her desk. She must have let Alex into the building; strange when she was scared of the man.

When he emerged from the elevator into the reception area, she was reviewing the cleaner's schedule. She looked up with relief written over her face. The cleaner looked pleased to see him as well.

"Riley, help me check this schedule. I think it's all been completed, but I'm not sure what should be done and when. Someone has to sign off on it before the invoice is passed upstairs."

"Riley," the cleaner pleaded, "tell her it's all been done, like always. I know my job. Nothing's changed. When are you back at work?"

"Next week, mate. Strictly speaking, I'm not working now, but show me the paperwork."

He took the schedule and checked off the necessary tasks as being completed and signed and dated the form. "There you go. All done and dusted. See you next week."

The cleaner gratefully departed and he handed the paperwork back to Diane for passing to the finance department.

"You're back next week?" Diane asked, sounding hopeful. He hoped that meant she had a new appreciation for everything he did around Blenheim House.

"I will be. An apology from those on Level four for their unjustified allegations would be appreciated, but I won't hold my breath. On another matter, I see on my security camera that

Alex, one of the Ferals, was in the building this afternoon. I was asleep at the time, but he tried to access the roof. What was he doing in the building?"

"That man! I didn't let him in. What time was this?"

"According to the recording, around two thirty."

"Two thirty… I was probably upstairs at that time. He must have come in while I wasn't at the desk. What did he want?"

"That's what I would like to know."

Riley walked to the front door and looked up and down the street. When you didn't want to see the Ferals, they were under your nose like a bad smell, but when you were looking for them, they were nowhere to be seen.

"If he comes back, don't let him in, okay?"

"As if I'm likely to. If he comes in here, I'm calling the police."

"Just kicking him out will do. If he causes any trouble, call me."

"And what will you do?"

Demand some answers, that's what. "I'll decide that when the time comes."

The ringtone on his phone interrupted the conversation. Colin.

"G'day, Riley. I'm outside. I've got your bike here. It's a bit sad. Where do you want it?"

Riley directed him around to the side entrance for the basement carpark and ran down the stairs to meet him. He activated the roller door to find Colin unloading the bike from the back of a van.

"Jeez, mate… you still look a mess. How're you feeling?"

"Have been better. Another couple of days should see me right. Not so sure about the bike though. That is going to need some professional help."

The front wheel had a buckle, and the front light was smashed.

"You're lucky it wasn't worse. You could've been squashed flat by a tram."

"You don't have to sound so cheery about it."

Colin laughed. "You have to look on the bright side, doancha?"

Riley couldn't argue with that.

Friday night. Who wants to cook at the end of the week? Riley didn't. He debated whether to contact any of the Skywalkers to see what they were doing, but after an internal debate, decided to slip down to the Colonial for a counter tea. That would be quick and easy. Jonathon might be on duty, but he didn't particularly need company. One of the pub standard meals, then back home in time for the end-of-week drama on telly would suit him just fine.

He fed Ginger, checked via the camera that nobody lurked on the floor below, and then took the elevator to the ground floor. Again, he checked the street in either direction before stepping down onto the pavement. Then he berated himself for being paranoid. The world had been on the crazy side lately but he didn't have to buy into that.

Twilight approached, and the birds in the street trees signalled that fact, screeching and calling to each other. He could see hints of colour in the sky, reminding him of the sunset he'd intended to watch. It wouldn't be the same from ground level. The views from above were one of the privileges of being a Skywalker. Whatever happened with the building and his job, he didn't want to miss out on that. A few people sauntered the street, but nobody he knew or recognised. It was a stock-standard Friday evening in the city. He told himself that a couple of times as he walked the short distance, hugging the sides of the buildings all the way.

He checked out the crowd inside the bar. A bunch of guys in suits occupied the table usually reserved for Skywalkers. They had slung their jackets over the backs of their chairs, and most of their ties were loosened and sitting at half-mast or were ripped off and presumably stuffed in a pocket or briefcase. Their raucous laughter indicated they had left work early and got a head start on the ale.

A couple of familiar people sat at the bar, but none he knew personally. One of them looked around on hearing the entrance swing door squeal, and gave him a nod of recognition. Riley nodded in return and made his way to the end of the counter where meals could be ordered. The bar might not have the ambience of the dining room, and the menu was not as extensive, but he wasn't in the mood for anything too complicated. He ordered a beef schnitzel with pepper sauce, and a schooner of ale on tap, and took his drink to a small corner table to sit down.

Not having anyone to talk to, Riley took out his phone and scrolled through his emails and his social media feeds. His mother had messaged him asking him to fix a wonky gate on his next visit. He sent her a quick response, and scanned the room again in case there were any new arrivals while his attention had been diverted. He hadn't let Jonathon know he would be in the hotel, so didn't expect his friend to come looking for him. It felt strange to be dining alone for a change.

The meal, when it came was smothered in the pepper sauce and accompanies by thick-cut potato chips, and a small bowl of lettuce, cut tomato and slices of cucumber that passed for a salad. He had almost finished the schnitzel when a familiar and unexpected figure passed his table, collecting empty glasses. Alex, feral by day and feral by nature. He nodded in Riley's direction.

"Hey, dude… you need to look behind you sometimes."

He didn't wait for a response, but headed behind the bar where judging by the clinking noise, he was unloading his tray of glasses. As Riley watched, he finished that task and patrolled the room again with his empty tray, collecting more glasses. Alex's dreadlocks were caught back in a hair tie, and although wearing his customary jeans, he also wore a black t-shirt emblazoned with the name and logo of the hotel. The straggly beard he usually sported had been trimmed to a neater configuration. He almost looked human.

What the fuck? Grabbing his phone from the table, Riley dialled Jonathon's number. It went through to voicemail. <Jonathon, call me.> He stabbed at the <END> button, and nearly threw the phone on the table. Didn't anyone answer their mobile these days? Alex passed by the table again. Riley couldn't help himself. He had to know what was going on.

"What are you doing here?" The demand stopped Alex in his tracks. He turned slowly, head tilted to one side as his eyes slid over Riley. The smirk indicated he found the question to be amusing.

"I'm picking up glasses."

"But why?"

The question provoked an eye-roll. "Because people keep emptying them and as the glassy in this establishment, that's what I'm paid to do. Drink up, I'll collect your glass when you're finished."

He sauntered off, and Riley could have sworn the other man was laughing. It was no laughing matter. He pushed the remains of his meal aside. He no longer felt hungry. Why had Jonathan employed someone who clearly meant him harm, and had been caught on his security camera? It didn't make sense.

He was still debating whether to stay or go when his phone rang. Jonathon. Riley skipped the pleasantries.

"What the fuck is the Feral doing in the front bar?"

"Riley! How are you feeling, mate? Where are you?"

"I'm feeling confused. I came down for a counter tea. What's going on?"

"Aah, I wasn't expecting you tonight. I thought you'd still be at home. Give me five minutes and I'll come and have a chat. There's something I should probably tell you."

23   Meeting at the Market

JONATHAN PULLED OUT a chair and sat opposite Riley. He evidently had no problem with leaving his back to the room. He leaned over the table, dropping his voice to an intimate level.

"He's on probation. He's the new glassy. If it works out, he can take on some yardman duties. It's a part-time gig for now."

"But... but, he's a feral. I have him on camera lurking on my staircase. He and his girlfriend are bad news. Anti-social at best, intimidating and aggressive at worst, perhaps more. They terrify the Blenheim receptionist. This morning, I found an image of him on my security camera. He was on the stairs leading up to the roof and it looked as though he was checking the door to my level. He's dangerous and not to be trusted. Why have you put him on the payroll?

"Yeah, well... that's what I need to talk to you about. He's under cover. We gave him another job. He's watching your back and keeping an eye on who comes near you."

Riley stared at Jonathon, trying to comprehend what he'd just heard. "Under cover? That's ludicrous."

"No, it's not. Alex turns up everywhere like a bad smell. He's hung around these streets for ages. Who's going to suspect him? When you get talking to him, he's not such a bad bloke."

"Who's the *we* you're talking about? You still haven't explained why he's working here."

"Jonathon flipped his hand dismissively, as though what he had to say was of little consequence. "All of us… the Skywalkers. We decided you needed someone watching your back and given his relative invisibility, he was an inspired choice. The promise of a job was the incentive to help us."

Riley shook his head slowly, puffing out his cheeks. Alex passed their table with a cheeky grin. He actually looked as though he was enjoying himself. "I suppose Jody has donned a trench coat and a trilby hat as well. You should have told me. What could Alex do if there was a real crisis? A puff of wind would blow him over."

Jonathon shrugged. "He could ring me and I would summon the cavalry."

"He wasn't there when someone drove their car at me, nor when I was harassed when riding my bike through the middle of the city. "

"Granted, he can't be everywhere. Those were unfortunate situations, assuming they were directed at you vindictively. You can't really be sure about that. Of course, those were the situations that you know about."

Riley looked at the man moving between the tables, even exchanging a few words with the customers. "How did Alex gain access to the building? I'm sure that on one occasion at least, he came in after hours when the front door was locked."

Jonathon looked sheepish. "I gave him my key, the one you gave me in case of emergencies. He needed to have 24-hour access in case anything serious happened."

The story got progressively worse. "You realise you put me in a precarious situation? If the boss found out the key was out of my possession, it would be instant dismissal. I'm already skating on thin ice."

"We've kept an eye on him, honestly. He's already saved your butt."

"What do you mean?"

"On Wednesday night, someone tried to access the fire escape at the rear of your building. They pulled down the retractable ladder; there were two of them. One stood watch while the other attempted to scale up the side of the building. Jodie and Alex were both watching. They shone a spotlight on the pair and Jodie activated a hand-held siren. The two men scarpered."

"Who were they?"

"I've no idea. They didn't get a photo, and the guys were dressed in black and wearing balaclavas. Another time, you were followed when you went to the supermarket. Alex and Jodie followed as well. When you stepped onto the escalator, they manoevred behind you and blocked their access.

Riley thought back over recent days—Alex greeted him only two days ago and the ferals seemed to pop up wherever he was. He'd wondered if they were following him, but the idea that they'd been asked to do so never occurred to him.

The thought that someone else had been observed following him, left him feeling cold.

"This has been a bit much to take in, but it can't go on for much longer. I need life to get back to normal. My job has been reinstated, by the way, thanks to Phoebe. I'm back on duty on Monday."

He filled Jonathon in on the events of the day, starting with news of the council meeting, recounting his discussion with Phoebe, and the subsequent meetings with Andy Nguyen and Eric Symes. "All in all, it's been an eventful day. I think I need to head home and crash. My brain can't take any more excitement today."

"I'm not surprised. Look, mate… I know you're not so happy about Alex and his girlfriend, but weird things are still happening, and until it's sorted, I reckon the arrangement should stand. There's another thing you should know. Alex and Jodie are staying in one of the staff rooms at the hotel."

Riley could hardly think straight. His head felt fuzzy, either the result of the drugs he'd taken or because their effect had worn off. His brain no longer had the capacity to work it out. Telling Jonathon he'd catch up with him in a day or so, he let himself out onto the street. Being followed home by a woman was the strangest feeling, but he didn't have the energy to think about that either.

The stiffness hadn't eased by the following morning. He peered at his face in the mirror and saw that the emerging bruising had added some interesting colour. He applied another layer of pawpaw ointment and hoped the healing started soon.

His phone rang mid-morning.

"Detective James Mullin here. I'd like to have a quick chat."

"I've told you everything I know."

"We need to clarify a few details. Can we come up?"

Andy Nguyen must have made good on his earlier promise to contact the police. Much as he would have liked to tell them to piss off, there was little to be gained from that approach. He could refuse to come down to the front door and let them in, but that would make him appear guilty of something. Cooperate, that was the strategy. Better to get the *chat* over and done with.

"I'll be down shortly."

The same detectives who visited before waited on the pavement as he approached the door from the inside. They moved forward on seeing him unlock it, but he remained standing in the doorway, blocking their access.

"Do you have ID on you>"

They looked at him in surprise. "Don't play silly buggers with us," Detective Ryan said tersely. "You know who we are."

"I'm not sure of anything anymore. Due to recent circumstances, I prefer to check and double check who gains access to the building."

"That sounds like either a guilty conscience or a touch of paranoia. What have you got to be scared of?"

"My own shadow at the moment," he said obtusely, hoping they didn't press him for an explanation.

The two men flashed their ID cards, and Riley locked the door behind them. He turned to face them. "How can I help you?"

"Can we go up to your level?" James Mullin asked. "That will be better than standing in this reception area."

That was ominous. It meant that they had more than a couple of questions.

"Sure."

Riley led the way to the elevator, held the door open for them to enter and followed them in. Eagle-eyed Steve Ryan spotted the security camera at the entrance to the stair well.

"Have a few security problems, do you? I wouldn't have thought many people would have access up here. Don't you keep the roof level door locked?"

"Yes, I do now, and no, I don't have a security problem. It's all just precautionary."

This time they ignored the view, and he led them into his flat. Ginger Puss looked up at the intruders and promptly asked to be let outside. Riley wished he could join him.

"We won't take up much of your time," James Mullin said. "We'd like to understand the nature of your relationship with David Barton. I understand you and he were associates."

"We were not. I assume Andy Nguyen has made that allegation. I have never even spoken to the man."

"Didn't you and he visit the casino together?"

"I've never been to the casino with anyone, let alone a bloke I didn't know. I'm not a gambling man."

Steve Ryan threw in a question. "How did you recognise David Barton on the roof the night he fell if you didn't know him?"

"I didn't recognise him. I wasn't even sure that I saw anyone, and I didn't know someone had fallen until the next day. It was a while after that before the local grapevine told me who he was."

The two men stared at him in silence and he resisted the urge to fill it. In the end, he couldn't help himself. "I don't know where Andy Nguyen got his information from, but there is no basis for it. The main person I know from that building is the building manager, Winston Ripley, but he has taken sudden leave to attend to family matters. If anyone knows what goes on in that building, I suggest you locate and ask him."

He felt a pang of guilt for dropping Winston into the investigation, but hadn't Winston done that to him?

"Just so as you know, we'll be checking with the casino to see if you are a registered patron. If there is anything to find out, we will. Are you sure there isn't anything else you'd like to tell us?"

Steve Ryan's attempt at intimidation was laughable. "Go ahead. There is nothing for you to discover. If you manage to locate Winston, tell him I'd like to have a chat with him myself."

The two men exchanged a glance, with some silent communication passing between them. "Thank you for your time," Detective Mullins said. "You know where to find us if you have anything further to add."

Riley accompanied them down to the ground floor to escort them from the building and to be sure that the front door was securely locked after them. You couldn't be too careful.

Thoughts about Winston occupied him on the journey back to the top floor in the elevator. Perhaps if he texted him rather than leaving a voice mail message, he might get a response. He made himself a cup of coffee and composed the text.

<Winston. The police have been here again. They are asking questions about you and David Barton.> SEND.

That was manipulating the truth, but if it got a response, it would be worth it. That done, he needed to do some grocery shopping. Maybe the Ferals would follow him, maybe the people in a black SUV, but he was beyond caring. Life recently had become ridiculous and he no longer wanted to give life to the drama. He didn't want to play that game.

He went through the usual routine of checking the street before leaving the building, telling himself he could still be cautious. No Ferals or anyone else was in sight. Perhaps everyone stayed home on a Saturday morning. He had a shopping list in his pocket and set off for the Central Market. He made a beeline for his preferred stalls for vegetables, fish, and meat, exchanging greetings with the stallholders.

His progress around the market aisles was relatively quick, finishing at Lucia's for brunch. It was possible to nibble on tastings of cheeses, sausages and salamis and various other titbits on passing the relevant stalls, but that didn't make up for serious food. His last purchase was for Kangaroo Island free range eggs, perched on the top of his other shopping. That done, he was free to indulge in coffee and brunch.

He dived on a free table in the food area, glad not to have to wait too long for someone else to vacate.

"That was swift footwork on your part. I had my eye on that table."

Riley looked up with concern that morphed into relief as he saw Charles and Christine standing beside him. He pointed to the free chairs at the table. "Why don't you join me. There's plenty of room."

"That would be wonderful," Christine said. "I feel as though we've walked up and down every aisle twice over and my feet are killing me. Sweetheart, can you order me a coffee?"

This last comment was directed towards Charles, who dutifully disappeared in search of the coffees while Christine sat down and arranged her shopping bags at her feet.

"I really should have brought the trolley, but you know, we were only going to buy a few things. It ended up being much more than that."

"It's a common story," Riley agreed. "If you're sitting here, I can order my food as well without losing the table." With Christine minding the table, he lined up at Lucia's and placed his order for a coffee, and scrambled eggs and bacon. Their respective coffees were delivered a short time later, and they caught up on local gossip while waiting for their food orders to follow. For Charles and Christine, a visit to the market was a treat rather than a regular event, and often coincided with their visits to Phoebe.

Charles looked at Riley's grazed face with open curiosity. "If it's not too rude to ask, what condition is the other bloke in?"

Instinctively, Riley put up a hand to touch his face, wincing slightly as he tried not to laugh. "It's actually looking better today. I came a cropper on my bike a couple of days ago. I caught the front wheel in a tram track and then went arse over tit." He belatedly thought about his choice of words. "Sorry, Christine. I didn't mean to offend."

"If that's the worst I ever hear, I'll be lucky. It looks painful."

"It was, but the stiffness is the greatest inconvenience. Love the pawpaw ointment. That's helping with the healing process." He eased his leg out straight under the table. "Have you been visiting Phoebe?"

"Yes. She's so excited about this recital," Christine said. "It has really put a spring in her step."

"It has," Charles agreed. "It's helped to take her mind off all the other silly business."

"You mean trying to get her to quit the penthouse and move into a retirement village. I reckon that would be the death of Phoebe. She'd die of boredom in a place like that."

"She'd certainly stir the old dears up a bit. Mother could never resist a bit of fun, as she calls it. Others might say she's not acting her age, or else sliding into an unfortunate dementia."

Riley laughed. "There's nothing demented about your mother. She's one of the sharpest people I know."

"In more ways than one," Christine muttered, turning her head to watch people passing by when her husband raised an eyebrow in response.

Riley spoke quickly, not wanting to get caught in the middle of a marital spat. "She told me a solicitor has been visiting her on behalf of Cornelia Mortimer, trying to persuade her to vacate the penthouse, with the not-so-subtle allegation that she could be declared mentally incompetent and would therefore require a different form of accommodation."

"I don't know what that was about." Exasperation crept into Charles' voice. "I have my mother's power of attorney, so obviously that is not going to happen. I contacted my half-sister, Meredith, to ask her what was going on. Cornelia refuses to acknowledge my existence, but Meredith and I have always had a cordial relationship. Our father used to take us on holidays together when we were kids, so we got to know each other."

He threw his hands out, illustrating his confusion. "She is positive that her mother never made any allegation of the sort. Cornelia has received a generous offer for the building and authorized a request be made to mother with mention of financial compensation if she agreed to relocate, but that isn't what was communicated by the solicitor. I tried to contact him to clarify what his instructions were and what he subsequently said to her, but he didn't return my calls, beyond relaying a message via an underling that his instructions are between him and his client."

Their food orders arrived in quick succession, and that interrupted their conversation. Eggs and bacon are best eaten hot. While he ate, Riley mulled over what he'd just been told. Surely, a solicitor was obliged to act on his client's instructions, and only those.

"Your mother has forwarded contact details to me for the solicitor you have engaged to represent her in any negotiations. I assume you don't have any doubts about his abilities?"

267

Charles paused eating with knife and fork in mid-air. "None at all. I wouldn't have recommended him to mother if I did. He's straight down the line. Do you have a problem?"

"I hope not. For a while I thought I might need help on an unfair dismissal matter, but that has probably been resolved. That just leaves allegations that I pushed that fellow off the roof of the Institute, so if that continues you could say I have a problem."

Charles nodded his comprehension. "And did you push this fellow off the roof? I assume it's the man who was mentioned at mother's birthday event."

"No, and yes. I did not push him off the roof; I didn't even know him, and it is the man who was mentioned that evening."

"Well, life is certainly full of excitement in the city," Christine said brightly. I don't think a retirement village would be nearly stimulating enough for Phoebe."

"Are you going to hear her play? Riley asked.

"We are. Luci badgered us until we purchased tickets. I've never seen her perform for anyone except family, and Charles was too young to remember her last performance. It should be filmed so we have a record of it."

"That's an excellent idea. I'd love to see it when you have a copy. Phoebe mentioned that she is hosting a small gathering after the event, so I said I would pop over for that."

"Lovely," Christine beamed. "No doubt, we'll see you there."

"In the meantime, I hope you don't get pinged for murder," Charles said dryly, "but if you do, Gordon's your man. I met him in my university days, and he knows his stuff."

Riley reflected on that as he walked home with his own shopping bags. Going to university had some definite benefits if it introduced you to influential people. Adelaide was like that. It didn't matter what you knew, more important was *who* you knew. That probably counted a lot when planning decisions were being made as well. He needed to broaden his networks. His immediate requirement was for a good bike mechanic. The front wheel needed to be fixed asap plus a couple of other things had to be replaced.

He contemplated his options for delivering the bike to a workshop while waiting at a crossing on Grote Street for the lights to change. Saturday morning traffic was always busy with people from the suburbs coming into the city to do their market shopping. He took a step back from the kerb as cars zoomed past in the outer lane, some of them too close for comfort. The black SUV was one of them. It could have been any SUV, and probably was, but there were two men in the front seats. They weren't looking in his direction, but the one in the passenger seat looked like Simmo, Lenny's mate. The clouds that shifted over the sun at that moment weren't the only reason for the chill that gripped his spine.

24   The Fire

THE STIFFNESS BEGAN to subside by the third day. Riley woke to the sensation of Ginger Puss kneading against one of his legs, after which the cat crawled up the bed and settled on his chest, purring contentedly.

Riley stroked the cat's head, savouring the lie-in and thinking over the events of recent days. The series of dramas made him wonder what the next week would bring. The police didn't have any evidence that implicated him, because there wasn't any. Their questioning had just been flying a kite in response to Andy Nguyen's allegations. If someone did push David Barton off the roof, they must be trying to deflect the guilt.

Sighting the black SUV yesterday had been disturbing. If that was Simmo he had seen in the passenger seat, was it too great a stretch to suggest that he and Lenny were responsible for the incident in the carpark and then again forcing him off the bike? Even to himself, he sounded paranoid.

Pushing a protesting Ginger aside, he slid out of bed and headed for the kitchen to put the kettle on. His phone lay on the kitchen table, and the screen indicated a message had been received. Winston. *You bastard. It's about time*. He swiped his thumb over the screen and opened the message.

<Sorry about the shit, Riley. It's out of my control. Keep your head down and watch your back. Don't know when I'll see you.>

That told him precisely nothing. He made his mug of tea and wandered outside. A tournament was taking place on the mini-golf course on the rooftop of the Birks department store building, and he caught sight of the movement of tiny figures in the distance. Perhaps someone had an early barbecue as well because he could faintly smell smoke. Phoebe's balcony was deserted, so it wasn't her. Bushfires were always a concern, particularly with the surrounding hills so close to suburbia, but the sky was clear to the east.

The smell became stronger. Whirling around, he looked towards Winston's flat on the roof of the Institute building. Curls of smoke crept out from under the roof, and drifted lazily towards him. The flat was on fire.

Fuck! Where was Winston?

He ran into his flat to grab his phone and dialled emergency as he ran back outside. He kept the phone jammed to his ear as the operator transferred him to the fire brigade. The depot was only a few streets away in the city, and within a couple of minutes he heard the sirens approaching. Simultaneously, a smoke alarm in the flat across the alley began to shriek. The smell was stronger now and smoke was more evident. Phoebe's balcony door opened, and she peered out, shielding her eyes against the morning glare.

Riley waved to her and called out. "It's Winston's flat; he's still not there. I've called the brigade."

She nodded vigorously in acknowledgement. He snapped a couple of pictures of the scene evolving on the other roof, and then took a selfie with the smokey fire in the background. No-one was going to place him at the scene of the fire if he had evidence of his location when it started.

The wailing siren of a fire truck stopped with a small whoop, indicating it had pulled up in the street outside the building. Another followed it. Riley knew they would have access codes and keys to the building. There was nothing further he could do. He had a garden hose, but the jet of water it produced wouldn't reach across the divide.

Two firemen in full safety gear appeared on the roof, talking into their radios as they assessed the situation. One opened the box on the wall of the main building containing the fire hose and after unrolling and connecting it, began to play water on the roof of the flat. More firemen appeared, and broke down the door to the flat. Thick, black smoke billowed out of the open door, and Riley could see the glow of flames.

The men knew what they were doing. In a short time, the fire was out. It must have been localized, but from what Riley could see, inside the flat was a mess. Winston wouldn't be living there again, nor for a while at least. Thinking of Winston prompted him to send the man a text.

<Your flat was on fire. Fire brigade here. Substantial damage. Suggest you check it out when safe to do so.>

He added a couple of photos, indicating the activity and the resultant carnage. Phoebe still watched from her balcony. Well, who doesn't love a fire-fighter? Not that she was the type to have one of those calendars of well-oiled pecs clutching cute puppies. The firemen were still in clean-up mode by the time Riley retreated inside, glad that he had previously shut his apartment door. He and Ginge didn't need to inhale whatever toxic substances were carried by the smoke.

He made a fresh mug of tea, seeing as the previous mug had gone cold, neglected in the excitement. While he drank that one, he pondered the obvious questions. If Winston wasn't in his flat, how had the fire started? He glanced at his phone screen, but there was no reply to his earlier text. Maybe the firemen knew.

He pulled on a pair of shorts and a t-shirt, and made his way down to street level, where a mob of people gawked at proceedings. It amazed him that on a quiet Sunday morning, so many people could suddenly materialize. He half expected to see the Ferals, but they weren't around. Usually, they were first on the scene. He approached one of the fire crew.

"Hi. I'm the one who called it in. Any idea how it started?"

The man paused what he was doing to give Riley a searching stare. "The investigators will be looking into that. You called it in, you say? What did you see, exactly? Who was up there?"

"Nobody. The flat's occupant is away for a while. I smelled smoke first, and then identified the source."

The fireman winced. "You look like you've been in the wars, mate. You must have upset the wrong people."

What did he know? Was he joking, or what?

273

The man laughed at his own poor attempt at humour. "No doubt someone will be in touch with you. The police will have some questions. It looks like an accelerant was used."

Police—I should have considered that. The last thing I need is police questioning me again about anything happening on the roof of that building.

Riley nodded to the man and retreated into Blenheim House. He'd heard enough. His apartment did smell of smoke when he returned. He turned on the ceiling fans and stripped his bed, throwing the sheets and bathroom towels into the washing machine. His phone rang as he hung the sheets out on his line, having first wiped over the line with a damp cloth to remove any residue.

Sophie. He answered the call and put her on loud speaker so he could finish his task with hands free.

"You seem to attract drama. I've just seen the news. There was a brief clip of some firemen attending a city fire, and you were in the background."

Television crews had been on the street, but he hadn't paid them any attention. "Yeah, it seems to be a new-found talent; one I could do without. It doesn't do me any favours."

"How is your recovery going? I should have asked about that first."

"Better than what it was. My face still scares dogs and small children but I'm feeling a little more human." He gave a synopsis of what he'd seen, and what the fireman had said on the street. "He said the police will probably be around to interview me. Now, they'll try to pin some long-distance arson on me as well."

Sophie laughed. She didn't sound as though she took the threat seriously. "You must have super powers that aren't immediately obvious. I can drive into the city and join you for a cup of coffee if you need some cheerful company. Perhaps you can practice heating the water with a single glare."

"Very funny. Yes, coffee would be good, but I think we should go out to a café. My apartment smells of smoke. Text me when you're outside, and I'll let you into the basement carpark. That will be easier than trying to find a park on the street. We can then walk over to Gouger Street. There will be several cafés to choose from."

"Be there in thirty."

Normally, Riley paid little attention to his appearance, but now rushed to make himself presentable. He shaved the sections of his face that weren't grazed and combed his hair. That done, he changed into a clean pair of jeans and found a black shirt in his cupboard that he thought looked if not cool, then at least passable. He arrived in the basement downstairs at the same time as the text arrived. She drove into the carpark after he raised the door, and parked in the bay normally reserved for tradesmen.

"This is great," Sophie said as she shut the car door. "Parking in the city without the hassles. You've won me."

"Don't get too excited. It only exists as long as my job does, and after that council meeting, who knows how long that will be."

"I'll make the most of it while it lasts. Lead on; you know the city options better than me."

As they emerged into bright light from the gloomy interior of the carpark, Sophie took note of his face. "If that's what looking better is, I'd hate to have seen you a couple of days ago. It must have hurt."

Riley put his hand up to his face, feeling the scabby surface. "Yeah, it did. I'm not in any hurry to repeat the experience."

They crossed the road in the direction of the Central Market, but Riley had in mind a couple of faithful standbys that were in the street on the other side of the market. If one was too full, they could always try the other.

As they walked, he filled her in on the events of the last couple of days. She didn't know the Ferals, so he skipped over them, merely saying that some of his mates were watching out for him. Explaining more would be too complicated. He told her about the visit from the detectives, his challenges in contacting Winston, and then the excitement of the morning with first spotting the fire, to chatting to the fireman on the street.

"Living in the suburbs must seem so boring given the life you lead. After listening to your stories, I'm not sure whether living in the city is a good thing or a bad."

"I love the convenience and the community here. Normally, it's a mundane sort of existence. I don't know what has happened recently. Mercury must be in retrograde, or something equally dastardly."

The conversation had taken then to the outside of the first of the cafés he had in mind, and although plenty of people were out looking for Yum Cha or other Asian cuisine, given the proximity to Chinatown, the café still had empty tables. They selected a window seat inside and placed their orders.

What's coffee on a Sunday without a sweet treat as well? Riley ordered a couple of slices of chocolate mud cake, warmed, and accompanied by generous blobs of cream. It was a substitute for breakfast, as he hadn't stopped to eat that morning. Sophie didn't appear to object, as she demolished her cake with enthusiasm.

"I didn't expect the street to be so busy at this time of a Sunday."

"You'll have to come in for Yum Cha one weekend. There are a few really good restaurants. Then you'll see why there are so many people here." He waved his cake fork at the people jostling outside on the pavement. "After Yum Cha, they come in search of coffee, so this place will be packed soon."

One unexpected figure caught his eye. He peered closely in case he was mistaken. "Hey, that's Winston's lady friend, the one who has a similar passion for vinyl records. Perhaps she knows where he is."

Sophie leaned forward, looking at where he pointed. "You mean that short, stocky woman? That's Katrina Dale."

"You know her?"

"Yes... sort of. She was at the council meeting the other night, but I've seen her around at industry events."

"Okay. I'm not sure where she lives, but she must have gone in to lend support to the protest. She was fairly non-committal when I spoke to her about the issue."

Sophie gave him a strange look. "Support the protest? You know who she is, don't you? She may have a thing about vinyl records, but that's way off beam to her interest in the city development. She's an investor and developer. She has lobbied hard for the re-zoning to be adopted."

Riley shook his head. "No, that can't be right. Winston met her at the Colonial. Look at the way she's dressed. If she were what you say, she wouldn't be hanging out with Winston. Are you sure you have the right person?"

"Squat figure, poor dress sense, doesn't quite look you in the eye, just walked past the window."

"The description fits. What you've told me doesn't make sense though. She doesn't look as though she has two cents to rub together."

"She has more than that, possibly because she's reluctant to ever spend her money, unless it's on an investment property. She definitely doesn't waste her money on clothes. She's ruthless in her business dealings."

"Do you think she's behind the bid to purchase Mortimer House? Would she be trying to de-throne Phoebe from her penthouse apartment?"

"Phoebe?"

Riley outlined the approaches made to Phoebe through the solicitor, and the underhand tactics trying to persuade her to leave.

"That sounds like Katrina. She doesn't have a sentimental bone in her body. She would happily sell her own grandmother, so forcing out someone else's nana would not be a problem."

"She won't find Phoebe a pushover. Charles, her son, is acting on her behalf and he'll look after his mother's interests. Katrina will have to find another building to buy. Just keep her away from mine."

"Forewarned is fore-armed. Unless you've got a pile of money in your back pocket, I'm not sure what you could do about it."

The conversation moved onto other things, but Riley's thoughts returned to what he'd learned about Katrina. Did Winston know what her plans were? Was that why he'd disappeared? He checked his phone discreetly in case Winston had responded in relation to the fire, but he hadn't. He was sorry he hadn't chased after Katrina to ask what she knew about Winston's disappearance, but given what Sophie had said, she was unlikely to tell him even if she did know.

They took the long way back to Blenheim House, wandering through Victoria Square. The place was buzzing with stalls for a food festival, and enticing smells filled the air. A pity they'd had their fill of cake. They settled on a Tom Collins cocktail from one of the up-and-coming gin distilleries instead, sitting on the grass in the enclosure to drink them. Riley had never tried one before, but was open to new experiences, particularly if it presented him in a more sophisticated light.

It tasted refreshing and more-ish, but they agreed that one was enough in the middle of the day. He wasn't in any hurry to end their stroll. It made a pleasant change to his usual Sunday, and he walked a little taller with his sense of ownership of the city and what it had to offer.

When they finally retrieved Sophie's car from the basement at Blenheim House, his mood had lifted significantly. Being with someone *normal* helped. They made arrangements to catch up through the week for another driving lesson, and when Riley tentatively suggested he owed her another gratitude dinner, she didn't acquiesce.

"Just try to stay out of trouble. I'll keep my eye on the news in case I hear of a murdering arsonist running loose in the city, who looks like he's been run over by a tram.'

"Very funny. If I were you, I'd steer clear of this bloke. Could be dangerous."

He wasn't sure on the protocol as he opened the car door for her to climb inside. Did she expect him to kiss her? How did these things happen? On the lips or just a peck on the cheek like he had after they had dinner? His earlier mood quickly morphed into gauche. He reached out and ended up tapping her lightly on her upper arm with a closed fist.

"I'll be seeing you."

She smiled in response, and gave him a bemused look that made him think she was aware of the quandary that had run through his head. Now he felt a total noob. Next time, assuming there was a next time. He would have to ask Phoebe for tips.

He watched the car disappearing up the street before retreating inside the carpark and lowering the roller door. When he emerged at roof level, he noticed that red and white striped barricade tape cordoned off access to Winston's flat. It wouldn't keep anyone out, but who would be up there anyway? Usually only Winston, unless maintenance people needed access to the roof area.

That posed the obvious question. Who could have poured an accelerant in the flat and why? The whole building could have burned down. With Winston away, normally nobody else would have access. It was more than his brain could cope with on a Sunday, particularly after the gin cocktail.

The shrieks in the distance alerted him to the fact that the golf tournament was still in progress on the Birks' roof. Good to see that some people enjoyed a normal weekend. Ginger had been sleeping outside in the sun since earlier that day, and now padded over to Riley, winding around his legs and demanding head pats while emitting a welcoming rumbling purr.

The washing he'd hung out earlier was already dry so he dragged it off the line and took it inside, beginning the tedious process of stretching the fitted sheet over the mattress and remaking the bed. He'd only just finished that task when his phone rang. The caller ID announced Jonathon as the caller.

"Riley, have you seen Alex?"

"Alex?"

"You know, the Feral. He wasn't at work last night and he and that girlfriend of his have disappeared, but they've left all their stuff in their room. It was part of the deal. I said they could stay for a week. If Alex proved his worth as a glassy, they could stay on for a basic rent. Jodie had her eye on a job in the kitchen as dish bitch, and I was going to give her a trial shift last night. They've disappeared, shot through, but left all their gear behind."

"That's typical, isn't it?" Riley tried to be reassuring.

"Maybe, but they seemed so keen. I'm surprised he left his guitar behind."

Riley agreed it was odd, very odd. It also meant that nobody was watching his back. There was nothing reassuring about that.

25 Phoebe's Soiree

RILEY HADN'T EXPECTED to feel eager at jumping out of bed to start work, but he did. Mindful of Alex's disappearance, he checked the footage from the security camera before heading down the stairs to tackle the early morning chores. He even whistled as he swept the steps and polished the brass. He half expected to see the ferals lurking in the street outside, but there was only a council street sweeper on his noisy machine, and the very early workers walking along the street on their way to wherever.

Even Ginger Puss was more active. The cat was outside on the rooftop when Riley returned upstairs, eyeing off a pigeon that foolishly sat on the parapet railing. His tail swished from side to side before he flattened himself into a slink, creeping towards the hapless bird. Just as he drew close enough to consider springing forward, the bird took flight, leaving Ginger to yowl in despair.

"Face it, Ginge, you were never going to catch it. Who wants a mouthful of feathers anyway? Tucker's better from Bruno. You coming?"

The cat appeared to understand perfectly, and stalked to the door of the stairwell, only the twitch to the tip of his tail indicating the angst he still harboured. Bruno greeted them both with a grin when they entered the café.

"Would you look at that; it's a man and his cat! I'd almost forgotten what that animal looked like. Your usual?"

Riley nodded and picked up a copy of the daily paper before seating himself at his usual table. Ginger stalked around the café, sniffing at furniture and the edge of the counter, and accepting pats from the customers who happened to be in the café.

"Are cats allowed in cafés? Isn't that against health regulations?" a customer asked.

"Cat? What cat? I don't see any cat," Bruno responded fixing her with a belligerent stare. She looked confused, gave a small shrug, then picked up her take-away coffee and after glancing once more at Ginger, left the café.

Maria popped out of the kitchen with a plate of chopped ham, which she gave to Bruno, nodding her head in Riley's direction. Her husband dutifully placed the plate on the floor at Riley's feet. Ginge gave up his sniffing antics and made a beeline for the plate, eating as though he hadn't been fed in days. Riley watched the cat eating for a moment before shaking his head and resuming reading the paper. It appeared that the cat brought him to the Daily Bean, rather than the other way around.

"What's this I hear about a fire yesterday?" Bruno asked as he plonked a flat white before Riley on the table. "How did it start? Was there much damage?"

"I've no idea how it started, but the fire brigade seemed to think an accelerant was involved. It was contained within Winston's flat. He won't be living there again, not for a long time at least."

"That's weird. Who would do something like that?"

"Who would do anything associated with that building. All I can tell you with absolute assurance is that it wasn't me."

"Winston must have crossed someone in a bad way. Why else would he have disappeared like he did?" Bruno wasn't expecting an answer to his question and hurried back to his coffee machine to deal with the waiting queue. His words sat heavily with Riley, but he didn't have an answer either.

This morning wasn't the time to ponder the issue. He finished his breakfast quickly, and after paying for his meal, scooped up the cat and hurried back to deal with his day. Diane surprised him by already being at her desk. She even looked affectionately at the cat.

Riley paused in front of the reception desk. "I didn't expect you here so early. You know I'm back on duty today?"

"Of course, I did. I'm used to the earlier start now. It means I can get a seat on the train, and I leave a bit earlier as well." She smirked. "I could come in even earlier and have breakfast next door like you and Ginger do. I'd love that."

Riley smiled weakly. To comment would just encourage her. "I'd better take Ginge upstairs, and then I'll check the log book for today."

"But you haven't told me about the fire! You were here… what happened?"

Riley paused at the lift door, then took a couple of steps back towards her. "There's nothing much to say. Early yesterday morning, I smelled smoke and realized it came from Winston's flat. I called the fire brigade and they were here really quickly. It didn't take them long to get it under control, but the flat's a mess. I've no idea how or who started it."

"Oh." She sounded disappointed. "I saw Stella in the street this morning, and she told me about it. That's the last thing he needs at the moment."

"He?"

"Nico Stravos. He's lost so many tenants recently and now there's a possibility that Excellerate will leave as well. They are his major tenant. He'll take a huge hit financially if they go."

"But..." Riley's brain whirred as he tried to make sense of what she was saying. "Why would Excellerate go? They have lots of students."

She shrugged. "I don't know the finer details. It seems Excellerate is in financial strife. Perhaps enrolments are dropping off."

"How do you know all this?"

She shuffled papers on her desk with a prim look on her face. "You're not the only one who has connections." Riley stood and waited. He knew she wouldn't be able to resist telling what she knew. "Stella hears a lot of things. The sister of one of the senior teachers is married to Nico Stravos. That's how Excellerate got the tenancy in the first place. I think a favourable deal was negotiated to get them to take up five floors in the building. Mortgage rates are rising, and if they move out, Nico might be forced to sell."

This information more or less confirmed what Winston had told him a couple of weeks ago, except that the way

Winston had phrased it, Nico was considering selling, jeopardizing the Excellerate tenancy. Whatever the correct story was, changes were afoot. He nudged the cat towards the elevator and pressed the button to summon the cabin. He didn't have time to concern himself with those matters this morning.

Riley received the call to come down to reception mid-morning. His heart sank when he realized that the two men waiting for him were detectives Mullin and Ryan. They didn't look any happier at seeing him than what he was at seeing them.

"Mr Monroe," Detective Ryan said in an accusatory tone, "you seem to pop up like a bad penny whenever there is a problem with the building next door. We'd like to ask you a few questions about the fire on the weekend."

Diane stopped typing and leaned forward, her elbow on the desk and her chin resting on her hand. Riley bet to himself that she'd probably taken the phone off the hook so it didn't ring and disturb her. Too bad he couldn't tell the cops any more than he'd told her that morning.

"I smelled smoke yesterday morning. When I looked around for the source, I realized it was coming from the building manager's apartment on the roof, so I called the fire brigade."

"What time was this?" James Mullin asked, pulling out a pen and notebook.

"About nine thirty."

"Did you see anyone in the vicinity of the flat?"

"No."

"Did you see anything suspicious."

"No, except for the fact that smoke billowing out from under the eaves was suspicious." The men stared at him, clearly not amused.

James Mullin exchanged a look with his partner before closing his notebook and sliding it into his jacket pocket. "You already have my card. If you remember anything else, give me a call."

"Sure." Riley gave them his most innocent smile. Just talking to these two men made him feel guilty. He remained standing in the reception area until the front door shut behind them, and then turned to go back to his morning chores. He was unlikely to call.

Phoebe's practicing reached a fever pitch over the next couple of days. Riley heard her in the morning, at odd times during the day, and then again in the evening. She played scales and some of her preferred warm-up pieces before focusing on the piece to be played at the charity event, plus another shorter piece in case an encore was requested. They sounded perfect to Riley's ear, but Phoebe appeared to be leaving nothing to chance.

Riley watered his potted trees and plants early Wednesday evening. Phoebe emerged onto her balcony, dressed in a fabulous gown of some sort of shimmery material. A velvet swing jacket hung on her shoulders. She gave him a little wave.

"I'm off now. Wish me luck."

"Break a leg, Phoebe. You look fabulous. I'll see you later to celebrate."

She blew him a kiss and disappeared back inside, drawing the curtains closed. He hoped the performance would be a success. She deserved the recognition after all this time. He made himself an easy meal of grilled salmon and steamed vegetables, with an end piece of fish sent in Ginger's direction.

He had a bit of time to fill in before joining Phoebe and her supporters at her post-performance soiree, so ironed his black shirt in readiness before settling down in front of the television with a book on his lap. If none of the programs took his fancy, then the latest Garry Disher mystery novel would keep him engrossed. He resisted the inclination to pour himself a nip of whiskey, knowing there would probably be plenty of alcohol on offer later in the evening. Ginger curled up on the couch beside him, purring contentedly.

He may have dropped off for a while; it was hard to be sure but a different program was on the television when he felt the book slide off his lap. After levering himself off the low-slung seat, he peered outside in the direction of Phoebe's apartment. All was quiet and in darkness. He checked the time on his watch. Ten past eleven. Surely, she would be home soon? She wouldn't want to stay up too late.

In anticipation, he pulled on a pair of black jeans and his freshly ironed shirt. In the absence of any suitable evening wear, he decided that cool black was the way to go and rolled up his sleeves. He needed a bit of facial stubble to complete the look, but he should have thought of that before his last shave. Anyway, if he grew a beard, it would be ginger, not dark. If he'd pierced his ears, he could have shoved an earring in one, something small but big enough to catch the light in an intriguing way.

Peering outside again through his open door, he could see that lights now shone through the curtains at Phoebe's apartment. As he watched, the curtains were drawn back and the sliding door to the balcony slid open. Lucinda stepped out and he could make out figures moving in the room behind her. She called out and waved in his direction.

"Yoohoo… Riley! Grandma says to tell you we're home."

He returned the wave. "On my way. See you shortly."

When he entered Phoebe's apartment after walking around the corner and accessing her private elevator, a general babble greeted him. With a glass of champagne in her hand, Phoebe beamed at everyone, and appeared to be on cloud nine. She gave a cry of delight when she saw him and bustled over to plant a kiss on his cheek.

"Riley, it was wonderful. I gave my best performance ever, and the guests loved it. I received a standing ovation."

"I'm not surprised. You practiced hard enough. Lovely flowers, by the way." A sheath of flowers consisting of yellow and purple Dutch Irises and a few other flowers in similar colours sat in a vase on her sideboard.

Phoebe turned and gestured towards an elderly gentleman standing to one side, but watching their interaction. "Tray Thornton presented them to me after my performance. Aren't they beautiful? Tray, this is my neighbour, Riley. He lives on the building across the way."

Tray looked out the sliding door towards Blenheim House before extending his hand with a smile that was polite rather than warm. "Phoebe's told me about you. It's good to finally put a face to the name."

The comment startled him. Why would Phoebe talk about him? Another guest claimed Tray's attention, and Phoebe blew him a kiss before hugging her birthday pashmina about her shoulders and turning to greet Colin, who had just arrived. Riley found Charles at his elbow. He wore a dinner suit being suitable attire for the function at which his mother played. He looked slightly flushed, as though he'd already had a few drinks that evening, but waved a bottle at Riley.

"Drink?"

"Thought you'd never ask. You must be very proud of your mother."

Charles filled a champagne flute and passed it to Riley. "Incredibly so. I never thought I'd see her performing publicly, as her career ended when I was too young to remember. I'm glad Luci was able to witness it as well. She'll have a good memory of her grandmother."

Lucinda appeared at his elbow, bearing a platter of canapes. "Are you talking about me, Dad?"

"You've got big ears. Yes, I was. I was saying how glad I was that you had this opportunity to witness your grandmother playing to an adoring public."

Lucinda tucked a strand of hair behind her ears with her free hand. "Even better… Tray arranged for it to be filmed. I'll deliver a copy to Grandma after it's been edited." She moved on with her platter, offering the small bites to other guests.

"Tray…" Charles said pensively. "It seems we have a lot to thank that man for. He's my mother's new best friend." He and Riley looked to where Tray stood chatting to a woman Riley didn't know.

"That's a good thing, isn't it? He's given your mother this recital opportunity, and he's given her moral support in this situation where approaches have been made to her to move out of this apartment."

"Sure, he's done all of that. Call me cynical or just overly protective of my mother. I keep asking myself *why?* What's in it for him?"

"Isn't he just helpful, and enjoys giving back to the community? I'm sure I read that somewhere when he was awarded that AO or whatever it was. Recognition for services to the community."

"My mother's not some charity. I keep my ear to the ground. Some people do nothing without self-serving motivation."

"Not jealous, are you Charlie?"

Charles gave a bark of laughter. Not likely. I don't need to butter anyone up, but for some strange reason, I'm rather caring where my mother's concerned."

Lucinda cycled back with a platter of sushi. Riley wasn't hungry, but took one anyway. If he was going to drink, he needed something in his stomach to counteract the alcohol.

"Grandma tells me there was a fire in Winston's flat on Sunday. There's been more excitement around this place than there's been in the last forty years. How did it start, do you know?"

Why does everyone ask me these questions? "No idea. I spoke to one of the firemen briefly. He mentioned the possibility of an accelerant, but I've not had any confirmation of that."

291

"Well, all I can say then is that it wasn't me," she said brightly. "There's only a couple left; take another. I'll bring out the party pies next. They're heating in the oven."

She swept off and Colin took her place. "I caught part of that conversation. You don't have any further information about the fire?

"None. I had a visit from the local constabulary, but I couldn't tell them much, and they told me nothing. Not very forthcoming when we're practically on first name terms now."

"Any word from Winston?"

"Yes, and no. I got a text message on Saturday apologizing for recent events and telling me to keep my head down. He didn't say when he'd be back. It didn't tell me anything useful. I sent him a text about the fire, but he hasn't responded about that."

"He'll be spitting to miss out on this do," Colin said, snaffling one of the party pies as Lucinda swept past. "Not like Winston to miss out on a free feed and a party."

"That's not all that's odd," Riley said, speaking quietly. He pulled Colin towards the open door to the balcony. "Sophie and I caught up for a coffee yesterday, and we saw Katrina in Gouger Street, you know… Winston's new lady friend. Sophie told me that despite her appearances, Katrina is some hotshot developer, and that she supported the rezoning proposal that was put before council."

"Back up a minute… you and Sophie? Is there something you're not telling me?"

"Don't get carried away. We're friends, that's all. She helped me when Ginger was poisoned, and since then has given me a driving lesson in case I need to go to the vet again."

"But you don't have a car."

"That's irrelevant to this discussion. Don't you think it's weird that Katrina's hanging around with Winston? Why didn't she say something to me when I raised the topic with her last week?"

"Maybe she's shy, or didn't like to be confrontational. You can be a zealot about this re-zoning issue."

"Colin, it's important."

"Yeah, I know, but it's progress, mate. You can't stop that happening. If you had your way, nothing would ever change."

"Well, it's definitely changed for Winston." They wandered towards the edge of the balcony where they could look down on the roof of the Institute Building. "Not only has his flat burned down, but I heard today that Nico Stravos is under financial pressure and the building will probably be sold. Winston won't have a job either."

"Geez, mate… that'll be tough for him."

They stood in momentary silence, looking down at the scene on the top of the other building. A faint movement in the shadows caught Riley's eye.

"What's that? It looks like someone's down there."

As they watched, the figure skirted along the wall of the elevator tower, and still keeping to the shadows, climbed over the police tape and made their way to the door of the flat. Only then did the figure look over their shoulder so that the light fell on their face.

"Bloody hell," Riley said. "It's Winston."

26   Winston Surfaces

"ARE YOU SURE? How can you be certain from this distance."
Colin squinted into the dark.

Riley whipped out his phone and snapped a photo of the
figure in the distance. "I've seen him on that roof often
enough. I'd recognise his loping walk anywhere." He tapped
out a quick message on his phone, attached the photo and
clicked <SEND>.

<Colin and I are watching you from Phoebe's balcony.
We need to talk. Come over.>

They saw him duck into the shell of the flat. A reply came
back a few seconds later.

<Not safe for me.>

They looked at each other. "What does he mean by that?"
Colin asked.

Riley lifted his shoulders in a confused shrug." I've no
idea. Nobody here's of any risk to him."

He messaged again. <Where can we meet you?> The
response seemed to take forever, but in reality, only took a
couple of minutes.

<White van. Lane between Mortimer House and here.
Fifteen minutes. Be careful>

"This sounds like cloak and dagger stuff," Colin said. "We can't go now; I've only just arrived."

It took supreme effort for Riley not to roll his eyes. "He's been incommunicado for over a week. There are questions he needs to answer. If I don't talk to him now, he might disappear for good. We can come back after we see him. Phoebe will understand."

Riley glanced at his watch. "It will only take us five minutes to walk down the lane to where this van is parked. That leaves us seven or so minutes to explain to Phoebe."

"I'm topping up my drink and grabbing another party pie before we go."

The number of people in the room behind them had swelled while they were on the balcony. Some of them lived on lower floors in the building, but others presumably were associated with different interests in her life. He heard Phoebe introduce one newcomer as Daphne, from my book club. He drained his champagne flute and tapped Phoebe on the arm, hoping not to draw attention to his conversation.

He spoke for her ears only. "Phoebe, something has just come up, and Colin and I have to leave for a while. We'll be back soon, I promise."

She looked at him searchingly, picking up on his heightened tension. "I won't ask you about it now. Tell me later, but be safe, Riley."

Impulsively, he kissed her on the cheek. "Always, Phoebe. See you soon."

He caught Colin's eye, and indicated the door with a nod of his head. As they made their way around the clusters of guests, Riley notice Tray Thornton watching him with a speculative expression. When their eyes met, Tray's face broke into a polite smile, and he raised his glass by way of acknowledgement.

Cool night air greeted them at street level, plus a distinct odour from the on-street skip bins. They paused at the entrance to Mortimer House and checked the street for activity before ducking down the lane leading towards the basement carpark for the Institute Building. Riley turned up the collar of his jacket and kept close to the side of the building as he walked. Colin didn't suffer from the same level of paranoia, but didn't have cause to either. He strode confidently down the middle of the lane. For one horrified moment, Riley thought he might start whistling as well.

The van was parked at the far end of the lane, and had been reversed in so that it could easily be driven out. There was no sign of Winston, but as they drew parallel with it, the side door slid open.

"Get in!" He spoke in a harsh whisper.

Riley pushed Colin towards the open doorway and clambered in after him. Winston slammed the door shut behind them. Two bench seats in the back of the van faced each other. Winston sat on one of them.

"It's dark in here," Colin muttered. "Can we put a light on?"

"No!" Winston looked over his shoulder towards the front windscreen. "Are you sure nobody followed you?"

"We checked, before coming this way. It's become a habit of late." Riley delivered the last sentence with the sarcasm he felt Winston deserved. "You've got some explaining to do. Why did you drop me in the shit, and why did you run away?"

"I'm sorry, Riley. I was playing for time. I knew any allegations against you would be dismissed soon enough, but while they were looking at you, they weren't looking for me. They noticed the locked door to David Barton's office, and realised that things had been moved. I wasn't careful enough. I didn't expect you would lose your job."

"Is that supposed to make me feel better? Where have you been? Why didn't you return my calls?"

"I can't tell you where I went. It's safe for me there, and I don't want to jeopardise that, nor the people who've helped me. It was best that I disappear for a while."

He peered over his shoulder again, clearly on edge. "I can't stay long, but I wanted to check the fire damage. I probably won't be able to come back, but all my stuff was in there. They burned my collection, all my vinyl. How could they do that?" His voice wobbled.

"Speaking of your vinyl, I learned something about your friend, Katrina yesterday. In spite of appearances and, besides an interest in ancient musical disks, apparently, she is a property developer of some repute. While I was drumming up support against the council's re-zoning proposal, she was actively campaigning for it. Why didn't you tell me?"

"I couldn't tell you what I didn't know, but that can't be right. She would have told me. Does she look like a property developer to you?"

Riley had to admit, she didn't. If Winston didn't know anything, there was no point in pushing it. "Who lit the fire, Winston? What's going on?"

Winston sighed heavily. "I've made myself some enemies. If I stayed, I was going to have David Barton's murder pinned on me. I would have gone down for sure. I couldn't go inside again."

Colin leaned closer. "Murder! I thought it was supposed to be suicide. Do you know who did it?"

"All I can tell you is it wasn't me. I know too much, so it wasn't safe for me to stay. Next, it might have been me ending up as a splat on the pavement."

Riley ran his hands through his hair as he tried to make sense of Winston's melodramatics. He was never sure of what was real and what was fanciful elaboration when listening to him.

"What made you think you were in danger?"

"It was made very clear to me. I learned things that put me at risk." Winston worked his mouth backwards and forwards as though performing a series of facial exercises. "I haven't told you this, but a few years ago, I was involved in a bad accident. It was my fault and two kiddies died. I went to jail for a couple of years. I deserved it, but I never want to go back."

Colin nodded. "I can understand, but this isn't news, mate. We might not know all the gory details, but we knew the rest. We love ya anyway," he added encouragingly.

The hint of a smile crossed Winston's lips, and disappeared as quickly as it came. "That episode in my life has left me in a vulnerable position. Others have picked up on that. It put me in contact with people I'd rather not know." His sigh was deep enough to almost rock the van.

"Working in the building, you hear and see things. I kept my mouth shut, but perhaps I wasn't discreet enough. Someone fiddled the books and syphoned off enrolment funds.

It jeopardized the business. The auditors had flagged there was a problem. There were late night visits to the building and people turned up in places where they had no right to be."

"I heard that money was disappearing," Riley said. "The finger was pointed at David Barton."

"Yeah, well he's not in a position to defend himself, is he? He was financial officer for the company, so it was a reasonable assumption, but it's more complicated than that. Family ties in the building are a bit incestuous. Did you know David Barton's sister is married to one of the staff members at Excellerate?" He looked at them quizzically before continuing.

"Before meeting me, Katrina had a relationship with that same bloke. The bastard didn't tell her he was married. *His* sister is the wife of Nico Stravos. It was through that association that Excellerate were leased the premises in the first place. There are no secrets in a situation like that. Katrina left him as soon as she found out. That's one of the things I liked about the woman—her strong moral values."

Riley and Colin were respectfully silent for a while. Neither of them was as confident as Winston on Katrina's moral virtues. So many questions remained unanswered though. Winston shifted uneasily and Riley sensed that he wasn't about to stay much longer.

"What prompted you to disappear?"

"I decided to speak to Andy Nguyen about the nocturnal activity I'd noticed, and the fact that lights were seen on the executive floor. That made him ready to believe that you had been up to no good that night when you rescued me. It seems I was overheard. I had a late-night visit from two blokes I'd rather not see again. I met them inside, and they owed me a favour. They warned me that they would be back the next day and if I knew what was good for me, I wouldn't be around. With that advance notice, they considered the favour repaid. I scarpered. They're a pair of mean bastards"

With a sinking feeling, Riley had a fair idea who Winston meant. "Do you mean Lenny and Simmo?"

"That's them. Thugs-R-Us. They'll work for the highest bidder. When they advise you to clear out, you don't stop to ask questions."

"Did they push David Barton off the roof? Was it them I saw that night?"

"I've no idea. I didn't see anything and that's the way it will stay. Not that they would have baulked at it if they'd been asked and paid appropriately, but I knew better than to ask."

"Who would have paid them? You must have some idea. Who did you see in the building?"

"I wouldn't know, mate. I didn't see anyone, just the lights."

Winston looked over his shoulder again. "I've hung around here long enough. You need to get out. I've gotta go."

"But… you must have some idea what or who's behind David Barton's death."

"It's complicated. Families mess you up. I'm keeping out of it. Better that way. Give my regards to Phoebe. Sorry I couldn't be there. Careful who you speak to. Don't trust anyone who might be there. Now, get out!"

They climbed out of the back of the van and Winston jumped into the driver's seat. "Steer clear of Lenny and Simmo and don't tell anyone you've seen me. That's safer for all of us."

"Wait, Winston… do you know anything about the Ferals? I haven't seen them around for a couple of days."

"Little fish shouldn't swim in a big pond," was all he said before slamming the door."

"What did he mean by that?" Colin asked.

"I've no idea, but whatever it was, it wouldn't have been good. We had better get back to Phoebe's. I can't stay long though. It's way past my bedtime."

They pressed themselves back against the side of the building as Winston threw the van into gear and roared off down the lane. He didn't have his headlights on, nor did he indicate before turning out of the lane. Riley couldn't be sure if it was an omission or a deliberate ploy.

"We need to get out of here," Colin said. "If those blokes are looking for Winston, I don't want to risk running into them."

Riley noticed that Colin didn't walk back quite as confidently as before, looking left and right at the corner, and over his shoulder a couple of times. *Now he knows how it feels.*

Laughter and conversation greeted them when they re-entered the apartment. More guests had arrived in their absence, and a couple of them were attempting to persuade Phoebe to play for them. Riley knew her arm wouldn't need much twisting. She still floated on the high from her earlier success.

She caught his eye as they came in, and Riley gave her a thumbs-up. She winked an acknowledgment before allowing herself to be swept towards the piano. The piece she played was another from her repertoire, shorter and suited to an audience with a drink in one hand and a canape in the other. Riley and Colin grabbed fresh drinks, and helped themselves to one of the mini quiches that Christine had just pulled out of the oven.

Tray Thornton leaned against the top of the piano, smiling supportively at Phoebe, and leading the applause. At one point, he closed his eyes and swayed gently as he immersed himself in the music. His patronage of Phoebe puzzled Riley. It was surprising that he had even heard of her. Not many people remembered her from her heyday. Obviously, Finn had told him about meeting Luci's grandmother, but even so, it confused him. Presumably, music spoke his language.

They pushed their way past the audience listening in respectful silence, to where a handful of people chatted on the balcony. Charles was there, and judging by his flushed appearance, he'd been steadily drinking since they left.

"Riley," he called, "where'd you get to? My mother's in entertaining mode. She's having the time of her life. She adores the limelight."

"As well she should. It's fantastic that Tray has given her this opportunity."

"Isn't it just."

The sceptical tone puzzled Riley. He raised his eyebrows in response. Charles dropped his voice.

"I've just had an interesting conversation with Gordon, the solicitor I engaged to deal with the approaches and veiled threats made to Mum." Charles nodded to the open doorway. "He's in there, listening to her play."

Riley waited as Charles took another mouthful of his wine, definitely a mouthful rather than a sip.

"Gordon has been doing some digging. After my conversation with Meredith, I became suspicious. If Cornelia wasn't applying the pressure, who was?"

"I thought the identity of the party making an offer on the building was confidential? That's what your mother told me."

"Yes, I heard that also. Meredith asked her mother who had approached her, and pushed for the offer to be put in writing. The listed purchaser is a holding company, but Gordon gave the company junior the task of chasing down rabbit holes to elicit who was behind the company."

"Isn't that difficult to do?"

"Much easier and quicker now with internet access and subscriptions to the relevant databases. He only found out late today, but didn't call me because he knew he'd see me here."

Charles stopped and frowned. "I hope the time he spent chatting to me and drinking my wine doesn't get itemized on my account."

"So… what did this underling discover?"

"It was a convoluted path, but it ended with a company in which the sole director was Marissa Thornton."

"But that's… she's…" Riley looked towards the people inside who were clustered around the piano.

"That's right. Tray Thornton's wife is the person who is trying to purchase this building. So why is he sucking up to my elderly mother, and offering her accommodation in his up-market retirement complex? You tell me."

27   What happened to the Ferals?

AS RILEY LEFT the soiree, aware that in a few hours he would need to be up again, the guests were thinning. Christine was in clean-up mode, while Charles glowered in a corner, still clutching a glass of wine. He was usually controlled and measured in his actions. Right now, Riley decided he was on the verge of being neither. Riley had persuaded him not to launch an inquisition with Tray until the evening was over, and certainly not until he had checked his facts. Nothing would be gained from spoiling the mood of the evening.

Colin had already gone home, muttering about not being able to cope with late nights anymore. In spite of the lateness of the hour, Riley didn't sleep well. Probably the effect of drinking alcohol late at night, but his brain kept ticking over, reviewing what he had learned in the last few days.

Strange things were happening at the Institute Building. Lenny and Simmo were confirmed as bad guys; Katrina wasn't who she appeared to be, even if Winston was ignorant of that fact; and Tray Thornton appeared to be a master manipulator. Someone had pushed David Barton off the roof. Which of these players, and why? Logically, it had to be Lenny or Simmo—or both, but at whose request? Odds on, it was Tray Thornton.

He dragged himself out of bed as the first hints of light hit the room. Still in his sleeping shorts, he wandered outside to check on the day. The roof of the Institute was shrouded in darkness, but he could still make out the cordon securing the entrance to Winston's flat. There was no movement from Phoebe's apartment, and after her late night, he didn't expect to see her before lunchtime.

He stood at the edge of the parapet, idly scratching his belly as the cool morning air lightly grazed his skin. Soft light cracked the sky in the direction of the range to the east of the city. As he watched, a band of soft tangerine that morphed into a dusky violet appeared. Muted clouds in shades of grey sat lazily on the horizon, while the hills below were still in murky silhouette. A golden glow focused behind them indicated where the sun would eventually appear. Silhouettes of city buildings stood out in relief in the foreground, some with twinkling lights in their windows.

His throat felt as dry as the Nullabor Plain. He wandered back inside and noted with a touch of jealousy that Ginger Puss still slept soundly on the bed. He flicked the switch on the electric kettle and began tidying the kitchen while waiting for the water to boil. The container of food scraps needed emptying into the green bin downstairs. He looked for old newspaper in which to wrap them up into a neat, non-smelling bundle. He kept old newspapers on the shelf under the coffee table until they threatened to slide onto the floor.

Riley spread a couple of newspaper sheets on the kitchen bench, and upended the scraps' bucket onto the paper. Carrot peelings, apple cores and onion skins spilled over the print, a dismal end for yesterday's news. As he wrapped the soggy bundle, he noticed it was the paper he'd bought a couple of weeks earlier containing the death notices for David Barton. Judging by the number of entries, he was sadly missed by many.

He'd only read the immediate family notice and the one from Excellerate before. Now another entry caught his eye. *Beloved brother of Annie, and brother-in-law of Derek. Until we meet again.*

Derek... that was the name of the teacher who took him up to Andy Nguyen's office. Winston had said that one of the teachers at Excellerate was married to David Barton's sister. The name wasn't common; Derek had to be the person he'd meant. Did Derek have an affair with Katrina Dale? What was the attraction with that woman? She must have attributes not immediately obvious to him.

He didn't have time to ponder the matter. Work called. Later, he stopped by Diane's desk, asking her nicely about her week, and complimenting her on her recent haircut.

"Suits you. I meant to tell you before."

She seemed surprised, but visibly preened before looking at him expectantly. "Something's put you in a good mood?"

"Aren't I always? Umm, I wondered... does your friend Stella know anything about a teacher named Derek having an affair with the woman Winston has been seeing lately?"

Diane's eyebrows rose towards her new haircut. "Why would she know something like that? What business is it of yours, anyway?"

"Humour me. You two are in the best position to know everything going on in your buildings. While you're at it, perhaps you could ask her if Derek and David Barton were related, and if they were on good terms."

She rolled her eyes and gave a small huff. "*If* I see her and *if* I remember, I'll ask."

"Thanks. New hairstyle makes you look years younger."

He didn't wait for any other retort, but continued down to his basement workshop, where he was fixing a wonky wheel on a luggage trolley. The wheel didn't take long to fix, and rather than progress to the next job on his list, he began to scroll through the Excellerate website. The business still promoted itself and sought new enrolments. On the *About Us* page, he found photos of the staff members, including both David Barton and Derek Hume. The reference to David Barton hadn't been updated.

Riley right-clicked on both images and downloaded them to his phone. Might be useful. That done, he gave Jonathan a quick call at the Colonial.

"Hey, Colin and I saw Winston last night. We spotted him from Phoebe's balcony as he checked on the damage to his flat and his precious vinyl, and we managed to have a brief discussion with him."

Riley repeated the substance of the conversation, and asked if Jonathan could shed any light on what they'd learned. "Did you know that Katrina Dale is some sort of property investor? Have you seen her in the pub with anyone other than Winston?"

"I don't keep track of who's up who, you know that."

"Sure, but I also know you don't miss much."

"I like to run a peaceful pub. My customers know I don't tolerate any funny business, but I don't ask questions when I don't want to know the answer."

"I'm just asking for your observations, not to break any confidences."

"Look, I've seen Katrina in here a bit, but she minds her own business. I've no idea what she does for a living. I always assumed not much, but what would I know? She used to come in here with some other bloke before she met up with Winston. I never knew his name."

"Just a moment. I'll email you two photos. Tell me if you saw either of these men with Katrina."

He put the phone on speaker before locating the two images in storage and sent them through to Jonathan. "You should get them any moment. One is wearing glasses and the other isn't." He heard a soft ping indicating a message received at Jonathan's end.

"Give me a moment while I check them out... I think so... yes, the bloke without the glasses. He was the one who came in with her a couple of times. They sat at a table at the back of the room. I never had anything to do with him."

The one without the glasses was Derek.

"What about the other man?"

"No... no, never seen him before."

"What about the Ferals? Have they turned up?"

"Yes, and no."

"What's that supposed to mean?"

"They're here, but not officially. Jodie is working in the kitchen, but being careful not to enter any of the public areas where she might be seen. Alex is lying low for a while."

"What happened?"

"Lenny and Simmo happened, that's what. Silly bastard should've gone to hospital, but he won't budge. They roughed him up and scared the shit out of him. He might be a cocky prick, but he's no match for blokes of their calibre. At the moment, he won't come out of his room."

"You mean, while he was watching my back, he wasn't watching his own. As security personnel, they were hopeless. Why did they target him?"

"To scare him off. He was treading on their turf. They don't tolerate amateurs. He wouldn't say much. You'd have to ask him yourself."

"I might do that. I'll slip down at lunch time. Hopefully, he'll talk to me."

"Bring him a bucket of Korean Fried Chicken and a six-pack of mango flavoured kombucha."

"What?"

"Yeah, I know. It's a contradictory diet but the guy lives on the stuff."

"Okay… if that's what it takes. I'll be down at the pub around one."

Lunchtime trade filled the bar and casual dining area when Riley walked into the Colonial Arms, carrying the bag of chicken in one hand and the kombucha in the other. He slipped inside the door and scanned the room for any sight of Lenny or Simmo. Neither of them was there, nor Katrina. He would have welcomed the opportunity of asking her a few questions. Jonathan wasn't in sight either, so Riley sent him a text message, asking where he could find Alex.

Two minutes later, Jonathan appeared at his side. "I'll take you there. He probably won't answer the door if he doesn't hear my voice. Follow me."

He led the way to a back staircase which took them up to the rooms on the second level. Jonathan had quarters up there, and a couple of other rooms were available for staff to use, subject to negotiation. He rapped on one of the doors.

"Alex, it's me. Open up."

"What do you want?" The voice was muffled. They didn't hear any footsteps.

"Riley from Blenheim House wants to speak to you. He comes bearing chicken."

Footsteps were heard, and the door opened a crack, wide enough for Alex to peer out. He didn't speak, but looked at them silently. His attitude was very different to the sassy strut when Riley had seen him collecting glasses in the front bar. The bruises on his face were ugly. Whatever happened, it would have hurt.

Riley held the bag of chicken to one side where it couldn't easily be grabbed. "Alex, I want to ask you a few questions. It won't take long. I won't tell anyone where you are. I need to understand what has happened to you and to a few other people around here."

Alex stared at him for a beat, then opened the door and stepped back. Jonathan slapped Riley on the back. "I've got things to do, mate, so I'll leave you both to have your chat. Catch up with you later." He took off down the hall, and Riley stepped inside quickly before Alex could change his mind. The door was slammed shut and locked behind him.

Now that he was inside, he felt a bit awkward. He should have planned in advance what he wanted to say. The room was simply furnished, with a double bed, a wash basin in one corner, a free-standing wardrobe, and a desk on which a television sat. Clothes were scattered around the floor, and the trash basket overflowed with takeaway food wrappings. The room smelled of stale cigarette smoke, which probably contravened hotel non-smoking policy.

Riley placed the chicken and kombucha on the desk, closer to him than to Alex. "Alex, I know you and Jodie see much of what goes on around the streets. I know Jonathan asked you to keep an eye on me when it seemed that there were people around who might cause me harm. From the look of you, it appears you were in the firing line instead. Can you tell me what you know about the death of David Barton, and what happened to you?"

Alex flopped down onto the bed, which Riley took as an invitation to sit on the chair by the desk.

"That pair of retards hijacked me when my back was turned. Bastards could never have taken me on if I'd seen them coming."

"Why did they do that?"

"Teach me a lesson, they said. They knew I'd been watching them, and on one occasion, I spotted them trying to access the fire escape to your building. I took their photo and pretended to be on the phone to the cops."

"So, they were coming after me?"

311

"Who else? I scarpered before they could catch up with me, but obviously they were just biding their time."

"Who were they working for? Why did they have it in for me?"

"We didn't stop to chat. The only person I've seen them talking to is that woman. She drinks here sometimes. She must live close by."

"You mean Katrina? The woman who's been seen with Winston recently?"

"That's the one."

"Did you hear any of their conversation?"

"I don't stick my nose where it has no business to be, not when I live on the streets. You can see why by just looking at me."

"Did you ever see her with David Barton?"

"The bloke who jumped? I wouldn't know him if I fell over him, which isn't going to happen now, is it? Winston is the only other person I've seen her with."

"Well, thanks," Riley said awkwardly. "It doesn't seem there is much else you can tell me, but you can always contact me through Jonathan if you remember anything else. I'm sorry for what they did to you."

"Why? It wasn't you that did it."

Riley didn't bother replying to that comment. As he left, he saw Alex tearing open the bag of chicken. He would have liked to talk things over with Jonathan, but he'd already run over his lunch hour. He needed to hurry back to work. Why did Katrina Dale keep cropping up? Nothing made sense.

As he expected, when he walked in the door of Blenheim House, Diane made a big show of looking at her watch.

"I know, I know… I'm late back. I had something I needed to do. I do heaps here in my own time, so get off my back."

"If you're going to be like that, I won't tell you what I've found out."

He had been heading for the elevators, but wheeled around at her words. "Tell me."

"First of all, an offer has been made to purchase this building. It won't be accepted of course, but I thought you might be interested."

"Who made the offer?"

"Some company called Sunstone Developments, if that means anything to you, but that's not all."

He leaned with his elbows on the top of the reception counter, with his chin resting on his hand. He knew Diane would extract maximum enjoyment in doling out the information, piece by piece. He would have to play the game and wait. "And?"

She leaned forward slightly. "The same company made an offer for Mortimer House."

He frowned. That must mean that Tray Thornton wanted this building as well. Sneaky bastard.

"And that's not all." Her level of glee noticeably increased. "They also made an offer on the Institute building. The company has overseas backing, with plans for a major development spanning these blocks, incorporating a posh hotel and office towers. They promised luxury accommodation would be made available in one of the towers at a favourable price."

"That's ridiculous. It will never happen, not here."

313

"You can't stop progress. It might be just what the city needs. Imagine working in a modern building with all the features. New buildings often incorporate gyms and swimming pools and elevators that don't shudder and clunk as though they are about to fall."

This was not the time to start an argument. "Did you find out anything about Derek?"

Now she sat back in her chair. Perhaps the information wasn't as exciting. "Not really. He's been in a black mood and difficult to get on with in the last couple of months. He and David Barton had a big fight before Barton died. It's been suggested that Derek discovered what Barton had been up to with fiddling the books, and that was what they fought about. They were brothers-in-law, so Derek would have been really embarrassed."

"Yes, I imagine so. That's all really interesting. I knew you two women would be the best sources of information."

"As long as you remember... I didn't tell you anything."

He put his finger to his lips and headed back towards the elevator. He knew how to keep a secret.

28   Who is Buying Up the City?

HE DIDN'T HAVE time that afternoon to ponder what she'd told him. The roller door to the carpark had jammed again, and a tenant was moving in on the seventh floor. He also had to meet with Eric Symes to give him the usual monthly report. The meeting was more strained than usual, given the events of the previous week. It might take them a while to retrieve the same professional footing they previously enjoyed.

Riley itched to ask him about the offer on the building, but not only was it none of his business, he also couldn't disclose the source of his information. As their meeting came to an end, he managed a slight conversational work-around.

"I hear that offers have been made to purchase Mortimer House and the Institute Building."

Symes straightened and placed his pen on the desk with a small clunk. "Is that so? I don't know what the intentions are of those owners, but Blenheim Pastoral is not for sale."

"I didn't imagine it would be," Riley said as he rose, suppressing his smile until he was out the door.

He worked past knock-off time, making up for the longer lunch hour. When he climbed the stairs to the roof level, Ginger Puss waited for him, expressing his displeasure at the delay. No cat likes to be kept waiting. After feeding Ginger, Riley heated left-over casserole made earlier in the week, and sat down to eat it in front of the evening news on television. After the late night the evening before, he wouldn't be long out of bed.

Glare shining through the window from the setting sun interfered with his ability to see the screen. He crossed to the window to pull down the blind, and noticed movement through the open curtains at Phoebe's apartment. Charles was visiting his mother. They were probably having a difficult conversation if Charles was telling his mother what he'd learned about Tray Thornton.

He didn't want to intrude, but thought that the information regarding the offers being made on all three buildings might be of interest. He had Charles' phone number, given to him some time ago in case of emergencies. Picking up his phone from the table where he'd thrown it on first arriving home, he sent Charles a message.

<Tray Thornton has made an offer on this building as well, plus the Institute.>

A few moments later, Charles came out onto the balcony, peering towards his flat with his hand shielding his eyes. Riley took a last mouthful of his casserole and went outside to stand at the point closest to Charles.

"What are you talking about?" Charles called.

"Heard today that Sunstone Developments is submitting offers to every building in site. According to my source, there's a huge commercial development planned around here."

"Come over here," Charles urged. "Tell me what you've heard."

A face-to-face conversation would be better than yelling across the alley. Anyone could overhear. Riley waved acknowledgement and headed for the stairs. When he stepped out of the elevator into the foyer area, the door to Phoebe's apartment was already open. Charles had a glass of red wine in each hand and shoved one at Riley.

"I need a drink, so I'm working on the assumption that you do too."

"Make mine a triple scotch," his mother said dryly. "I feel such a fool."

"Why a fool, Phoebe? Tray was very convincing. After all, his son is dating your granddaughter. Why wouldn't you believe his intentions were honourable? We all did."

"Yes, but he made me think I still had credibility in the music world, and that people wanted to hear me play."

"And they did. Haven't you seen today's papers? There was a brilliant review in the Arts & Culture section."

"Tray probably paid for that too."

"You're doing yourself an injustice. I didn't see it, but Diane said there was a mention of your performance on the channel Nine breakfast show. You wait... you'll be asked to do magazine interviews next. Front cover perhaps. Whatever his motivations, he's put you back in the public eye."

She sniffed disdainfully, but Riley knew from the set of her shoulders and the glint in her eye that she was already imagining those things.

"What's this about mass offers to buy up half the city?" Charles turned the conversation back to the matter that interested him.

"My spies tell me that Sunstone Developments has put in offers on these three buildings, being Mortimer House, Blenheim House and the Institute Building. The company has overseas' backing, and has major development plans."

"Who are Sunstone Developments?"

"I don't know. I assumed it was the company owned by Tray Thornton, or rather his wife."

"No, that's Southern States Projects. I've no idea who this mob is. Perhaps he has two companies, you know... his and hers."

Riley snorted. He knew some people had his and hers bathrooms, but his and hers companies sounded too ridiculous. "Can your solicitor do his magical research and find out who's behind it?"

"I'll ask him. There was no mention from the bloke who approached Mum that there were two offers on the table. Presumably he didn't think that was relevant detail, or else he's planning on playing one against the other for the highest commission."

Riley took a gulp of his wine. If there were two separate parties vying for the properties, that would push the prices up and make the owners more inclined to sell. Even Blenheim Pastoral wouldn't hold out forever if the offer was good enough. He was about to lose his job, his home, and the landmark building that was his grandfather's legacy.

He pinned his hopes on the one thing in his favour. "As long as your mother is resolute on her decision to stay here, this building can't be sold. If the proposed development is reliant on acquiring all three buildings, this one is the key as it is a corner site, and is between the other two. That's why Tray Thornton has been trying to get her out."

"I'm staying. The only way I'm leaving is in a box." Phoebe folded her arms, as though that settled the matter.

"Blenheim Pastoral wouldn't rush into a sale either, at least I don't think they would. I'm not so sure about Nico Stravos. I hear that a few tenants have left the Institute Building, and now that Excellerate is experiencing financial difficulties, they might quit the business and leave as well."

"Why are the tenants leaving?" Charles asked.

"I think they've got better offers elsewhere."

"Hmm... I wonder if those better offers are in buildings owned by Tray Thornton."

"I wouldn't be surprised. I'd be curious to know what Nico's intentions are. He would probably think it's none of my business."

"No harm in asking," Charles said. "The worst that can happen is that he tells you to bugger off."

Riley drained his glass. "I might do that. I haven't got his number but I'll message Winston and ask him for it. Failing that, I might be able to ask Andy Nguyen."

"Let me know how you get on. Tomorrow, I'll get the solicitor onto searching the background of this new company."

Charles poured himself another glass of wine, but Riley shook his head. He hadn't forgotten his intention to have an early night. His kissed Phoebe on the cheek and left mother and son to their discussions and the rest of the bottle of wine.

Before he went to bed, Riley texted Winston. <I need to speak to Nico Stravos. Can you give me his mobile number?> Hopefully there would be a reply by morning.

The return message waiting on his phone when he woke up was not what he wanted to read.

<Whatever you're doing, leave me out of it. I don't want to be involved.>

That meant he would have to try speaking to Andy Nguyen. He did check hopefully with Bruno in case Andy was a regular customer and if so, what time did he usually come into the café, but with no luck. He would have to try the direct approach. He waited until mid-morning, when he thought he could legitimately take a break. His calendar for the day was clear, and Diane hadn't lined up any impromptu tasks requiring his attention. She didn't look up from her screen as he slid out the door to walk around the corner to the front entrance of the Institute Building.

Stella's face reflected surprise when he fronted up to her counter. She evidently remembered the reasons for his last visit to the building.

"Wait here. I'll check if Mr. Nguyen will see you."

She didn't even make a pretence of finding out whether or not he was in. His welcome was not a given in this building. Still, after conferring via the internal phone network, she informed him that Mr. Nguyen would see him and that someone would be down shortly to collect him. "Please take a seat."

He expected that Derek would appear when the door of the elevator pinged open, but instead it was a young woman who he had not previously seen. They stood stiffly side by side in the elevator cabin as it carried them up to the fifth floor, making him sense that before she was sent on this errand, some sort of adverse remark had probably been made. Lucky, he came with a tough hide. Come to think of it, it got tougher every day. Being trawled by thugs could do that to you.

She took him directly to Andy Nguyen's office and rapped on the door softly to attract the attention of the man hunched over a pile of papers on his desk. He shoved them aside and gestured to Riley to sit down. There was no offer of a handshake as once might have been the case.

"Thank you, Joanne. No need to shut the door."

The young woman departed with a curious glance thrown in Riley's direction before leaving the room. Andy Nguyen leaned back in his chair, with his hands together in a steeple in front of him.

"This visit is unexpected. What can I do for you?"

"Thank you for making the time. I'm trying to contact Nico Stravos, the owner of this building and wondered if you had his mobile number."

The faintest of frowns betrayed Andy's response. "Why would you want that?"

Riley had anticipated this question, and still argued within himself how he should respond.

"I know offers have been made to acquire Mortimer House, and Blenheim Pastoral. I believe the same approaches have been made in relation to this building. Transactions involving these three buildings will have significant impact on a few people. I wanted some indication of his intentions, assuming he is able to discuss the matter."

Andy rose and shut the door. "Where did you get this information?"

"I have my sources. Offers have been made through external solicitors, and it would be helpful for the parties concerned about the proposals if they were fully informed. Presumably Excellerate has a registered lease protecting your tenancy, so of course any sale would be subject to your continued occupation."

If he made Andy believe that his information came from external sources, which mostly it had, then no suspicion would fall on Stella as being a source of information. He didn't want to give the impression either that he was aware of Excellerate's financial difficulties.

"Who has made these offers, if indeed they have?"

"I believe one has been made by Tray Thornton, via one of his development companies. I have yet to learn the identity of the second party."

The other man stared at Riley clearly processing this information. He exhaled heavily before replying. "I would be most interested to learn the identity of this second party. I can give you this phone number, on the condition that you keep me informed about the progress of your enquiries."

"You could always ask him yourself."

"I could, but for personal reasons, I prefer not to have that conversation."

Riley guessed that he didn't want to answer any questions about his own intentions in relation to his occupancy of the building. "Sure. I can do that. I'll let you know after I speak to him, but it might not be for a day or so."

Andy picked up his phone and scrolled through the screen before writing a mobile number on a post-it note. He tore off the slip and passed it over. "Do not forget. I want to know."

Riley nodded and rose from the chair. Getting the number hadn't been as difficult as he feared. When he left the office, Joanne half-rose from her seat at her workstation.

"It's all right. I can find my way out."

He was aware of eyes following him as he made his way to the elevator and then waited for the cabin to arrive. As the doors slid closed after he'd entered, he noticed Derek walking towards Andy's office. Remembering the man's attitude on the last occasion he'd been in this office, Riley was glad they hadn't actually crossed paths this time.

Lunch comprised a toasted sandwich outside on the roof. A ham, cheese and tomato was his go-to when he had run out of culinary ideas. Ginge followed him outside and sat on an adjoining chair at the outdoor setting. Riley contemplated calling Sophie to arrange another driving lesson. His injuries were healing, and turning his head and flexing his arms was no longer such a painful experience. He decided to leave that call for the evening, rather than interrupt her working time. Instead, he would call Nico. If he thought about it for too long, he would get cold feet.

The call was picked up promptly.

"Yes?"

"Nico? Hi, it's Riley Monroe here. I manage the Blenheim Pastoral Building in the city."

"What do you want?"

"I won't take up much of your time. You may have heard that this section of the city is being re-zoned to allow denser development. It has increased the value of these older buildings. Already, offers have been made to purchase Blenheim House and Mortimer House. This has implications for those of us who live and work in those buildings. Tray Thornton is one of the interested parties. We wondered if similar offers have been made to you, to acquire the Institute Building, and If you are considering selling? It's an attractive proposition for developers."

Nico snarled a response. "You can tell your friends and whoever else wants to know I have no intention of selling. I won't be strong-armed into it either. You can tell that mob and their henchmen the same."

"Which mob? What have they been doing? Are the Thorntons luring your tenants from the building?"

"Thorntons? Who the hell are they? What are you talking about."

Riley wasn't sure who was more confused. "They own Southern City Projects. I thought you said they were applying pressure tactics."

"I switch my phone off and ignore the lot of them. Tenants leave; they do that. No problem. I find more. My wife oversees property management. It's her headache, not mine. Her brother works in the building. He can keep an eye on it for me."

"Her brother? You don't mean Winston?"

Nico snorted. "Don't be bloody ridiculous. Her brother's a teacher with that education mob, deadbeat that he is. I married his sister, not the family. He's a drain on society."

"Not a fan, then?"

"Can't keep it in his pants, and can't keep money in his pockets. The casino's his second home. That's why he's a loser."

Riley let Nico's family problems wash over him. The fact that he didn't plan on selling the building was a relief. It meant the redevelopment proposal could effectively be staved off for a while, even if it was inevitable at some point in the future. Even he was realistic enough to understand that.

"Thanks, Nico. You've been most helpful. If you change your mind about selling, can you let me know? I'll text you my contact details."

"No promises. Like I said, I'm not planning on selling."

Riley disconnected the call, and sat for a while reviewing what he'd just heard. He hadn't discovered who was behind Sunstone Developments, but that didn't really matter if none of the building owners wanted to or were able to sell. He texted his contact details to Nico. But decided to call Andy Nguyen later. He'd over-run his lunch break already. Diane would be on his back before long.

With that weight lifted, his mood lightened, so much so that he decided to hoist the blue flag. He could update the others at the Colonial that evening, and catch up on any other news as well. By afternoon tea time, he could see the green flags in response, plus Bruce and Colin had Lowered their flags a smidgeon, not enough to attract attention but enough to signal their response.

The pub special this night was bangers and mash. With the addition of peas and lashings of gravy, it reminded them all of childhood meals and was always a favourite. The sausages were made in the Barossa Valley, using a recipe from the early days of German settlement. Once a cheap food, now the sausages had assumed gourmet status, and were sold for a hefty price at the Central Market.

Riley was the first one at their customary table, but the others arrived soon after. The evening followed the usual pattern of gossip and banter, fuelled by generous helpings of food and drink. He and Colin recounted their meeting with Winston, and Bruce gave them his usual report of the antics in Government House, complete with caricatures of some of the key players in political life.

They all knew about Phoebe's success, because it had been published in the daily paper, and the Skywalkers' grapevine had done an effective job.

"And the best thing is, she doesn't have to move," Riley explained. For now, none of us do because the building owners don't want to sell. Skywalkers survive to live another day." They all raised their glasses to that.

"How are you feeling now, Riley?" Colin asked "You're looking more human, if that's possible," he added jokingly.

"Still got the bruises, but the soreness is easing. In another week or so, the grazes should be mostly healed." Riley gave a dramatic sigh. "Where was my security tail when I needed him most, speaking of which, is our friend emerging in public again?" The question was directed towards Jonathan.

"Tentatively. Unlike you, he's not yet fully human again. He's not ready to emerge on the streets as yet."

The others looked enquiringly at them both, but Riley waved a dismissive hand. "It wasn't only me who fell afoul of Lenny and Simmo, assuming that's who I can blame for the state of my face." He didn't want to say more than that, knowing Alex's state of mind.

"There's another strange thing I learned this week. Winston's girlfriend, actually supported the rezoning proposal, and not only that, she is a hotshot property developer." He emphasized the word *girlfriend* with air quotes. "She might look the quiet, unassuming type, but she had an affair with some married bloke before she met Winston. She dropped him because the affair didn't agree with her moral values."

"You can never trust the quiet ones," Jonathan said to no-one in particular.

"I'm not sure, but I think it was one of the teachers at Excellerate. According to Nico Stravos, this bloke regularly loses at the Casino, so that might be a more realistic reason for her moving on."

"What scepticism! What does this bloke look like? I sometimes drop in at the Casino if things finish on time at Parliament House."

Mark was known for enjoying the blackjack table, and with the Casino being located above the Railway Station, next door to Parliament House, it was easy for him to indulge occasionally. Riley flipped open his phone and brought up his copy of Derek's photo. Mark took the phone from him and peered at it closely.

"Yeah, I've seen him there. Sometimes with a woman but more recently on his own. Sometimes wins, but mostly not. If he's a teacher, don't know where he gets his money from. Must be syphoning off the kids' college funds."

"What did the woman look like?"

"Don't remember. Nothing startling."

That sounded like Katrina. Strange woman. Her choice of companions was equally confusing. Riley let it go. Nothing to do with him, anyway.

Later, while walking home after cautiously checking the street activity, he remembered he hadn't contacted Sophie. Too late now. He would do that first thing in the morning. Now that he was confident of retaining his job, it was time to make positive changes in his life.

29 Unexpected Meeting

SATURDAY MORNING PRESENTED a much-needed opportunity for recharge and reflection. The events of the last few days took some processing, both in implications for the present, and for the future. He hadn't caught sight of either Lenny or Simmo through the week, and that had to be a good thing. Not good news about Alex, though.

Riley slipped over to the Central Market early to stock up on eggs, cheese and some vegetables before buying the paper and sitting down to read over a cup of coffee and toasted ham and cheese croissant from Zuma Caffe.

Back home, he shoved the week's washing in the machine and sat down to call Sophie. "If it's not too forward and if you have the time, can we schedule another driving lesson for tomorrow?"

"Sure, I can do that. The afternoon would be best for me. How is the body recovering?"

"It's good. Still a bit tender in places, but you'll notice some improvements over the last week. Leave time for afternoon tea. We can have a proper catch-up then. It's been an eventful week."

"Isn't every week eventful for you?"

Riley laughed. "I can understand you thinking that, but I should be boringly low-key from now on."

"I'm not sure if that's a good thing or not. I'll see you tomorrow, and hopefully nobody tries to run you over this time."

His spirits lifted as he disconnected the call. Banter was not usually his style, not with women anyway, but Sophie made him feel relaxed. He no longer became anxious at the thought of calling her. That had to be progress.

His bike was still out of action, so he caught the tram down to Glenelg for an obligatory visit to his mother. He knew she was pleased to see him, but as usual, her greeting was brusque.

"What have you been doing to your face? Have you been fighting? Riley, that's not like you."

"Came off the bike. It's nearly better. Have you ever known me to get into a fight?"

"I guess not. You were always a timid little boy. Wash your hands and sit down at the table. I've made those rissoles you always like."

He loathed the dry, tasteless balls of overcooked mince, but dutifully ate them before broaching the matter of the car. "Mum, I haven't progressed far with the driving lessons yet, but it might help if I had a car in which to learn. Do you think I could take Dad's car to make it easier for me to get my hours up, once I'm more proficient?"

"You'd have to pay for registration and maintenance."

"Absolutely. I wouldn't expect otherwise. It will make it easier for me to take you shopping or to any appointments you have."

"And that woman is still teaching you?"

"She is, yes. I have a lesson tomorrow. When I'm more competent behind the wheel, I'll make arrangements about getting the car picked up."

His mother moved on to a discussion about the lawn needing to be mowed, and some weeding taken care of, so he assumed he had her agreement. She was a woman of few words. He probably took after her.

His mobile rang late afternoon. Riley checked the screen, but he didn't know the number.

"Hello?"

"Riley Monroe? I'm calling for Andy Nguyen. He wants another discussion about the matters you raised with him on Thursday. Can you come over to the Excellerate Office?"

"Now? It's Saturday."

"Yeah, don't I know it. We have a few things to catch up on. It's easier to do some strategic planning when the students aren't around."

The voice sounded familiar but Riley couldn't put a name to it. "Who is this?"

"Derek Hume. I'm here with Andy."

Riley reviewed his plans for the rest of the day. Bring in the washing, put the makings of some pea and ham soup in the slow cooker… nothing that couldn't wait. "Okay. I'll be there in five minutes. How will I get in?"

"I'll meet you at the front door."

"Fine. I'll see you shortly." He shoved his phone in his pocket and headed down the stairs to the elevator on the floor below. There was minimal activity in the street when he emerged at street level. Weekend activity didn't feature strongly in this part of the city, other than people passing through to somewhere else. The only person he did see, and surprisingly on her own, was Jodie. She sat on the edge of a planter box, scrolling through her phone. Presumably, Alex still hid in their room at the Colonial.

"Hi Jodie."

Her head jerked up, her face registering surprise. He realised then that he'd never spoken to her before. She gave a slight smile before resuming her scrolling. It gave him his second warm, fuzzy for the day.

When he arrived at the front of the Excellerate premises, Riley could see Derek lurking inside the sliding door. A moment later, the doors slid open, and Derek gestured to him to come inside.

"Good of you to come. We need to go upstairs."

Riley followed him to the elevators. The cabin already waited at the ground floor so the doors pinged open straight away. They entered, and Derek pressed the button for the ninth floor.

"Isn't Andy's office on the fifth floor?"

"It is, but we're meeting on a different level."

That surprised him, as he thought Excellerate only occupied the first five floors, but perhaps they had negotiated additional space. The doors opened and he stepped out into a cavernous room.

If Excellerate had leased another floor, no fit-out had been provided. A few packing boxes were stacked against a wall, and other than that, there was only a table and a couple of chairs in the room. He couldn't see Andy Nguyen.

"Where's Andy?"

"He'll be along soon. Come and sit down."

Something was not right, but he wasn't sure what that was. His gut instinct was to leave. "Look, this should wait until Monday. I can come back and meet with Andy then."

He caught a faint movement from the corner of his eye before being grabbed from behind. A rope noose was dropped over his head and tightened around his arms.

"What the fuck?"

"You were told to sit down."

The voice wasn't Derek's. Twisting his head, he saw Lenny and Simmo standing behind him. In panic, he tried to shrug off the rope and bolt for the stairwell, but his legs were kicked from underneath him. He landed on the floor with a thump that knocked the breath out of him.

The two men loomed over him. Lenny held the other end of the length of rope, which he now wound around Riley's arms in a second loop. The pair of them grabbed him on either side and hauled him to a standing position, then frog-marched him to the chair. He kept his legs stiff and tried to resist, but one of them kicked him behind a knee, causing that leg to buckle. He sat, and Lenny used the rope to secure him to the chair. In the process, they pulled his arms behind the back support and secured them at the wrists with cable ties. The hard plastic of the chair back bit into the flesh of his hands.

A second rope formed into a noose was slipped over his head. The other end was threaded over an aluminium beam supporting the modular ceiling panels, pulled taunt, and then tied to the back of his chair. If he tried to escape, he risked choking himself. He was effectively immobilised.

"That's us done for now," Lenny said to Derek. "The rest is up to you."

"What's this about? Where's Andy?"

Lenny and Simmo turned and headed for the elevator. The cabin still sat at their floor and the door pinged open quickly. As they entered, Lenny sent a leering grin in Riley's direction.

"You've been lucky up until now. I think your luck just ran out. Have fun."

The doors closed, leaving Derek and Riley alone.

"What's going on? Why have you brought me here?"

"It's simple. Your interference has cost me a lot of money. You need to pay for that."

As best he could with the restriction to his neck, Riley looked around the vast empty space for any clues about what Derek meant, as well as anything else that might be of use in freeing himself. He tried to twist his head sideways to test if that loosened the noose. The rope dug into his neck. There was nothing obvious for him to use, even if he wasn't trussed like the Christmas turkey. "What do you mean?"

"We've got some time, so I'll tell you. You've stuck your nose in where it's not wanted. You've actively campaigned with the owners of these buildings not to sell. You've interfered with my family. My crazy brother-in-law is now attempting to cut my wife out of her share of the family money if she doesn't leave me."

"You can't keep me here. There are cameras in the elevators for a start. People will know you've brought me here."

"Do you think I'm stupid? I disabled them. Nobody knows you're here. Those two aren't going to talk."

"Lenny and Simmo... the realisation floored him. It was you! You got them to intimidate me and try to make me another road statistic."

Derek actually laughed. "That wasn't me. That was Katrina. Lenny and Simmo are her pets, not mine."

"What do you want from me?"

"You're going to ring Nico. You're going to tell him that there have been changes. The adjoining buildings are now under contract. He's in Port Lincoln. He doesn't know what goes on in the city."

"What difference will that make?"

"If Nico doesn't sell, I miss out. That fool is asking questions He's coming to Adelaide to investigate. He wants a meeting with Andy. He can't do that. You've got to stop him."

Riley shook his head, trying to make sense of the jumble of information. "What difference does it make to you if Nico sells... or not? What's Katrina got to do with all this?"

"Katrina wants this building. She has plans. I owe her money. If Nico sells to her, she'll wipe the debt. It's up to me to persuade him. She's got me by the short and curlies."

"You had an affair with her."

"I'd hardly call it that. She manipulates people when they're useful to her and then spits them out. She's nice at the beginning, but it doesn't last long. You do what she asks, or else. Lenny and Simmo see to that."

Derek stood up. "Where's your phone?" He walked behind the chair on which Riley sat and patted his pockets, finding and retrieving the mobile. He placed it on the table in front of Riley.

"I can't make a call if I'm trussed up like this."

"I'll put it on speaker. That way, I can hear both sides of the conversation. He absolutely can't come to Adelaide. Andy is asking suspicious questions. I've got you to thank for that as well. I've got to throw him off."

He leaned over the table, breathing into Riley's face as he did. Whatever his last meal was, it didn't smell pleasant in a regurgitated format. If Lenny and Simmo didn't get him, he might die of asphyxiation.

"If you convince Nico that others are selling, he'll listen to you. Tell him that if he doesn't sell now, he'll be locked out of the market. His building won't be attractive to tenants and he'll lose Excellerate. They are already struggling to pay the rent. Now is the time to lock in his capital gains."

"Nico won't listen to me. I'm not a property guru."

"He'll listen if you tell him that you have inside information from that girlfriend of yours. Tell him a heritage order is about to be slapped on the building. When that happens, the redevelopment options will be severely restricted and the value will drop. No developer wants the cost of a heritage building."

Riley had no idea how he would get out of this situation What would happen if he refused? Would Lenny and Simmo come back? Ginger Puss would wonder where he was. His cat would starve and Sophie would be confused when she turned up for their lesson. She would think he'd changed his mind without telling her.

"How do you unlock your phone?"

Riley told him the unlock code. It seemed the best way to keep the situation under control.

"I'll dial the number, and you can talk to him. No funny business. I'll hear every word. If you give him any hint of what's going on, you'll end up spread over the laneway."

Riley's guts tied themselves in a knot. He wouldn't go anywhere without a fight, but for now, he had to keep the conversation on an even keel. He nodded, and Derek dialled the number and held the phone up in front of Riley's face. The ring tone sounded for about six seconds before switching to voicemail.

<You've reached Nico Stravos. I'm not here. Leave a message.>

Riley glanced enquiringly at Derek. The other man gestured at him, mouthing "Leave a message."

<Hi Nico, this is Riley Monroe. You remember, we spoke yesterday. Look, since then more information has come to light. I've learned that in the face of good offer, Blenheim Pastoral and Mortimer House are going to be sold. Also, based on inside information, I've learned those two buildings plus the Institute are earmarked for heritage listing. When that happens, their appeal to a developer will drop immediately. If you want to make the most of the current inflated value, I advise you to accept the offer currently on the table. Call me if you need more explanation."

Riley glanced at the other man, assessing his response. Derek disconnected the call and slid the phone over to his side of the table.

"Bugga. Hopefully, he gets the message soon. And calls back. You have to be more persuasive."

"So, we wait?"

Derek got up and began to pace. "For now. I don't want to be here too long. I've got other places to be."

"Look, if you need to get home to your family, I know how to keep my mouth shut. You can untie me and I'll go home as well. When Nico calls back, I'll tell him what you instructed."

"Nice try, but I don't think so. We stay here until it gets dark. If he doesn't ring back in time, hopefully, your message has done the trick."

There was something Derek wasn't telling him. The only option that Riley could see was to keep him talking. "You had some financial difficulties? It sounds like Katrina knew how to exploit that."

"Money's never been my strong point. With all the stresses I've been under, I needed some sort of outlet. I made the mistake of borrowing. It was all too easy."

"Borrowing? You mean mis-appropriating funds? From Excellerate?" That was a guess, based on the rumours he'd heard. "Was David Barton involved?"

Derek snorted, a disdainful sound. "That imbecile interfered. He couldn't help himself. He discovered I had forged his signature and withdrawn funds from the business. I had to cover my losses at the casino. I was going to pay it back when I could."

"Wouldn't the signature be picked up somewhere—at the bank for instance?"

"We met at Uni. It was a game then. We took turns in doing assignments and would submit for each other. I learned to copy his signature."

Riley looked at Derek with dawning horror. "You pushed him over the edge."

Derek shrugged, as though it was of no consequence. "He was going to ruin everything… tell my sister, tell my wife, tell Nico… I didn't have any other choice. He would have destroyed me. I'd have lost my job, my children…"

To say nothing of a jail term. Riley kept that thought to himself.

Did you have something to do with the fire in Winston's flat as well?"

Derek looked pleased with himself. "I did well to keep it contained to just the flat, don't you think? He knew I was in the building the night David died. He took the film from the security cameras and stashed it. I couldn't risk it being found, so I set fire to his place. With his history, he knew enough to keep away. Lenny will take care of him if he doesn't."

Derek walked to the window and peered out at the sky. "It won't be long before night sets in," he said cryptically. Walking back to the table, he seized the other chair and straddled it, facing Riley. "I'll wait until it's fully dark, and then you're taking a little trip. There will be a note in your pocket, confessing to the murder of David Barton, and saying that you and he had a fallout over money that he was syphoning from Excellerate."

"You're crazy. I'm not going near the edge."

"After you've had your skull caved in, you will. No-one will notice the difference after a fall."

The man was batshit crazy. All Riley could hope was that Phoebe noticed something happening and called the police. The likelihood of that was low, particularly if it was dark. He had to keep Derek talking while he figured out his options. He turned his head as best he could and scanned the horizon. The sky was softening with dusk-like colours. Night approached, and with it possibly his end. He could taste bile in his throat.

His shoulders ached from being pulled back into an unnatural position. He tried wriggling his hands to see if doing so would make it possible to slip one or both out of the ties. It didn't.

"Derek, you don't have to do this. The threat of Lenny and Simmo is enough for me."

"Oh, but I do. You're the fall guy and that's the final piece in this puzzle. With you taking the rap, I don't have to keep looking over my shoulder."

"With Katrina pulling the strings, and Lenny and Simmo on the payroll, do think you will ever be able to stop doing that?" He tried to sound calm and controlled. There had to be some way to reason with the man.

"Shut up. You're giving me a headache."

Derek kept pacing towards the window and back again, with his level of agitation clearly increasing. Riley tried to shunt the chair around slightly so he could keep an eye on the other man. That way, Derek couldn't attack him from behind. Perhaps he could kick him in the kneecaps? The rope around his neck tightened as the movement increased the tension, forcing him to lift his chin higher. Any tighter and he wouldn't be able to breathe. His options did not look good.

A soft ping announced the opening of the elevator doors. Riley swivelled his head as best he could without straining the noose. Winston stepped through the open door, followed by Jonathan and Bruce.

"Is this a private party, or can anyone join in?"

30 The Rescue

WINSTON STOOD WITH his hands on his hips, eyebrows rising towards his receding hairline. Derek's jaw dropped, but he recovered quickly. He shoved out a hand, warning them not to approach "Careful, he's dangerous. I had to restrain him. He's admitted he killed David Barton. The two of them had a fall-out over money."

"I don't think so," Winston said. "I reckon you've got that story arse-about."

Mark slipped behind Riley and removed the noose from around his neck. "Been having a fun time then?" He began the task of untying and unwinding the rope that bound him.

Riley blinked furiously to hide the insipient tears of relief that threatened appear. "I don't know why you're here, but I could kiss you. This bloke's off his rocker."

The second elevator door pinged open to reveal two other men—detectives Mullin and Ryan. Derek dashed for the door leading to the stairs, and they heard his footsteps clattering either up or down. It was difficult to tell.

"Aren't you going to follow? Riley asked, looking at the detectives.

"Uniform guys are downstairs. They'll nab him. There's nowhere else for him to go. In the meantime, we've got a few questions for you."

Riley stood slowly, rotating his shoulders and massaging his wrists. "Did he go down or up? What if he climbs up to the roof?"

Winston snickered. "Then there's only one way down, and he's too much of a coward to take that route."

The two detectives exchanged a glance and disappeared in the direction of the stairwell. No doubt, they would be back to quiz him later. Riley turned to his rescuers. "How did you know where to find me?"

Johnathan spoke up. "Jodie. She saw you enter the building and then a short time later, Lenny and Simmo came out, smirking. She didn't know what was going on, but came back to the Colonial and told me. We couldn't gain access to the building to check on you, so I rang Winston to ask his opinion. He said it could be bad news and he would meet us here to let us in."

"But I could have been anywhere in the building."

"The floor indicator on one of the elevators was lit up for Level 9, so we took a punt on that."

Riley sat down again. His knees had the shakes. "He wanted to push me off the roof. He was going to pin David Barton's death on me."

"Winston said you were likely to be in trouble."

"I tried to warn you to stay clear, Riley. Derek has always been mad and bad, but I didn't expect him to do this. I wouldn't have come near the place but knowing my vinyl had been incinerated was the final straw."

Riley wasn't sure how he felt about coming second in consideration behind a record collection. "Can we get out of here? I've had enough of this building for one day."

Mark pressed the button on the wall to summon the elevator, and they moved as a group to stand in front of it. "Jonathan called me while he was waiting for Winston, and I called my mates on the force, in case you're wondering," he said. "They knew those two detectives had been working on the David Barton case and let them know. That's why they turned up."

When they emerged at ground level, they found a couple of cop cars outside the building and Detectives Ryan and Mullin were questioning Derek. Other uniformed police officers stood inside the door. Derek was handcuffed, and looked at them defiantly without speaking. Riley paused, taking in the scene. He felt like spitting in Derek's face, but turned and headed for the front door.

James Mullin called after him. "Hey, we need to speak to you."

Riley didn't bother turning around. "You know where to find me. Speak to me later."

Mark placed a hand in the small of his back and ushered him through the door and out onto the footpath. "I reckon you need a drink, mate."

"I do, but right now, I just want to go home. Can I catch up with you all later?"

"Are you sure you'll be okay on your own? Perhaps one of us should come with you.?" Mark looked worried. "We'll at least walk you to your front door. I know Lenny and Simmo will be picked up, but I'm not sure when."

Privately, Riley was relieved at that suggestion. He was in no hurry to encounter those two again. They walked with him around the corner, stopping at the front of Blenheim House.

"I'll call you if I need to talk, okay? I'll catch up with Jodie at the first opportunity. I owe her my life." He noticed the quick look they exchanged. "And all of you, of course. If you hadn't turned up when you did, I'm not sure I'd still be here."

"It's okay," Jonathan said. "We understand. You know where we are if you need us."

Riley watched them walk down the street before swiping his fob key and letting himself inside. Upstairs, Ginger Puss snoozed on one of the outdoor chairs and greeted him with a soft chirrup. He stroked the cat under the chin, and it stretched its neck out, purring contentedly. Oh, for the simple uncomplicated life of a cat. He would never know if someone had deliberately poisoned Ginger, or if the cat had found and eaten something he shouldn't. Aside from that mishap, Ginger had it good.

He wandered over to the parapet and looked out to the north, towards the river and the entertainment precinct. He could see the spire of St Peter's Cathedral in the distance. Night was falling, and lights in various colours had sprung up around the city. On the surface, everything looked normal. He wasn't sure if he knew any more what normal was. His thoughts strayed to the leather gloves, now sitting in his outdoor storage bin. On second thoughts, he wasn't likely to ever use them. He retrieved the gloves and threw them in the bin.

He fetched himself a plate of cheese and crackers, and nip of scotch, and brought the bottle outside as well. He sat with Ginger, contemplating the scene at his doorstep. Thoughts of what could have, no probably *would* have happened played on an endless loop. He couldn't find the off button. It was a long time before he stirred himself and went to bed, lying there until what seemed to be the early hours of the morning.

He stood under the shower for an extraordinarily long time in the morning, washing the events of the previous afternoon away. After that, he made himself an indulgent breakfast of scrambled eggs, smashed avocado and smoked salmon. Even Ginger Puss got some of the smoked salmon. He washed it down with a cup of freshly-ground Mahalia coffee, purchased from the Market the day before. After that, he began to feel more relaxed and under control.

Steve Mullin rang mid-morning, and after a brief discussion, Riley agreed to come down to the city police station on Monday morning to make a statement. The detective assured him that Derek, Lenny and Simmo were all in custody. Katrina Dale was also under investigation. Charges may be pending.

By the time Sophie texted him to say she was only five minutes away, he had finished making notes of his experience the previous afternoon, in preparation for his interview, and also had a brief nap to make up for the lack of sleep. He had woken feeling rested, with the knowledge that the worst was probably behind him. Sure, there would be a court case in which he would have to give evidence, but that would be months away.

Sophie pulled up at the kerb, and jumped out to attach the learner plates.

"Great day for a lesson. Get in. You can drive from here today. The city traffic's quiet."

"Are you sure? Your car... inexperienced driver... who knows what might happen?"

She laughed. "That's what makes life interesting. If I didn't think you would cope, I wouldn't have suggested it."

He didn't argue, but slid behind the wheel. His progress was cautiously slow, but she was right. When he relaxed, followed her instructions, and accepted her advice that he could do it, he did. She directed him through the city and into the suburbs to the south, then taking the ring route around the park lands that surrounded the city streets and back to the front of Blenheim House again. He climbed out of the driver's seat with a sense of satisfied accomplishment.

"You're joining me for afternoon tea? My shout."

"Of course. Lead on. Take me somewhere new where I haven't been before."

This was his territory. They wandered along the Mall, full of weekend shoppers and tourists and continued into Rundle Street. He led her to a wine bar in the East End, that served wine by the glass at one end, and coffee and cake at the other. They found a quiet booth against the wall and slid in on the benches, facing each other. Riley ordered them each a serve of Crepes with seasonal berries.

"How's your week been?" Sophie asked. "No more fires, I hope. You sounded a bit mysterious on the phone."

Riley stirred his coffee, even though he hadn't added any sugar. It gave him thinking time as he collated his thoughts.

"I know you said I attract drama, but it's been more eventful than usual. Phoebe's presentation was a great success; Winston emerged briefly from hiding and warned a mate and myself to watch out for the bad guys before disappearing again; the bad guys roughed up one of the street ferals who I thought was a bad guy, but actually wasn't; and yesterday the bad guys caught up with me and one of them threatened to throw me off the roof of the Institute building. Other than that, it's been the same old, same old."

"Whoa… backtrack and start from the beginning! I saw the write-up about Phoebe in the paper, but explain the rest to me in words of one syllable."

Their order of crepes arrived, so he waited until the waiter retreated before giving a more detailed summary of what had happened.

"So, Tray Thornton isn't the upright civic citizen he appears to be."

"It appears not. He and Katrina Dale have been on top of this re-zoning issue for some time, and although competitors, both were making spectacular redevelopment plans, based on that event. Obviously, something like that will happen in the future, but not as soon as I feared. It means I have a job for a while yet as well as somewhere to live"

"Actually, you probably have more time than you think." She scooped up some strawberries and cream and jammed them in her mouth before they slid off the fork. "In all your

348

drama last week, you probably didn't take note of what was happening elsewhere."

Riley paused, holding his fork in mid-air and looked at her enquiringly.

"Are you aware that the Minister for Planning resigned his portfolio last week? No? I thought not. He has a major health issue and is leaving parliament immediately. A new minister has been sworn in, and it is well-known that he doesn't support the re-zoning proposal. Ultimately, he's the one who has to sign off on it, and I don't think that will happen. Not on his watch, anyway."

Riley didn't know whether to laugh or cry. All that drama for nothing. One man lost his life, and others were manipulated or terrorized. This in a city that was considered by some people in the other states to be bland and uneventful.

They ambled back along the Mall after coffee, pausing to watch various buskers. A juggler threw flaming batons. An elderly Chinese man played an eerie-sounding stringed instrument. A young woman strummed her guitar, and sang songs of unrequited love and yearning for change. They stood in the late afternoon sun and listened as her voice soared and echoed against the adjacent buildings. Song finished, Riley threw some coins in her basket and reached for Sophie's hand as they turned and continued their stroll.

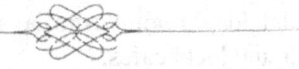

If you enjoyed this book, and I hope you did, please leave a review on the site from which you purchased it, or alternatively my website.
www.emilyhussey.com.au/home/dorothy-shorne

Dorothy Shorne

Currently semi-retired and living in
Adelaide, Dorothy Shorne has had a
varied career. She built modular houses
in Central Australia on remote
aboriginal settlement, opened various businesses, and was
involved in the development of Sydney Airport when it was
operated by the Federal Airports Corporation.

The airport job was ideal, given her pre-existing interest in
aviation. She obtained her private licence whilst living in
Alice Springs. She has worked as a property consultant
throughout her working life, with the last role being with the
Level Crossing Removal Project in Melbourne.

A solo mother by choice before Hollywood decided it made a
good story line, earlier time and resources were focused on
bringing up her son. Now she can turn thoughts to other
interests, writing being the foremost.

She is a published romance writer, and loves the short story
format in a range of genres. She now lives in a beachside
suburb in Adelaide, South Australia, and much of her writing
takes place in the local cafes.

Also by Dorothy Shorne

Rites of Passage Series
From This Day Forward
Naming Ceremonies
The Last Farewell

Writing as Emily Hussey
Red Centre Series
Journey to the Heart (Prequel)
The Red Heart
Trust Your Heart
Follow Your Heart

Tales from Harrow
Wild Spirit (Prequel)
Wild Destiny
Wild Tempest
Wild Fire

Stand-alone Stories
Ambition & Passion
Maison Angelique
Romance in the Stone

Sandy Bay Series
Secrets in Sandy Bay
Escape to Sandy Bay
Return to Sandy Bay

Writing as Rowena Wylde
Plan B: Secret Donor Baby